THE GHOST OF JOSIAH GRIMSHAW

Praxos Academy

SG TURNER

The Ghost of Josiah Grimshaw

A Praxos Academy Novel
by SG Turner
Published by Chill Out Press
Copyright SG Turner 2012

For more information about SG Turner and upcoming books, please visit:
www.chilloutpress.com/sgturner

❦   I   ❦

Lightning shattered the darkness. Not even Emma's thick purple quilt could shut out the light as it filtered through to her closed eyelids. A low echo of rumbling thunder made its way across the North Sea towards Andilyse Island, and she shivered. Suddenly something landed on top of her head, and she shrieked. The sounds of laughter emanated from the bed across the room.

'Lana, you cow,' shouted Emma as she threw back the covers and tossed the pillow back at her sister who just shook her head and giggled.

'It's only a storm. There's nothing to be scared of.'

'There is everything to be scared of,' she replied as she cowered beneath the quilt again.

'Oh come on, Sis. We're quite safe here. This house has been standing for hundreds of years; it's not like it's going to collapse is it?'

'It nearly did the last time,' Emma croaked.

'That was like sixty years ago, Em, and none of the houses collapsed. The only thing that took the brunt of the storm was the pier.'

'And the church.'

'Exactly. None of the houses. Stop being such a coward. You're fifteen! It's a storm; it's rain, it's not the end of the world.'

'It was for all those poor people.'

'Oh stop being so dramatic. Things were different back in the 50s, Em. We're safe, now stop worrying.'

The sound of the front door slamming downstairs made both girls jump. Emma glared at Lana before they both hopped out of bed and ran to their bedroom door which they opened, looking down over the railing.

'Dad?'

Peering up at them from the bottom of the stairs stood an attractive grey-haired man in his early 50s, taking off his soaking coat.

'Shhh, we don't want to wake Greg and Lucy,' he said as he summoned them downstairs.

'Oh Patrick, they should be in bed too,' whispered a voice from the kitchen as the two girls skipped down to find out what was going on.

'You know what they're like, Audrey,' he said as he hung his dripping coat on the stand in the hallway. Tutting, his wife promptly removed it and placed it in the sink in the downstairs cloakroom before going back to kiss him.

'What's happened, Dad?' asked Emma as she sat huddled up to her sister on the bottom step. A clap of thunder made her jump, and she shivered, her eyes wide open with apprehension. Lana rolled her eyes and put her arm protectively around her sister.

'Let's have a cup of cocoa,' Audrey said, recognising the look on her husband's face. There was bad news.

While they waited for the milk to heat up on the stove, Lana went into the lounge looking for candles as the lights continued to flicker, constantly threatening to go out for good.

'I've found some,' she said, setting them down on the kitchen table with a box of matches, 'just in case,' she smiled. 'So what's going on, Dad? Why did you have to go out so late?'

'He's the Chief Constable... it's his job,' answered their mother as she poured steaming milk into the four mugs, before stirring them as quietly as she could.

Lana stood beside her, adding a spoonful of sugar to her mug before passing the calming drinks to her family, who stood sipping the chocolatey goodness silently for a moment.

Rubbing his forehead, Patrick put his cocoa down on the table just as the rain began to clatter loudly on the roof tiles.

'Oh no,' whispered Emma as she pulled her feet up towards her bottom and rocked back and forth in her seat.

Patrick put his hand on her shoulder, 'it's okay sweetheart. It's just a storm. It'll pass. Everything will be all right.'

'Well then why did you have to go out in it, Dad?' she asked.

'I was called out to the old Grimshaw farm... Josiah was seen wandering close to the pier again.'

'What? In this weather? Does he have a death wish?' said Lana without thinking as her mother tutted, glancing towards Emma. 'Did you find him? Is he okay?'

'I'm afraid he's nowhere to be seen. And in these conditions, it's impossible to send out a search party. We can't send out the lifeboat without risking the lives of everyone else, I'm afraid. He's a silly old man. He should never have been left alone in this storm. Everyone on the island knows how it affects him.'

Audrey patted her husband's hand, 'there'd be no stopping him, love. He's just looking for her.'

'Well, maybe he's finally got his wish.'

'Daddy?' said an innocent child's voice from the stairs.

'Oh, we've woken the kids,' said Audrey as she stood up and went to check on her two younger children.

'Hey, sweetheart. Sorry we woke you. Come on, let's go back to bed,' she said to her family. 'There's nothing we can do now. We should all try and get some sleep.'

❦

'YOU AWAKE, SIS?' ASKED LANA LATER THAT NIGHT.

'Of course I am. There's no way I can sleep in this,' said Emma as she snuggled deep into her quilt.

'It'll be over soon.'

'I hope so. It's been going on for hours. I just hope old Mr Grimshaw is okay.'

'Yeah, I know. Do you know why he was out?'

'No, I haven't got a clue who he's looking for. I was going to ask Mum before Lucy came down.'

'We'll find out tomorrow. Try and sleep Em,' Lana said as she rolled over and closed her eyes.

Emma let out a deep sigh and pulled the cover back over her head. ''Night Lana.'

The next morning Emma sighed as she peered over the edge of the cliffs towards the view below, wondering if Mr Grimshaw had been found yet.

Pieces of driftwood, big and small, scattered the beach, along with masses of seaweed that covered the expanse of sand and pebbles. The calmness of it all belied the furious storm that had battered the island the night before.

Squinting, she spotted something unusual among the debris, and a breath halted in her throat. 'Oh my God,' she whispered as she turned back up the garden path to the house and ran as fast as she could, shouting, 'Dad! Dad!...'

Patrick appeared from the back door, putting on his coat, his eyebrows knitted together, 'What is it? What, love?' he asked as she bounded towards him.

'There's someone... someone on the beach. It looks like a body, Dad.'

'Stay here, love,' he asserted as he ran towards the cliff edge to take a look.

Sure enough, there was a body strewn on the sand below. It wasn't moving.

'Is it Mr Grimshaw, Dad?' she cried from beside him.

'Emma, you mustn't see this. Go back indoors, tell your mother what's going on and then stay put.'

Pulling out a mobile phone from his inside pocket, Patrick called for an ambulance as he began the climb down the steep path that led directly to the beach. Emma, who had quickly run inside and told her mother what was going on, soon appeared, following closely behind.

'Emma!' he said, 'go home.'

But his daughter confidently shook her head, 'I'm not a child any more, Dad, I'm fifteen, and I'm coming. You might need help.'

Shaking his head, he said, 'At least stay behind me. You shouldn't have to see this.'

She nodded as they reached the bottom of the cliff and ran towards the body.

As Patrick checked for signs of life, Emma couldn't resist peering at the pale young man whose dark brown hair plastered his forehead. He wore a dark blue velvet trimmed suit jacket, a shirt that was once perhaps white and loose-fitting black trousers with black leather brogues, all of which were soaked through and ripped in places. Little pieces of drying seaweed were dotted all over him. His eyes were closed.

'Is he... is he... dead, Dad?'

'He has a pulse,' said Patrick, 'it's weak, though. Come quickly, Audrey, he's still breathing!' he yelled as he spotted his wife climbing down the pathway with her medical kit.

'I've spoken to the ambulance, and they're almost here...' she said, out of breath, 'mind out the way, love and let me have a look at him. Do you know who he is?' she asked as Patrick and Emma stepped back to let her do her job.

'Never seen him before. Do you recognise him, Emma?' he asked as she shook her head.

'Patrick, the ambulance is arriving over at the far end of the beach. They might need a hand getting the vehicle a little closer. Can you go and give them a hand? We're okay here, love. Emma can help me.'

Emma's eyes widened as she looked at her mother, and she gulped.

'Help me with this love,' she said while Patrick ran to the other end of the beach. 'Emma, I need your help with this,' she repeated.

Crouching down, Emma did as she was told and held the boy's head in place while Audrey inspected him for injuries.

'Well I can't see any visible wounds to the body, but that's not to say he doesn't have any internal injuries. We need to keep his head and spine perfectly still until they bring the stretcher. His breathing is very slow. What happened to this poor boy?' she said more to herself than to Emma. 'It's okay now, love, you can let go. I've got him.'

Emma released the boy's head and swallowed hard as she returned her arms to her side, but just as she did so, he suddenly moved and grabbed hold of her.

Gasping, Emma jumped and froze.

'Mum,' she cried as the boy's eyes opened wide and he looked right at her.

'Shhh,' said Audrey, 'it's all right, dear. You're safe now. Please stay still. Can you tell me your name?' she asked softly.

The boy said nothing; he just continued to stare at Emma, who began to fidget nervously.

'Em, calm down, please. You must be calm for our patient.'

The boy's grip on her arm strengthened, and she looked down at it, wondering what to do.

The arrival of the ambulance crew solved her problem, as they swiftly and carefully attended to him, placing him on the stretcher and carrying him back towards the ambulance. As they carefully put him into the vehicle, the boy suddenly groaned, before he yelled out, 'Em!'

Audrey looked at her daughter, 'I thought you didn't know him?' she asked.

'I don't, I've never seen him before. I don't know him, Mum, honestly I don't.'

'Em!' he yelled again, struggling against the equipment that was keeping him in place.

'Emma, you're going to have to come along for the ride. If having you here is the only way to calm him down, then so be it,' said Jeff, one of the Medics.

Audrey nodded and ushered her inside before she went to close the doors behind them.

'But Mum?' she said.

'There's no buts. We need to get this boy to the hospital as soon as possible; you're going with him.'

'Tell Lana where I am, please. Tell her to come.'

Audrey nodded to her daughter, finally closed the door, and the ambulance began to drive away, with the boy gripping on to Emma's hand.

$\mathcal{H}$ 2 $\mathcal{H}$

'I can't believe you left me at home,' said Lana, pouting outside the hospital after she'd cycled all the way there.

'You wouldn't have come anyway. I followed Dad to the beach down the cliff pathway. You know, the cliff that you're terrified of. You'd never have gone down there. Besides, I had no choice. He wouldn't let me leave. It was weird.'

'Yeah, I guess so. Do they know who he is yet?'

Emma shook her head and ran her fingers through her long brown hair. 'He's sleeping now. Are you going to come up and see him?'

Lana grinned, 'Of course! You know how I love a mystery,' she said, practically dragging her towards the entrance to the island's only hospital.

Emma smiled at her sister and shook her head as Lana pulled her through the electric doors. They walked straight up to their father.

'Dad,' said Lana, 'Any news?'

Shaking his head, Patrick placed a protective hand on both his girl's shoulders. 'Afraid not girls. We don't know who the boy is, and there's still no sign of old Josiah. It's not looking good. The coastguard has been scouring around the island all morning.'

'That's so sad?'

'Dad?' asked Emma.

'Yes, sweetheart, what is it?'

'Who was Mr Grimshaw looking for?'

Patrick was just about to answer when the walkie talkie he carried in his belt during working hours went off.

'Do you copy, Chief?'

Turning slightly away from his girls, Patrick held the gadget to his face, 'Ten-four, Duncan. What's going on?'

'It's Josiah Grimshaw. The Coast Guard pulled his body out of the water about a mile off the coast. He's alive, but it's touch and go at the moment. Over and out.'

'Well I never... erm, Roger that, Duncan. I'm at the hospital. I'll await his arrival. Over and out.'

Placing the walkie talkie back onto his belt, he turned and smiled at the girls, 'this might be a good day, after all. Why don't you girls go on up to our mystery boy? If he wakes up with you there, it might help to calm him. I'll be up again in a bit after I've checked on Josiah.'

Nodding, Lana and Emma gave him a quick hug before heading to the stairs where they ran up to the second floor and tiptoed into the boy's room.

'Oh... I was expecting a kid,' whispered Lana. 'He's not much older than us. He's cute.'

'Lana... for goodness sake,' said Emma as she tried not to laugh, 'but I guess so,' she added with a half-smile.

⚜

HALF AN HOUR LATER, A FAINT GROAN ESCAPED HIS LIPS, MAKING the girls jump.

'Em?'

'He wants you, Em. He just groaned your name,' said Lana with a smirk as she tiptoed to his bed and looked down at the handsome young stranger.

'Grow up, Lana,' she said as she shook her head.

'Em... is that you?' he muttered with his eyes closed.

'Well, come and speak to him then,' Lana demanded.

Reluctantly, Emma stood and walked slowly to his bedside, pushing Lana to one side.

'Erm, it's me. It's Emma,' she whispered.

He held out his hand towards her. Emma's eyes opened wide, and she turned to look at her sister who pushed her forward. 'Go on then.'

Inching her hand forward, she gently placed it in his. He squeezed it and opened his eyes. When he saw her he smiled, 'Em, is that you? I knew you'd come back to me.'

'But... but how do you know who I am?' she asked and he smiled.

'I could never forget you. I've been looking for you for so long.'

'You have?' Emma felt her cheeks burn while Lana sniggered behind them.

'Who are you?' She asked. He looked hurt.

'You don't know who I am?'

Emma slowly shook her head, and he coughed.

'Please, may I have some water?' he asked with a hoarse voice.

Lana stepped out from behind Emma, filling the small glass from the pitcher on a tray at the end of the bed. She handed it to Emma, who carefully placed the straw to the young man's lips.

'Thank you. Are you sure you don't know who I am?'

Again, she shook her head, 'I'm sorry, but I've never seen you before.'

'That's impossible. You're my Em,' he whispered sadly. 'I finally found you after all these years, and you don't even know who I am,' he coughed again, wincing in pain.

'Are you in pain?' asked Lana. 'Shall I fetch a nurse?' she said, heading for the door.

'I... I, Em?' he gasped as a coughing fit hit him full force.

'I'm sorry, I don't know what to do,' she panicked, bringing the straw in the glass of water to his lips again but his body began convulsing, and so she stepped backwards in shock.

The door opened, and a doctor in a white coat, followed by quite a butch nurse rushed in.

'Please wait outside girls,' she commanded.

Lana and Emma did as they were told, watching just before the door closed in their faces.

'What the heck was all that about?' asked Lana.

Emma looked at her sister and burst into tears.

'Em? I'm sure he'll be okay, Sis. Don't worry, he'll be fine,' she said, not quite as reassuringly as she'd hoped.

Pulling her sister away from the room, the two girls found a small sofa just down the corridor opposite a large window that looked across to Carlton Point, the highest point on the island.

Patting the seat next to her, Lana smiled as Emma sat down and leaned her head on her sister's shoulder.

'I wonder why he thinks he knows you. I wish we could find out who he is,' she sighed just as Patrick appeared at the top of the stairs at the far end of the corridor. Before he noticed them, he walked into the boy's room, only to walk out moments later holding his hat close to his chest with his head lowered.

Spotting them, he smiled sadly and walked quickly towards them.

'Dad?' asked Emma.

But their father just shook his head, 'He's fallen into a coma. It's not looking good, I'm afraid.'

Emma's bottom lip quivered. Noticing, Lana took her hand in hers and squeezed.

'And Mr Grimshaw?' Lana asked.

'He keeps drifting in and out of consciousness,' he replied, shaking his head sadly, 'it's the same situation as the boy. Touch and go. I must get back to work. Are you girls going to head home?'

Emma shook her head, 'I want to stay here a while longer. I'd like to stay with him, if that's okay, Dad?'

'Course it is, sweetheart. I'm sure he'd like that. I'll see you at dinner,' he said, kissing each of them on their cheeks before placing his hat back on his head. He walked back down the corridor towards the stairs.

'I can't stay, Em. We arranged to meet Scott this morning, remember?'

'You go. I think I'd rather be on my own here anyway.'

'You sure?'

Emma nodded, 'I'll walk home later on.'

Lana said goodbye and wandered down the hallway, turning to watch her sister calmly walk back into the strange boy's room alone.

❦ 3 ❦

Outside, the harsh sunlight made it hard to believe that such a ferocious storm had unleashed itself on the island the night before. Apart from the debris piled across the beach, the only other proof of the event lay fighting for their lives in two different hospital rooms.

Lana removed her leopard print cardigan and shoved it into the handbag she wore across her chest before shovelling around to find her favourite over-sized black sunglasses. Putting them on, she flung her bag across her back, climbed onto her bike and pushed away from the hospital, onto the main road.

Scott had been waiting for 25 minutes and was just about to leave when he saw a lone figure cycling uphill towards the castle ruins where they so often met.

'Hey!' he shouted, 'You're late!'

Lana stuck out her tongue childishly and grinned at her and Emma's best friend who stood waiting impatiently. As she pushed the pedals the last few metres, the blonde-haired boy removed the small rucksack from his back, again, and dropped it to the floor.

'Sorry,' she huffed, 'you'll never believe what happened,' she gushed.

'Where's Em?' he asked.

'Give me a minute; I'm getting to that...' she said as she

climbed off the bike and let it drop against the crumbling walls of the ancient castle.

'This unconscious guy was found on the beach this morning. Dad and Emma were the first ones down there to help him, and when he opened his eyes, he recognised Em. He won't let her leave his side. It's seriously weird.'

'Who is he?' asked Scott as they walked through their favourite archway and sat on the fallen stones where they'd sat a thousand times before.

'Nobody knows, but he sure seems to know Em.'

'So where is she?'

'He fell into a coma at the hospital, and she doesn't want to leave him.'

Scott smiled, 'She's such a softie, your sister.'

Lana pretended to be offended, 'And I'm not, you mean?'

'I think you know the answer to that,' he replied as he shoved her shoulder playfully.

'Well, I guess I'm not quite as soft-hearted as she is, I suppose.'

'You reckon?' he laughed.

Lana rolled her eyes and looked through the archway towards the rolling green hills and numerous wind turbines beyond, 'Did you hear about old Mr Grimshaw?'

Scott nodded, 'Did they find him yet?'

'Yeah. He's in the same condition as the young guy. Weird, huh?'

'I guess. Let's hope they both make it.'

Lana nodded and stood up, 'Do you wanna go for a ride?'

'Sure,' he said as they wandered back to their bikes. 'Where do you want to go?'

Lana shrugged her shoulders.

'We could try and get up to Carlton Point?' Scott said with a straight face.

'You are joking, right?'

A chuckle escaped his lips, and he nodded, 'Yeah, I know, I know. I wouldn't put you through that. Don't worry; we'll stay on low ground.'

Before he knew what hit him, Lana gave him a swipe with her handbag, nearly knocking him to the ground.

'Haha, hilarious Scottie.'

'Don't call me that,' he laughed before hopping on his bike, 'Come on, I'll race you!'

'Hey, so not fair,' she laughed as she raced along behind him.

But just as she reached him, she heard him curse as his mobile began ringing.

'That'll be Mum, she said she'd call me if she needed my help today,' he said, slowing down.

'Aww but it's a Saturday, Scott.'

Raising his eyebrows, he pulled the phone out of his pocket, 'Hey Mum… yeah okay. I'll be there in fifteen.'

Clapping the phone shut, he turned to Lana, 'Jeanie had a bit of an accident and had to pop down to the hospital, so Mum needs my help in the shop.'

Lana's angry expression vanished, 'Oh, is she okay?'

'And there I thought you weren't a softie,' he laughed, adding, 'yeah, she'll be fine. She just cut herself on broken glass. It's a nasty cut and needs a few stitches. I'd better go, though. Maybe see you later?'

Lana nodded and shooed him away. 'Go,' she said with a smile, 'I'll see you later.'

Staying put on the side of the road, Lana watched him cycle away into the distance. She didn't want to go home, and she certainly didn't fancy going back to the hospital, so she hopped back onto her bike and took a leisurely ride towards the old churchyard. As she approached the crumbling remains of the building that was destroyed in 1953, she kept a close eye on Carlton Point which stared back down as if goading her.

But instead of pulling up at the churchyard, something made her continue cycling. It was if they weren't her legs pedalling. She just kept going. Breathless, her heart thumped in her chest as she came to a slow about halfway up the steep hill. Stopping, she climbed off and pushed her bike to the grassy expanse to the side of the pathway, letting it fall to the ground. She followed it and sat down for a few minutes, getting her breath back.

The wind picked up temporarily and with it came a gentle sound. It sounded like someone calling out her name. Turning to look up towards the very top of Carlton Point, Lana couldn't see anyone. It's just my imagination, she thought. It's just because my heart is beating like God knows what. But the sound continued persistently: 'Laaaanaa..... Laaaanaa.... Laaaanaa...'

'What the...?'.

Standing, Lana did a full circle squinting her eyes before chuckling nervously, 'Very funny, Scottie. I know it's you. You can come out now!' she yelled.

But nobody appeared.

She fidgeted with her fingers, nervously. She planned to climb back on her bike and cycle away, but her legs moved in another direction: towards the summit.

No, she thought, no.

But it was no good. She no longer had any control over her body, and she continued walking until she reached the pinnacle of Carlton Point. Lana was terrified. She'd always had what she thought to be an irrational fear of heights, just like Emma had an irrational fear of water. There was no explanation to either phobia. Then why am I here? Why did I climb up?

At the very top of Carlton Point was a small circular patch of ground surrounded by an ancient stone wall. On one side of it was the pathway she'd just walked along, although steep, there were no scary edges as such. But the other side was an altogether different story. She'd seen it in pictures, and from afar, but she'd never seen it up close.

Standing dead centre as she let her handbag fall to the ground, Lana closed her eyes just for a second. I'm not here, she thought, I'm in bed having a nightmare. But the gentle breeze told her a different story. She gulped hard and opened her eyes, her limbs incapable of moving further. But she was no longer in the centre of the circle. She was now looking down at a sheer drop hundreds of feet below.

She could hear her heart beating, feel it thudding in her chest. She couldn't open her mouth; it was too dry. All she wanted to do was scream, but she couldn't even do that. Please, God, don't let me die, she thought.

A sudden massive gust of wind took her feet from beneath her, and she was forcefully pushed from the top of Carlton Point, falling silently and peacefully to the rocky hills below.

❦ 4 ❦

She'd fallen asleep with her head leaning forward on the bottom of the bed. She woke with a start, a cry slipped from her lips, startling herself. Her hands flew to cover her mouth, and a tear fell down her cheek.

A strange feeling overcame her and Emma searched the room for Lana.

'Lana?' she asked.

'Em?' said the voice from the bed.

Emma gasped. Wasn't he supposed to be in a coma, she thought.

'I'm here,' she said without thinking, moving closer so he could take her hand.

'It's me, Em... it's Joe, don't forget me. I've always loved you, you know.'

Emma blushed, 'I... erm... I...'

Joe smiled, his dry lips cracking, 'I knew we'd be together again, Emelia... ' he sighed and as a final breath of air whispered through his lips, so did his life.

'Joe? Joe?' she cried, 'Wake up, Joe...'

The door opened, and the doctor rushed in. After a few moments that seemed to last for ages, he turned to face her.

'Emma,' he nodded. 'He's gone. I'm so sorry. I knew he wouldn't come out of the coma.'

Emma looked at the doctor strangely, 'But... but he did. He just spoke to me,' she exclaimed.

The doctor walked over to the monitoring system and shook his head, 'I don't think so, dear. There's nothing here to suggest that he woke from his coma. He's gone now. He's no longer suffering.'

Emma sniffed, 'What will happen to him?'

'Until the police can locate his family, he will be kept in the mortuary. I'm sorry, Emma, I know you seemed to have developed a bond today, but he's gone. It's time you went home,' he smiled as he patted her arm gently.

'I... I want to go and see Mr Grimshaw if that's all right?' she said, not quite knowing why she wanted to go and see the old man.

The doctor nodded and directed her to his room, 'But, you do know that he's in a coma too, don't you?'

Emma nodded, thanked him and walked down the corridor to Mr Grimshaw's room. As she pushed open the door, she expected him to have company, but the room was empty, except for old Mr Grimshaw who lay pretty much the same way the young boy had done — linked up to all kinds of machines that beeped quietly in the background.

Pulling up a chair, Emma sat beside the bed and closed her eyes. A strange sensation flooded her body, like a feeling of deja vu. She shivered, wondering what Lana and Scott were up to when a sense of foreboding filled her. She rubbed her arms and shivered again, before closing her eyes, letting the gentle sounds of the hospital lull her to sleep.

❧ 5 ❧

It didn't feel like death was upon her. In fact, Lana felt strangely alive as her body fell slowly to the ground. Slowly? Yes, she was falling slowly, far too slowly. Lana looked down and watched as the ground below her seemed to hover. She held out her arms and felt her feet gracefully touch the floor like a ballet dancer about to pirouette in the air. A shocked giggle erupted from her lips as she twirled and looked around, before glancing upwards to see how far she'd fallen. But it wasn't a fall, she thought, I should be dead.

Suddenly, the full extent of what had happened hit her. She took a step back as if someone punched her in the stomach. Oh My God, she thought, gulping. I've just fallen from Carlton Point and survived. Not a scratch. Nothing. It can't possibly be right.

'Oh No,' she whispered, 'I must be dead.' Her hands flew to her mouth, and she retched, heaving, throwing up the chocolate Rice Krispies she'd had for breakfast. Sitting down on a mossy rock, she put her elbows on her knees and breathed in and out deeply.

Hang on; if I'm dead, surely I wouldn't throw up this morning's breakfast? She searched around for her body, and it was nowhere to be seen. She pinched herself over and over until her arms were pink and sore.

And then she couldn't help it. She began laughing and laughing until her stomach muscles ached. But after about five minutes, she stopped abruptly. A sensation in her abdomen caused her to curl over in agony. Writhing on the floor for what seemed like an age, tears rolled down Lana's face. Eventually, the pain dissipated, and she was able to sit up.

Scrambling at her long black T-shirt, she pulled it up and peered down at her stomach. There, etched on her skin, was what appeared to be a tattoo. Lana's eyes opened wide, and she began to cry, loudly.

'What the hell?' she sobbed, 'What's going on?' she shouted as tears streamed down her cheeks, causing black mascara to smear across her face. 'What's wrong with me?' she said as she fell to the floor in a heap.

'Emma, I need to get to Emma,' she whispered, pulling herself together as she scrambled upwards and ran around the back of Carlton Point until she eventually reached her bicycle.

'My bag... where's my bag? Oh no,' she whispered as her gaze was forced upwards towards the pinnacle. Her shoulders slumped as she realised where her bag must be. 'No, I can't do it. I can't go back up there.'

But Lana soon changed her mind as she remembered that her bag was full of her many treasured things: her favourite animal print cardigan; expensive perfume, Juicy Tube lip gloss, pink camera, etc. She couldn't just leave those things up there. Reluctantly, she dropped her bike once again and began climbing upwards.

But that's when she realised something had changed. The fear that she'd felt since she was a baby had gone. She walked with newfound confidence. The confidence that her fear of heights had left her. It had gone for good.

When she reached the top, Lana held her arms high above her head and twirled around and around, laughing. She located her bag and took out the camera, taking pictures of everything that she could see from such a height. All the places where Scott, Emma and herself spent much of their time: the old churchyard, the castle ruins, the new church which they visited on special occasions, but best of all, she could see the one place she'd always wanted to see for herself but had never had the courage to: the mainland. She could just about see mainland England.

'Woop, Woop!' she shouted as she eventually put the camera back in her bag and went over to the spot where she'd fallen. Lana looked down. It didn't even make her dizzy. Without thinking, she climbed up onto the stone wall and held out her arms, 'I'm on top of the world!' she yelled as loud as she could, laughing. When another gust of wind pushed her from behind, Lana didn't even flinch. She let it take her because deep down she knew she would land on her feet, in one piece, safely. And that's exactly what happened.

But the pain in her abdomen brought her back to reality. 'Mum and Dad are going to kill me,' she whispered as she bent over, wincing. How the hell am I going to explain this, she thought as she walked back around to her bike, climbed on it and headed downhill.

People milled around the hospital just as they had before, minding their own business. Lana walked up the stairs, past the nurses' station and into the room where she'd left her sister earlier. The sight of nothing but an empty bed startled her.

'Oh no,' she whispered, 'Excuse me,' she asked one of the orderlies cleaning the floor outside, 'Can you tell me what happened to the young man who came in in this morning?'

'I'm sorry, love. He died a little while ago. Your friend was here when it happened.'

'My friend?'

'Yes, love, the girl with the long brown hair. You know, with the intense green eyes,' he smiled.

'Oh, you mean Emma. That's my sister,' she replied.

The man looked at her quizzically, 'Your sister?'

Lana smiled, 'Yes, my sister.'

The man looked a little awkward before adding, 'She's still here. She's down with the old man who was brought in earlier. Grimshaw, I think his name is.'

'Oh? Okay, thank you. Can you tell me which room?'

After he told her where to find Emma, Lana thanked him and walked away.

'Em?' she whispered as she opened the door to Room 12 and saw her sister sleeping in a chair next to the old man.

Tiptoeing inside, she gently closed the door behind her and

wandered across to look at Mr Grimshaw. He looked terribly sick. He's so old; she thought, poor thing.

When his eyes shot open, Lana nearly had a heart attack.

'Jeeesus!' she cried.

'Wh...what the...' shrieked Emma who jumped up from the chair.

'Em... Em... is that you, my love?' said the old man.

Emma groaned, 'Oh no, not again.'

Lana raised her eyebrows at her sister once she'd calmed down. 'What is it with you today?'

'Em... Emelia?' he croaked before closing his eyes again, quickly returning to his unconscious state.

The door opened, and a nurse popped her head around the door.

'Everything all right, girls?'

Emma nodded while Lana shook her head.

'Well, which is it?' she said as she walked into the room and checked on Mr Grimshaw. Lana was about to say something, but Emma tugged at her arm and shook her head.

Smiling sweetly, Lana told her everything was fine.

The middle-aged nurse pulled a funny face and walked out, closing the door behind her.

'What's going on, Emma?' Lana asked, placing her hands on her hips and tipping her head to one side.

But before she could tell her, Emma asked, 'Are you all right, Sis?'

'Wh...why do you ask?' she stuttered.

'Well, you've got panda eyes for a start and, I don't know, I just had this horrible feeling earlier. Weird really,' she said, shrugging her shoulders before she proceeded to tell her sister about what had happened while she was out.

'... and he told me his name was Joe. Just before he died, he called me Emelia.'

'Well that's a relief, knowing that he was just confusing you with someone else, isn't it? Oh, and I'm sorry he died. I know you, you know, connected with him or something,' she said as she peered at herself in the small Union Jack mirror she carried in her handbag before wiping her face with a wet wipe.

Emma's face dropped, and she rubbed at her eyes, 'Yeah, I guess I did. But, but, why did Mr Grimshaw ask for Emelia too? That's just weird.'

'Or just a coincidence, perhaps?' Answered her sister as she snapped the mirror shut and put it back in her handbag, content that she looked human again. Sitting opposite Emma, Lana immediately started tapping her fingers on the bedside table.

'Okay... what is it? What aren't you telling me, Lana?' said Emma, who leaned forward to scrutinise her.

Lana looked away, then up to the ceiling and down to the floor, but she could no longer keep it to herself any longer, and she stood up, lifting her T-shirt slightly, revealing what looked like a tattoo.

'Oh My God, Lana... Mum is going to KILL you!' she exclaimed as she jumped up and bent down to have a look. 'A tattoo? That's what you did today? Are you insane? Okay, don't answer that.'

But Lana shook her head aggressively, 'No, no, no, no' she said, 'I didn't do it. It wasn't me.'

Emma raised her eyebrows, 'I didn't do it? That's your excuse? Sorry, Sis, but our parents aren't going to buy it. Where did you go? I didn't even know we had a tattoo artist on Andilyse,' she said, absentmindedly shaking her head.

Lana grabbed her sister's wrist, forcing Emma to look up into her eyes.

'Oh My God... somebody did this to you? But how? Did they assault you or something? Oh Jeese, Lana. Are you all right?'

Lana nodded and gulped, 'I think you'd better sit back down, Sis. You're never going to believe what happened to me this morning.'

❦ 6 ❦

Poor old Mr Grimshaw died during their conversation, and they hadn't even noticed. He'd taken his last breath when he'd uttered those word, 'Em, Emelia'. Similar words said by the young stranger before he'd passed away earlier in the day.

Emma cried when the nurse walked in to check on his condition, only to discover he was already dead. It was the same nurse who'd walked in on them earlier. She hadn't been pleased that the girls hadn't called for her. As she ushered them out of the room, she'd tutted and shaken her head, but seeing the tears falling down Emma's cheeks; she'd taken pity on them and reassured them that Mr Grimshaw was in a better place now.

'Come on, Em, let's get out of here. I think you've dealt with enough today. Let's go and get some fresh air,' persuaded Lana as she took her sister's hand and led her away from the second floor, down the stairs and out into the bright sunlight.

'Oh, I forgot I don't have my bike here. I came in the ambulance this morning,' Emma sighed as the tears continued to flow.

'We can manage', said Lana as she made Emma sit side-saddle on the frame between her and the handlebars, like children.

Emma managed a giggle as they went on their way, away from the hospital, away from death.

'I still can't quite believe what happened to you today,' she shouted as Lana pedalled, out of breath, up a gentle hill back towards their little house.

'I know, it's crazy,' she panted, 'I still can't believe it myself. Were it not for the tattoo; I wouldn't. I can't believe what's happened to you today either,' she laughed and then realised it wasn't funny and shut up, 'Sorry.'

'It's okay. It's all bizarre. You know, I don't want to go home just yet.'

Lana stopped pedalling and pulled over, letting Emma hop off.

'What do you wanna do then?' she asked.

'I want to go to Mr Grimshaw's house,' she whispered.

'Oh... but why?'

Emma shrugged her shoulders, 'I dunno, I just do. I just have this feeling, you know?'

'Uh oh.'

'What?'

'I had one of 'those' feelings this morning, remember, and look what happened to me?'

The girls chuckled and started walking, Lana pushing the bike along between them.

'Okay, let's go over to Mr Grimshaw's, but let's go home first and pick up your bike.'

Mr Grimshaw lived in an old farmhouse, isolated from neighbours, about a twenty-minute ride from their house. He had no family to speak of, and so the house was empty, apart from an old, half-blind mutt that wouldn't stop barking when they first arrived.

Approaching the gate, the little shaggy-haired black dog howled at them before it started wagging its fluffy tale uncontrollably.

'Hello boy,' said Emma as she bent down to pet him on his back. He soon rolled over, though, making the girls laugh as she tickled his tummy.

'The poor thing, what's going to happen to him now?' said Emma while Lana shrugged, looking around.

'Maybe we should take him home with us?'

Lana immediately shook her head, 'No way. It's a mangy mutt, and we don't need a mangy mutt getting in our way. The house isn't big enough for the six of us, let alone a dog as well.'

'Lana, you're so cold-hearted. The poor thing has just lost his owner. He's all alone.'

A movement towards the back of the house caught Lana's eye. 'I'm not quite sure about that. Look, Em, there's someone out the back,' she whispered as she began to walk quickly around the side of the house.

'Wait for me,' said Emma as she ran after her, leaving the dog who laid down to enjoy the sun on his belly. 'Great guard dog you are,' she laughed as she glanced back at him.

'Shhh,' whispered Lana, holding her finger to her lips, 'There's someone just gone in through the back door.'

'Well, maybe it's the police or something?'

'Don't you think I'd recognise him if it were? Are you forgetting Dad is the Chief Constable? We know every last police officer on this island, Em.'

'Well, what did he look like?'

'Medium height, dark brown hair, wearing a weird blue jacket, loose-fitting black trousers and black shoes.'

A vague recollection flashed across Emma's mind, but she shook her head and followed Lana who was peering through the back window into the kitchen.

'I can't see... I'm going in,' she said as she carefully squeezed through the door that was already ajar, without making a noise.

'Lana, we're trespassing, you know?'

'No, we're investigating a possible break-in,' she said as they both crept through the kitchen and screwed their noses up in disgust at the rubbish strewn everywhere and the piles of dirty dishes scattered across the worktop and sink.

'Jeese, did he never clean this place?'

'Lana, the poor man is dead. Show some respect.'

Ignoring her, Lana continued to walk through into the dining room, which had the same amount of old pots and plates everywhere. She moved as quickly as she could through the house until she reached the front door, which was firmly closed. Crouching down and peering through the letterbox it, she just saw the back of a man disappear into the distance.

'Damn, we lost him,' she said, turning to find that her sister wasn't behind her. 'Emma?'

'I'm in here.'

The living room was a little tidier than the other rooms she'd seen, for starters, there was room for a couple of armchairs and a television. The décor looks like something out of a museum; she thought as she wandered back through to look for her sister.

'Where, Emma?'

'In here,' she said as she poked her head out of a door just beyond the stairs. 'You need to see this.'

It was a tiny room, immaculate, with a small rocking chair by the hearth. And all around on every wall were old photos. Every one of the same woman. A beautiful woman with wild long dark brown hair, high cheekbones and huge expressive eyes. 'Em, she looks a little bit like you,' Lana breathed.

❧ 7 ❧

The mangy mutt sat happily sleeping beneath Lucy's feet at the dinner table while Lucy sat beaming. She'd always wanted a pet, and now her dream had come true. She was going to call him Henry.

'You can't just change his name,' said Greg, their 12-year-old brother, matter-of-factly. 'He already has a name. He'll never come to you unless you use his real name.'

'But we don't know what he's really called, so his new name is Henry,' said Lucy as she sucked a piece of spaghetti through her lips.

'Henry? But that's a horrible name. I want to call him by his real name,' he replied.

'That is his real name. It's his new real name,' she replied with a scowl.

'Lucy, you're such a child.'

'I am not. I'm eight. I'm nearly as old as you are.'

'You'll never be as old as me, Lucy Jo. I'll always be the eldest,' he said, sticking out his chin.

'Well that's not strictly true is it?' interrupted Lana with a smirk, 'I do believe that both me and Emma are heaps older than you, Greg.'

'Yes but you don't really count, do you?' he said, instantly regretting it, biting his lip.

'What? Because we're adopted?' Lana coughed into her glass of Doctor Pepper.

Greg looked like he was about to cry when Emma interrupted them, 'We might be adopted, but we're still your sisters, Greg. And we love our little brother and sister, don't we, Lana?" she said eyeballing her across the table.

Lana chuckled and nodded as Audrey looked across at her husband and smiled.

'Who wants pudding?' she said, standing up quickly as the kids all cheered and she began clearing the plates away.

'I'll help you, Mum,' said Lana as she stood up, but a sudden pain in her abdomen caused her to bend over, dropping the plate she'd picked up. Leftover spaghetti bolognese splattered all over the floor.

Henry rushed over and began cleaning the floor happily.

'Oh Lana, you should be more careful,' said Patrick before he realised she was in pain. 'What is it, sweetheart? What's wrong?' he asked, rushing to her side as he helped her over to the little sofa in the kitchen corner.

Lana shot a look of help to Emma, who instantly realised what was going on.

'It's okay, Dad. I'll take her upstairs. She's just got, erm, women's pains, you know?' she lied.

Patrick stood upright and blushed, 'Oh, okay. Shall I bring you a hot water bottle up, love?' he asked, and Emma smiled.

'No, Dad, I'll be okay. Thanks though,' muttered Lana through gritted teeth. 'Perhaps some painkillers, though.'

Audrey was already standing on a stool reaching into the cupboard where they kept such things. Tossing a packet of Paracetamol down, Patrick caught it and handed it to his daughter before they disappeared upstairs.

'Thanks for that, Em,' said Lana as she curled up on the bed.

'Is it the tattoo thing again?' she asked as Lana nodded, feeling uncomfortable while rolling up her sweatshirt to reveal the inky pattern that was moving across her abdomen.

Emma gasped, almost falling backwards as she watched the so-called tattoo move slowly around her sister's torso until eventually, it came to a halt on her lower back.

'It's stopped,' she whispered.

'Are you sure?' asked Lana with tears in her eyes.

Nodding, Emma tiptoed forward and bent down to have a closer look. 'There... there are words...'

'What do you mean, words?'

'Words, among the pattern. It says something,' she said, gently touching her skin and following the letters with her finger. 'Provehito In Altum,' she whispered, 'I think it's Latin.'

'Prove in what?' said Lana as she unsuccessfully tried to look over her own shoulder before giving in and getting up to go to the full-length mirror inside the wardrobe door.

'I can't read it back to front,' she huffed. 'What the hell is it, Emma? What's happening to me?'

Emma, who was gazing at her from her own bed, squinted her eyes slightly, 'Are you sure you're telling me everything? I mean, this all sounds a bit, you know, crazy?'

'You don't believe me?' shrieked Lana, 'Oh My God, Emma,' she added, shaking her head before sitting down on the edge of her bed.

'It's not that I don't believe you. Of course I believe what you've told me, it's just that, well, I'm wondering whether someone erm, well, drugged you or something and maybe did that tattoo when you were unconscious or something. Maybe we should tell Dad? If there's someone out there drugging young women, well...'

Looking across at her sister, Emma stopped talking as she noticed tears falling down Lana's cheeks. This was serious. Lana never cried.

'I... I don't know. I remember falling off Carlton Point, Em, I do and this? It just appeared, how can a tattoo crawl all over your body? It just doesn't make any sense,' she spluttered.

Emma stood up and walked over, sat down beside her and took hold of her hand, 'It's okay, Lana. We'll figure it out.'

Lana attempted a smile, 'Please don't tell Dad. He won't believe me, Em. You're the only one I can trust with this.'

'Okay, I promise. Now let's have another look at your back. I wonder what the words mean?' she said as Lana stood and lifted her top to reveal those three written words 'Provehito in Altum'.

'Can you take a photo with my camera so that I can see it properly?' asked Lana as she watched Emma scrutinising it.

A couple of minutes later, Emma had uploaded the image to her laptop, and both sat staring at the downloads. It wasn't just the image of the tattoo but the photos that Lana had taken at the top of Carlton Point. Proof that she'd been there.

'I'd forgotten all about them,' she exclaimed with her eyes wide open, and she turned her head to look at Emma. 'See? This is absolute proof of what happened.'

Emma stared back before turning towards the laptop and flicking through the pictures of the view. She opened her mouth to say something, but nothing came out.

'Do you believe me now, Sis? I mean, I know you said that you believed me before but do you, like, really believe me now?'

Emma said nothing. She just nodded and swallowed. She knew that Lana would typically have been terrified at the mere thought of climbing to the top of Carlton Point, and yet there she was. A photo she'd taken herself with her arm outstretched, standing, smiling at the highest point on Andilyse Island. It was clear that she was alone. And she looked ecstatic.

As they continued to flick through the images, they eventually came to the tattoo.

There was no doubt about it; it was beautiful. The words looked like they'd been there forever, there was no scarring, no redness and the pain had almost entirely gone. The words just seemed to hug the curvature of her lower back.

Above the short phrase was a symbol that looked like an eye with wings. Although they both thought it was vaguely familiar, neither could identify it.

'Let's look up the words,' Lana said, breathlessly, as Emma typed them into Google.

'Oh look,' exclaimed Lana, 'It's 30 Seconds to Mars. Provehito in Altum is their motto! Oh, do you think I have some connection to the rock band? I love Jared Leto,' she swooned.

Emma merely laughed and continued searching until she found what she was looking for. A literal translation. Provehito in Altum was Latin for 'Launch Forward Into The Deep'.

'Oh... okay... but what does it mean?' asked Lana with a deep yawn.

'I honestly don't know. But don't worry. We'll find out.'

Later that night, Emma listened to the gentle sounds of her sister's breath as she slept. Occasionally the sound would quicken, and Lana would thrash around below her duvet before calming down again peacefully. Emma, on the other hand, couldn't sleep. She thought about Lana's strange moving tattoo as well as Carlton Point, but that wasn't what was keeping her awake. It was the boy on the beach and Mr Grimshaw. Both had died right in front of her. Why had they both called out to her? And who was Emelia? And, although she hadn't seen him herself, who was the stranger poking around Mr Grimshaw's house?

8

Darkness was all around her. The silence punctuated only by the sounds of an owl in the distance. Lana shivered while her eyes adjusted to the blackness surrounding her. Standing deathly still, she listened. Sticking out her neck slightly, she could just about hear the gentle rock of the shore not too far away. It sounded familiar. It seemed like the bottom of the garden.

She turned and just made out the back of the house, but it wasn't the same somehow. The rose garden that her mother had spent so many hours tending to wasn't there. Instead, a massive expanse of ivy-covered the whitewashed walls. Only two pairs of wellies, instead of six, stood under the lean-to next to the door.

Underneath her feet, Lana's toes squelched in the mud, where there should have been a lovely lawned area. Why am I not wearing any shoes? She thought before she suddenly realised she was also wearing pyjamas. What's going on? Oh, it's just a dream. She smiled as she walked down the garden towards the cliff edge.

Glancing down across the dim moon-lit shore below, she gasped at the sight of a small hot air balloon drifting towards her. It wasn't like the ones she'd seen on TV, this one was much smaller, almost like a miniature one but the balloon part was beautiful. As it came closer and closer, she could make out the intense blues, reds and golden colours that intertwined within the intricate pattern of the fabric.

Lana stepped backwards as she watched it gracefully land halfway between the cliff edge and the house. Skipping across to get a closer look, she noticed a slight gurgle sound came from the little basket beneath it.

As she approached silently, she peered down, gasping at the sight of a tiny baby with dark skin and a flash of dark hair. It giggled at her, kicking its arms and legs out playfully.

Leaning in, Lana noticed something on the pretty blanket that enveloped the baby. It was a symbol — an eye with wings.

❃   9   ❃

Lana woke with a start. A strange feeling bubbled up from her toes to her stomach as she remembered yesterday. A faint groan lingered on her lips as she felt across to her lower back, the dream all but forgotten.

As Emma was snoring, she decided not to bother her for a while. Instead, she grabbed her favourite pink and fluffy black nightgown and crept out of their room, gently closing the door behind her before quietly walking down the stairs, careful to avoid the creaky step that always woke her sister.

As she strolled down the hallway, she peered into the living room and smiled at Greg and Lucy, who were glued to the TV, sitting on the floor watching silly cartoons. Of course, Greg would deny it if you ever mentioned it to his friends. But Sunday was the only day they were allowed to watch morning television and so they could always be found there.

Listening to the sound of her mum's voice, Lana walked into the kitchen just as Audrey was saying goodbye to someone on the phone.

'Morning, Love,' she said as she leaned over and kissed Lana on her forehead. 'Are you feeling better?'

Before she could reply, the kettle boiled, making an awful gurgling sound before it switched itself off. Picking it up, Audrey filled the old teapot and replaced the lid. 'Do you want a drink? I've got some green tea if you're still suffering from your period.'

Lana smiled, remembering the lie her sister had told the night before. 'No, I'm feeling much better, thanks. I'll just have a cup of normal tea, please.'

'Is Emma still in bed?'

Lana nodded.

'That's unusual. She's always up before you. I hope she's not coming down with something,' she sighed as she gave the teapot a bit of a shake before pouring the tea into two mugs.

'I think it's more to do with old Mr Grimshaw, Mum, and that boy dying. She was pretty upset about it.'

Smiling sadly, Audrey nodded, 'Of course, yes. Poor thing. Dealing with death quite often, I forget how stressful it can be.'

'Have you heard anything yet?'

Her mum looked across the table quizzically.

'The boy?' said Lana.

'No, nothing. The police are looking into it, but so far he's been unclaimed. They've sent photos to the mainland, and they're doing some facial recognition thing on the computer this morning. They're hoping someone might recognise him.'

'How do you think he got here, Mum if he's not a local?'

Audrey took a sip of tea. 'He might have been on a boat that got caught in the storm. That's the likeliest explanation.'

'Mummmm... Greg won't let me watch Tracy Beakeeeeerrrr,' yelled Lucy as a kerfuffle ensued from the living room.

Audrey rolled her eyes and stood up, 'Why don't you take a cup of tea to Emma? I'm sure that will have woken her up,' she smiled as she went to sort the kids out.

'Morning, trouble,' Lana smiled as she opened the bedroom door to find Emma sitting up in bed, rubbing her eyes.

'Trouble? That's your name, not mine.'

Lana laughed, 'I suppose you're right. Here, I brought you some tea,' she said, handing it over before plonking herself down on her bed.

'What time is it?' asked Emma.

'Just gone ten. It's not like you to sleep in?'

'I didn't get to sleep until really late. I couldn't stop thinking about, you know, yesterday.'

Lana smiled before standing up and taking off her dressing gown. She lifted her pyjama top, turning to look at her back in the mirror. The tattoo was still there.

A brief knock on the door made her almost jump out of her clothes, and she pulled down the top just in time as Audrey opened the door and peered around.

'Morning, Love. Are you all right? You slept late this morning.'

'I'm okay, Mum,' she replied as she leaned forward to let her kiss her on the forehead.

'Now that you're both awake, I've got something to tell you.'

The girls looked across at each other expectantly.

'I was waiting for confirmation about accommodation before I broached the subject, but I've just spoken to one of your Dad's old friends, and it's all confirmed...'

'What is, Mum... what's confirmed?' asked Lana impatiently.

'Wait, I'm getting to that,' she smiled, before carrying on, 'Your work experience. Your Dad and I thought it would be good for you both to go...' she paused for effect, '... to London,' she said, almost squealing.

Lana jumped up with a smile so wide, that it almost reached the outer corners of her eyes.

'Holy.... sh.....sugar,' she exclaimed with a glance in Audrey's direction, 'I thought I was going to work in the gallery with Lady Denton. How did you do it? Where are we going to stay? Where are we going to work? When are we going?' she said with barely a breath in between.

It was then that Audrey and Lana realised that Emma was very quiet.

'Emma? Whatever's the matter? I thought you'd be over the moon?'

Swallowing hard, Emma looked across at them both and burst into tears.

Lana watched as her mother rushed to her side, 'Emma Jane, why on earth are you crying?'

Placing her thumb to her lips, Emma was about to bite her nail when Lana practically dived on top of her.

'Ahem... oh no you don't. It took me ages to get you to agree to have that nail art; you're not going to bite it all off now. It took hours to do,' she said, smiling and trying to make light of the situation.

Emma hesitated and put her hands down by her side.

'What is it?' her mum asked again.

'It's just... it's just, how are we going to get there?'

Lana and Audrey both realised the problem at the same time. They sighed together, their shoulders drooping.

'No, Emma. I've had enough of this. You can't let your fear of the water stop you from experiencing something so, so awesome. You have to get over it already.'

Emma dropped her head to one side and scowled at Lana, her mouth forming a sharp pout, 'And this is from the girl who would never go anywhere near the bottom of the garden because of the cliff edge or Carlton Point until... until...'

Lana's eyes grew wide, and she tried to shake her head without her mum seeing.

'What are you talking about? Until when? Until what?'

Lana managed a little chuckle before swallowing hard.

'I... I went up to Carlton Point yesterday, on my own,' she managed to utter.

'Oh, but that's... well that's... I don't know what to say, Lana. That's just incredible. Well done,' she said as she leaned forward and hugged her daughter tightly.

Emma's head bowed before she shook it. 'But that's not the same. Lana's fear was never quite as bad as mine.'

'Nonsense Emma Jane,' said Audrey, 'You two were always as bad as each other. You both have, had, have, oh whatever, such an... an irrational fear...'

'Exactly, Mum. Irrational fears. And if I can get over mine, then surely Emma can get over hers and I won't let a silly thing like fear of the sea stop me from going to London,' she said as she stood up with her hands on her hips. 'Come on, Em. It's London. It's only a few hours by boat. You'll be completely safe, and I'll be with you. Look...' she said as she approached her sister's bed, crouched down and took Emma's hand, 'I'm sorry for being so pushy, but this is such an amazing opportunity, Sis. Let's do it together. Please?' she asked.

Looking from her sister and back to her mother, she realised there was nothing she could do. She had to do it. Not just for Lana but herself. If Lana could get over her fear, then she would try her hardest to do the same.

'Okay, I'll do it,' she whispered as Lana jumped up and cartwheeled onto her bed.

Audrey shook her head and laughed out loud.

'Scott is going to be so jealous,' giggled Lana.

❧ 10 ❧

Emma, Lana and Scott stood at one side of the newly dug grave, waiting patiently while Father Hawkins said a few words as Mr Grimshaw was laid to rest. Quite a few people had turned up to the funeral, even though nobody had known him that well. He had no family. An only child, his parents had passed on many years before, he had never married, and he appeared to have no close friends. Both Audrey and Patrick were busy working, so the girls decided to attend the funeral on their behalf. After all, it was the least they could do, considering he had died right in front of them.

'Why are we here?' whispered Scott, as Emma stepped forward to drop a couple of large daisies onto the earth as the hole in the ground was slowly covered.

'Shhh,' said Lana as she frowned at him, 'We were there when he died, Scott. We're just paying our respects,' she said sensibly.

Scott looked at her as if she'd gone mad. 'We didn't even know the old man.'

Emma turned and scowled at her best friend, and as she did so, she thought she spotted a movement behind a large tree in the distance.

Following her gaze, Lana and Scott both turned to see what had caught her attention.

'What is it?' asked Lana.

'Nothing, I just thought I saw someone watching us. It's probably just the shadow of the tree.'

'Thank you for coming, Emma, Lana, Scott,' said Father Hawkins with a nod before he turned back to the others as they all headed out of the churchyard.

'Can we get out of here now?' asked Scott, as Emma crouched down to whisper goodbye to Mr Grimshaw.

'Okay, okay,' she said as she stood up and turned, linking her arms through his and Lana's.

'Did you see that?' Lana asked, squinting behind her.

'What?' asked Emma.

'I could have sworn I saw someone hiding over there.'

The three unlinked arms as Lana broke free and walked quickly towards the huge overgrown tree. She saw a person bolt, so she sped up, running across the grass, followed by Emma and Scott in pursuit across the graveyard.

But the far end of the graveyard gave way to a long drop to the sea below. Without even a moment's thought, Lana launched herself off the highest point.

'Lana!' cried Scott as he fell to the floor close to the edge with his arms outstretched. But as he looked down, expecting to see a horrifying sight, he was greeted by Lana running steadfast across the beach towards the shore.

'What the...? How the...? Lana?' he whispered.

Emma stood by his side, not saying a word.

'You knew? You knew she could... she could jump like that?'

Emma nodded, 'I'll let her tell you all about it. But for now, come on, we'll have to climb down the old path over there,' she said, as she grabbed his arm and pulled him back up to his feet, before dragging him towards the edge.

The two ran as fast as they could, tumbling down, their backsides getting covered in sandy dirt and moss as they reached the bottom of the cliff.

'Which way did she go?' said Scott breathlessly.

Emma looked one way and then the other, but she couldn't see Lana anywhere.

'Lana?' she yelled.

'Over here,' came a reply from the other side of a huge boulder that stood blocking access from the beach.

Emma looked on as Scott took off his shoes and waded into the water around the rock until he'd vanished from sight.

When he popped his head back around to see what she was doing, he suddenly realised.

'Sorry', he mouthed, 'Do you want me to carry you?'.

Afraid of stepping foot anywhere near the water, she shook her head, 'I'll... I'll wait here,' she said as she kicked at the sand beneath her feet.

He nodded and disappeared again.

On the other side of the boulder, Scott followed Lana's footprints towards a well-covered cave, 'Lana?' he asked as he peered into the darkness.

'I'm right here, Scott,' she said quietly.

'I can't see a thing. Look, what's going on? Can you come out?'

'Erm, just give me a minute.'

Scott stepped outside and looked around, taking a deep breath, inhaling the fresh salty air and waited.

After a few minutes, Lana appeared looking confused. She kept glancing over her shoulder as if someone was following her.

'What's going on, Lana?' he asked.

'I found him hiding in the cave,' she said with a nod behind her.

'Found who?'

'Him,' she said, rolling her eyes upwards.

'Erm... I hate to break this to you, Lana, but there's nobody here but you and me.'

Lana laughed, 'You're so funny, Scott,' she chuckled until she noticed his expression.

With her eyebrows raised, she slowly turned towards the young man who hovered behind her and gulped loudly.

'Let's just go back to Emma and maybe everything will be explained then.'

Tutting, Scott shook his head as the two of them walked silently back towards the rock boulder.

'Lana? Scott?' said the voice from the other side.

'It's okay, Sis. We're here. We're coming back over now.'

Emma sat on the beach some distance from the shore, with her knees under her chin and her arms wrapped around herself.

As they waded through the water back towards her, Emma watched as the two of them looked at each other suspiciously.

'Well? Did you find whoever it was?'

Sharing a strange look, Scott said no, and Lana said yes.

'Well, which is it? What on earth are you two talking about?'

'I did find someone, Sis... but Scott can't see him.'

Emma slowly stood up, brushing dry sand from her black jeans and grey converse.

'It's... it's the boy from the hospital.'

'But... but... he's dead.'

'I know,' whispered Lana as the hair on the back of Emma's neck stood on end.

'He... he told me that his name is... Joe, Josiah. Josiah Grimshaw.'

'It's the most bizarre thing I've ever heard,' said Audrey to her husband later that night. 'Apparently, his body has just vanished from the morgue. But not just that, all his medical charts have gone too. It's as if he never even existed.'

Patrick was pacing up and down the living room; occasionally, his footsteps would stop as he spoke. 'His file has disappeared from the station too. I can't explain it. Some of the guys are saying perhaps we should just forget about him.'

'Well, perhaps it's a sign, love. Maybe we should just forget...'

Lana and Emma were sat at the top of the stairs listening in to their parents' conversation. It had been the strangest day of their lives, well, perhaps the second most bizarre after Lana's tattoo incident. Josiah had spoken to Lana and explained that it was really him, Josiah Grimshaw, the old man. When he waded into the sea during the storm, he was knocked out by a strong wave. Waking up on the beach the next morning, he was a young man.

'I thought I was dead. I opened my eyes, and there she was, my Emelia. I thought she must be an angel, come to take me with her to heaven,' Joe had explained on the beach earlier while Scott and Emma looked at each other with worried looks in their eyes as they watched Lana have a conversation with herself. Well, it had certainly looked that way to them.

'And then I remember being in the hospital in two different

rooms. I can't explain what happened. All I remember is that girl, who I thought was Emelia, was there. She held my hand. But then I realised it wasn't her. They just looked a little similar, that's all. The next thing I know, I'm in the other room, I felt so terrible, so old. And then when I woke up again, I couldn't feel anything. I just felt – I don't know, surreal, I guess. I felt like I was floating. That's when I realised I must be dead. I went home and saw my reflection in the mirror, and I couldn't believe my eyes. I was young again. It was me, Joe. Not an old man, not Josiah as everyone else called me. But Joe, that's what she called me. I wandered around town for a while, hovering, but no-one could see me. When I returned home, that's when you two came to my house, and I realised you could see me. It spooked me, it did.'

'It spooked you? But you're the dead guy, Joe,' Lana had chuckled as she became more and more at ease with him.

He'd smiled at her before continuing, 'That's why I ran; because it scared me. But then I became curious why you could see me and no-one else could. So I went to the graveyard to watch my funeral. Thank you for coming, all of you. I was touched,' he said as he put his hand to his heart and smiled at her before turning to the others. 'Please tell them how much it meant to me.'

'I will,' Lana said as she looked over her shoulder to Scott and Emma who continued to be deathly quiet. She smiled.

When she turned back to Joe, he'd gone.

The three of them stayed on the beach for a couple more hours, Lana explaining what she'd been told before she gained the courage to tell Scott what had happened to her at Carlton Point.

'Wow,' he'd said as she'd lifted her top slightly and revealed the beautiful tattoo that adorned her lower back.

'It says Provehito In Altum. Launch forward into the deep, but we've no idea what it means.'

'Maybe it's got something to do with the fact that you can now launch yourself from major heights or something?' Scott suggested.

The girls both nodded their heads, 'You might be onto something there. It kind of makes sense, doesn't it?' said Emma.

'But what is all this about? The tattoo, Carlton Point, seeing dead people?' asked Scott as he threw pebbles across the sand in front of them.

'Whoa hang on a minute, I've only seen one dead person. I certainly don't want to be seeing any more, thank you very much,' Lana said, waving her hands above her head. 'No way, no thanks.'

Suddenly the sound of distant thunder made Emma jump.

'Oh God, I'd not even noticed the clouds coming in. It looks like we're in for another storm. I'm outta here,' she said as she stood up and immediately began walking towards the long windy path that would lead them back up to the churchyard where they'd left their bikes.

'Hang on, wait up!' Yelled Scott and Lana who followed behind her. Just as they caught up, a few spots of rain began to fall, and Emma shivered as she looked up towards the sky. It was getting darker and darker, the clouds moving overhead far too fast for her liking.

As they scrambled up the pathway, Emma ran across the grass as fast as she could until she reached her bike. But the rain, which had started lightly, was threatening to unleash its force on top of them. Scott and Lana shared a familiar look.

'Let's head for the church,' Scott suggested, 'and wait out the storm'.

So for the next hour and a half, Emma sat huddled in between her best friend and her sister, inside the cold little church, listening to the rain beat down on the slate roof as the thunder clapped overhead. Attempting to take her mind off her fear, the others talked about the bizarre events that had been happening.

One of the things that Emma loved about the church was that when the sun did shine, the light that came through the stained glass windows was beautiful. She was so pleased therefore when the clouds finally moved on from overhead, heading back out to to the North Sea, and the church was suddenly lit up by all kinds of gorgeous colours and patterns.

Her face lit up along with it as she stood and stretched her legs, turning to Scott and Lana with a smile. Neither of them said a word; they just followed her to the open door and looked out at the most spectacular rainbow that stood proudly across the island.

Emma took a deep breath. Even though she was frightened of the heavy rain, she appreciated what was left behind - a scent of freshness filled the air and a slight chill carried across the ground.

'Come on, let's head home,' Lana said as she gently pushed her sister out into the fresh air.

They climbed onto their bikes, sheltered from the water in the entrance to the church and pushed themselves away, waving to Father Hawkins who had been solemnly walking around the church grounds under a large umbrella which he closed as they disappeared out of sight.

What they didn't see was Joe, standing in the distance beside his freshly laid grave, looking out across the sea sadly.

❧ 12 ❧

It was time.

Emma was sweating profusely, the hairs on the back of her neck stood on end, and nausea rolled around in her stomach, threatening to erupt at any moment. Audrey had done everything she possibly could to try and calm her stomach down, but nothing had worked, not even the ginger tea. Emma would simply have to put up with it. She would have to face her most significant fear head-on.

They sat at the port, waiting for the ferry that would take them directly into London. On it was their father's friend and former colleague, Declan Alexander. Emma and Lana would be entirely in his care for the next few weeks, and they had no idea what to expect. They knew nothing about him, other than that he and Patrick worked in the police force together a few years ago. Their parents hadn't even told them what they would be doing for work experience.

'We'll leave it up to Declan to explain when you get there,' they'd said mysteriously.

Lana glanced across at her sister as they sat with Scott sipping a hot cup of tea inside the little terminal building, while Patrick and Audrey took Lucy and Greg for ice cream.

'I still can't believe you're leaving me to go to London while I stay here and do work experience on my own,' sulked Scott.

Lana was beaming, 'I know! Isn't it awesome?' she laughed.

He raised his eyebrows.

'Well, at least you're going to be doing something fun. It's not like you're going to be working in your parents' shop.'

'Fun? I'm going to be working on the Nutters' farm. How is that fun?'

'Aww come on Scott, you love animals,' Lana said, jabbing him on his shoulder, 'Besides, Charlie and Keira are lovely. They'll go easy on you.'

Charlie and Keira Nutter ran the island's largest organic farm.

'Yeah, they might go easy on me, but I doubt Lottie will,' he said blushing slightly.

Suddenly, Emma stood up, her hands covering her mouth, and she rushed towards the toilets.

Scott raised his eyebrows again, 'That's the third time she's thrown up since we've been here.'

'I know, I'm sure she'll be all right,' said Lana a little unconvincingly, 'I'd better go and check.'

In the bathroom, Emma was heaving inside one of three little cubicles.

Lana opened the door to the one next door, stood on the toilet and peered over to look at her sister.

'Are you okay, Sis?' she whispered. Emma responded with a groan before she flushed the loo, grabbed a handful of toilet paper, wiped her mouth and put the toilet seat down so she could sit.

'No!' yelled Lana, making Emma stop abruptly, mid-crouch. 'Don't sit on it. It's a public toilet. It's disgusting.'

'I don't care,' groaned Emma as she continued to crouch before her black jeans made contact with the toilet seat cover.

Lana's face screwed up in disgust and she silently gagged. 'Come on, Sis. Come on out of here. We're not going to see Scott for a few weeks, don't you want to spend our last half-hour with him?'

'Of course I do, but I feel so sick Lana...'

'Nonsense. This is completely and utterly psychological, Em. You're making your body sick because of this irrational fear you've got going on. You need to control it, and you won't feel sick again.'

'Tell her to go out and get some fresh air,' said a familiar voice from the third cubicle.

'Yeah, I tried that earlier, but she wouldn't go out,' replied Lana.

'Huh? What are you talking about?' asked Emma.

'Oh, it's Joe. He says you should go outside and get some fresh air.'

'Joe? Is Joe in here? These are the ladies toilets. Tell him to get out.'

'He can hear you, Emma. Besides, I think he's gone,' said Lana as she hopped down from the toilet and checked that there was nothing gross on the bottom of her shoes. Content that they were as clean as they could be, she pulled open the cubicle door and looked down at her sister.

'Come on you; Joe has a point, let's go outside. It'll make you feel better. Being stuck in a public loo certainly isn't going to. In fact, it's making me feel nauseous. Come here,' she said as she pulled her to the sink, grabbed a load of paper and used it to cover the tap before she turned it on and gently dabbed Emma's fore-head with some cold water.

'Ooh that's nice,' she said with her first smile that day. 'Thanks, Sis. I'm sorry for being like this. I wish I could help it, but I don't think I can. But don't worry, I'll do it. Just bear with me, okay?'

Lana was touched and smiled, 'I knew you could do it.'

The sound of an approaching ferry horn welcomed them as they stepped outside with Scott in tow. Emma breathed in deeply, trying to ignore the smells coming from the sea, focussing instead on the fresh air.

'It's here, girls,' said Patrick as the rest of the family made their way towards them. 'How are you feeling? Do you think you'll be all right, love?'

Emma nodded at her father and smiled weakly as he gently ruffled her hair like she was a child. She rolled her eyes at him, and he laughed. 'Oh look, there's Declan,' he said as he pointed towards a very handsome guy who was waving energetically at them from the approaching boat. A boat that appeared to be rather small for a ferry, thought Emma as she gulped, trying to calm her nerves.

As it docked, the family watched as just two cars drove off the ramp and onto the island. Over the tannoy came the announcement that the ferry would be leaving in precisely 30 minutes.

Declan walked confidently towards them with the biggest grin plastered across his face.

'Patrick, my man!' he said, making the kids giggle, 'Great to see you, mate. How have you been?'

'Really good, look at you, you've barely aged at all. That London air is still doing you some good,' Patrick said after they'd hugged each other.

'Wow, Audrey, you look exactly the same as last time I saw you. You look like an angel,' he said as he leaned forward and kissed her on her cheek.

'And you, Mister... you must be Greg. We've never met, but I'd have known you anywhere. You're a chip off the old block, you are,' he said as he shook Greg's hand, 'and what a mighty grip you've got there,' Greg's chest visibly rose as he enjoyed the compliment.

'And this little lady is obviously Lucy Jo. Well, Miss Lucy Jo, you look just like a little angel with them golden curls. You're going to be a real heart breaker, you are, aren't you?'

Lucy giggled and blushed, nodding. The rest of the family burst out laughing.

'Well at least she knows she is,' chuckled Audrey.

Finally, Declan turned to the two elder girls and held out his hand, shaking Lana's hand first before moving over to Emma's. 'Lana Beth and Emma Jane. It's an honour to meet you both finally. Your Dad's told me a lot about you, and I have to say, me and Saleena are certainly looking forward to the next couple of weeks. I hope you are too?'

Lana nodded with a huge grin, while a familiar nauseous feeling overcame Emma and she put her hand over her mouth.

Declan glanced across at Patrick who said, 'Emma's the one with the fear of water,' just as her face began to change colour, again.

'Oh right,' he replied and stepped towards her. Moving her hand away from her face, she looked up at him.

'Look at me, Emma. Focus on me, don't think about the nausea, just concentrate on something else, anything else. Think about a real nice memory, that's it; keep thinking until you've got that memory stuck firmly in your mind.'

Lana smirked at Scott who was trying not to laugh.

'That's it, have you got it. Are you visualising it now?'

Emma nodded as she thought about her 15th birthday when she'd been given a brand new road bike in matt black, with purple tape on the handgrips and purple tyres. She remembered the first time she'd gone out on it, on her own, cycling down to the nearest wind turbine, where she'd stopped and sat for ages, just admiring her new bike with the whooshing sounds constantly whirring behind her. She sighed happily at the thought.

'Now, pinch your thumb and your forefinger together, like this. Do this whenever you start to feel dodgy again, okay, and it will pass. Your mind will be filled with thoughts of that good memory instead. How do you feel now?'

Emma's face changed, the nausea practically gone. She broke out into a grin, 'How did you do that? That's amazing,' she said in awe as Patrick and Audrey shared a smile over her shoulder.

'It's just a simple mind trick, that's all, but it works. Keep on doing it,' he said with a grin. 'Now, have we got time for a cuppa together before we're on our way? Oh, sorry mate, nearly forgot to say hello to you,' he said as he clapped his hand on Scott's back, almost knocking him over.

'This is Scott,' said Lana, 'he's our best friend.'

'Well, good to meet you, Scott. Don't worry; I'll take good care of them while they're away.'

Scott blushed just ever so slightly as the group walked back towards the café.

Twenty minutes later, Declan was stood holding both girls hold-alls as they said goodbye.

'Oh! I almost forgot,' said Audrey as she tucked her hands into her large handbag. 'Now, I know we've always said you don't need mobile phones on the island but...'

Lana and Emma both beamed at their mother as she presented each of them with a phone.

'... in London, it's another matter altogether. If you need us, we're just a phone call away. I've already put all our numbers, including Scott's, in them for you,' she said as Lana took her phone with the bright pink cover and hugged Audrey tightly. Moving to her father, she turned and hugged him tightly too as Emma put her dark purple phone in her handbag before following suit.

'I'm going to miss you girls so much,' whispered Audrey, 'you're growing up so fast. It won't be long now until you're leaving us altogether...' she said, wiping away a tear from her cheek.

'She's right, you know. Work experience now, weddings tomorrow...' Patrick added with a chuckle.

'Erm, I don't think so, Dad,' laughed Lana as she and Emma gave Greg and Lucy a quick hug before following Declan onto the boat.

'Don't forget to bring us a present back!' yelled Lucy with a grin as she waved frantically.

'Be careful, girls. Look after them, Declan!'

Declan turned, smiled and waved. 'I'll guard 'em with my life, Audrey. I promise you that. See you in a few weeks.'

As the boat chugged into motion, the two girls stood alongside their temporary guardian as they waved. Suddenly, Emma looked down into the churning waters below, and her fear came back with a vengeance.

Over the sound of the engine, Declan shouted, 'Finger and thumb, Emma, finger and thumb.'

❧ 13 ❧

They'd been travelling for four hours, and although Emma had managed to sleep through much of it (thanks to Declan's mind tricks), she woke with a start when she heard a loud horn in the vicinity.

She turned and found Declan reading a newspaper to one side of her while Lana sat on the other. She was by the window, utterly mesmerised by all that was happening along the Thames.

A sudden urge to throw up made Emma jump up, 'Erm, just need some fresh air,' she said.

'Do you want me to come with you?' asked Lana, but her sister shook her head.

'No, I'll be fine. Thumb and forefinger, thumb and forefinger,' she muttered over and over as she walked away. She opened the door that led outside, and a blast of cold air immediately made her feel a tad better. Finding a seat at the back of the boat, she sat down and breathed deeply, pushing her thumb and forefinger together so hard that her fingers turned white.

She forced herself to look up from the floor at the water that surrounded the small ferry boat. Thumb and forefinger, thumb and forefinger, she repeated in her head while she tried to think happy thoughts. But something was preventing her. It was as if a brick wall had been erected between the water and her pleasant thoughts. Slowly she felt the fear seep further into her bones, creeping from the soles of her feet right through her stomach to the top of her head. A wave of nausea came with it, and she had no choice but to rush to the side of the boat, where she held on for dear life and vomited with her eyes tightly closed.

Forcing herself to open them slowly, she watched the water as it churned up and down, around and around by the slow chugging of the ferry. And that's when a voice entered her head and told her to jump.

'What the...,' she whispered, 'I'm not going to jump.'

But the voice had different ideas, and soon Emma found herself sneaking a look around her to make sure no-one was watching as she climbed over the handrail.

Her face was as white as a sheet, but her body didn't seem to care as she threw herself from the boat, into the cold waters of the Thames estuary.

Hitting the cold water winded her. Breathing was almost impossible, and she found she could no longer move her body as she began to sink further and further down below the surface. With her eyes wide open in terror, she watched as the boat continued without her. Powerless to do anything, she simply watched the murky water around her, waiting for her terrible fate. Death by drowning. Her biggest fear. One that she was sure was about to come true.

Nobody would know until it was too late. She had made sure no-one was watching as she threw herself in. Although death beck-oned, confusion reigned in her head. Why had she done it? Why?

Suddenly, something began happening to her body, and she felt a newfound strength fill her lungs, almost as if she could breathe underwater without actually inhaling it. Her arms and legs began to move gracefully through the water, and she swam along the bottom of the estuary. She felt as though a great weight lifted from her and she laughed beneath the water, somersaulting and dancing like a water baby.

A strange itchiness began in her feet, slowly making its way to her ankles. Emma bent over and lifted the bottom of her jeans, only to find something black winding its way up her legs. A momentary shock of fear pulsed through her and she catapulted herself from the bottom of the Thames upwards until she broke the surface of the water. Scanning the numerous vessels that sailed around her, she concentrated all her efforts on finding her ferry boat.

When she spotted it in the distance, she dived back under the water and swam with such speed that when she surfaced again, she realised she had swum much too far. Laughing, momentarily forgetting about the strange thing climbing her body, she reversed, swimming back towards it. Swimming alongside, she started to think about how she was going to get back on board, but before she could give it another thought, her body threw itself upwards, and she landed, feet first, exactly where she had started, on the deck of the boat.

Sitting back down, she closed her eyes for a minute. 'I'm dreaming. None of that really happened to me,' she told herself. But when she opened her eyes, she wasn't alone. Sitting beside her was none other than the ghost of Josiah Grimshaw.

She closed her eyes again, took a deep breath and re-opened one and then the other. He was still there. The young man she'd seen die in hospital.

'H...ello Joe,' she whispered.

His face lit up as he turned to look at her. 'You can see me? You can see me now?'

Slowly she nodded.

'But why? You couldn't see me earlier on. I've been on the boat with you and Lana all day.'

Gulping, she scrutinised him, 'You have?'

'I...I... just came back outside when I saw you.... jump out of the water.'

'You did?'

He nodded.

'So it did happen,' she squealed, turning to him and attempting to hug him, but her arms went right through him, and she almost tumbled to the floor.

'Sorry,' he said, 'but if it hadn't happened, surely you wouldn't be soaked to the skin. Aren't you cold? You must be freezing.'

As Emma's teeth began to chatter, she realised that she was a bit chilly and her clothes were sopping wet. Now what? She thought. I can't very well go inside like this, Declan will go mad.

'Erm, Joe?'

'Yes, Emma?'

'Can you do me a favour?'

Ten minutes later, Emma had managed to creep back inside without Declan noticing her. Lana met her in the toilets.

'What's going on?' She said, 'For some reason, Joe told me to bring your bag into the toilets... Oh My God, you're soaked. What happened? Jeese Emma, are you all right? You look like you've been for a swim. Hang on a minute, you look amazing, how is that possible? For the past five days, you looked like you were about to die and now you look like, like...'

'Like what, Lana?' laughed Emma.

'Like a new woman.'

'I feel exactly like that, Lana, I feel like a new woman. My fear, it's gone. It's completely and utterly gone!' she exclaimed as she took off her wet jeans and wrung them out over the sink.

Lana gasped.

'What?'

Pointing, Emma slowly looked down. She'd forgotten about the black thing in the water. She, too, gasped when she saw that a tattoo-like thing was still winding itself up her legs. Soon it had reached her belly. A sudden pain made her bend over, and she winced, holding her stomach tight.

'Oh, God... that's agonising.'

Lana watched in shock as the tattoo then began winding itself around Emma's back, finally stopping in exactly the same spot that her tattoo had. Like hers, it hugged the curvature of her spine. Emma stood up as the pain eased. 'Wh... what does it say? Does it say Provehito In Altum? Look, Lana, look.'

Leaning down, Lana read the words aloud, 'Lux In Tenebris Lucet,' she said. 'And it's the same tattoo as mine with the eye and the wings; it's just the words that are different.'

'But what does it mean?'

'I haven't got a clue, Em, I'm no Latin expert. Maybe Declan will know?'

'No! We can't ask him?'

'Why not? It's not like he'll have any idea why we're asking.'

'I suppose not.'

A voice came from inside one of the cubicles, 'it means light shines in the darkness.'

'Josiah Grimshaw... this is the ladies toilets, what have I told you about that. It's creepy.'

'Sorry, I didn't see you get undressed, honestly. I've been behind the closed door the whole time.'

Lana suppressed a laugh as she looked at her sister, 'So what does that mean? Light shines in the darkness?'

Emma shrugged as she put a black sweater on over her purple jeans, 'I don't know. I don't know what any of it means. I've just been for a swim in the Thames, Lana, the Thames! I could almost breathe under the water, and I swam like a... like a dolphin or something. It was amazing. But I have no idea what it all means. Even though I feel so totally exhilarated, all of this is scaring the living daylights out of me. What are we going to do?'

Lana raised her eyebrows and sighed, 'There's nothing we can do. Not at the moment anyway. We're in London for the next few weeks, and we will just have to get on with our work experience. We can figure everything out when we get home, okay?' She said as she hugged her sister, 'I'm so glad it's happened to you too, Em. Now we're even more like true sisters.'

The girls smiled at each other as they walked out of the toilets carrying Emma's bag, complete with sopping wet clothes inside.

$\maltese$ 14 $\maltese$

Declan didn't say a word when they returned to take a seat next to him. Instead, he just looked up at them and grinned before pointing out the window.

Lana gasped at the sight unfolding in front of her. It was breathtaking. It was the Thames Barrier.

'Wow,' she muttered, her eyes wide in amazement, 'It's amazing. I can't believe we're actually here.'

'It is a great city,' said Declan, 'I think the three of you'll find it a real eye-opener.'

'Don't you mean the two of us?' asked Emma.

Declan's eyes shot wide open before he laughed, 'That's what I said, wasn't it?'

'No... you said the three of us.'

'Must have been a slip of the tongue,' he winked.

Lana glanced at her sister, her eyebrows raised before she shrugged casually and continued to stare out the window.

'It was built to stop London from being flooded by storm surges and particularly high tides,' said Declan.

'It was the storm, the great storm that influenced its creation,' whispered Joe as he seemed to shiver.

Lana and Emma tried hard to ignore him.

'Has it ever been used?' asked Lana.

'Oh yeah, it's been closed loads of times,' answered Declan.

'When was the most recent?'

'This year, they closed it for the Queen's Diamond Jubilee pageant.'

'Really? How come?' asked Emma.

'Oh, not because of anything serious that happened. It was to reduce the flow of the river due to the number of boats that took part.'

'Did you see it, did you take part?' Emma asked.

Declan laughed, 'I saw it, yeah, but I didn't take part. Not exactly.'

'What do you mean, not exactly?'

Declan just shook his head, 'You ask a lot of questions, Emma. Just enjoy the views,' he said, pointing outside again.

From then on, they all sat quietly, as they passed landmark after landmark.

Even Josiah's mouth stayed open as he took in the sights to the city. A city he'd never visited, not as a young man nor an old one. He spent his entire life on Andilyse Island.

Emma was tempted to close his mouth for him but thought better of it while Declan was so close. Plus, her fingers would probably go right through him anyway.

Declan chuckled to himself.

Turning to see what was so funny, Emma thought she noticed him look away from her suddenly. Was he pretending to read the newspaper?

'This is it, girls. This is where we get off,' said Declan as he folded his newspaper and stood up. 'Are you ready for your first adventure in London?'.

The girls grinned and nodded as they followed him off the ferry. Lana kept tripping up because she kept focussing on the views surrounding her.

'Watch where you're going, Lana,' tutted Emma as Declan took their largest hold-alls off them.

'We have a little bit of a walk so I'll carry these for you. Just follow me,' he said, and then he was off, walking so quickly that they had difficulty keeping up.

Emma had to keep grabbing Lana's arm to stop her from being

too distracted as they rushed on behind him, occasionally bumping into passers-by.

With London bridge now far in the distance and the London Eye on the other side of the Thames pulling her in, Lana's stomach fluttered with butterflies. Breathing deeply, she took in the sweet scent of candy floss and smiled. She was on cloud nine. For years she'd dreamed of this moment, and now she was here. She was really here. She happily sighed as Emma dragged her out of her daydreams.

'We're going to lose him if you don't snap out of it. Come on,' she said sharply.

'Oh, for goodness sake, let me enjoy the moment. We're not going to lose him. He's right there, erm....'

'Oh, great. See? Now look what you've done,' snapped Emma as she scoured the crowds trying to spot the familiar well-built man with his cropped brown hair and slightly broken nose.

'We've lost him,' wailed Emma just as a firm hand squeezed her shoulder reassuringly. She turned to see Declan grinning at her.

'Sorry girls, I just thought you might like some of this,' he said smiling as he presented them both with candy floss on a stick, bought from a vendor who was now pushing his candy floss cart across the road.

'Aww thanks, Declan,' said Lana with a massive grin.

Emma blushed and took it reluctantly.

'Oh, it's okay if you don't like it, Emma. Not got a sweet tooth like your sister, then?'

Still blushing, Emma shook her head as Declan took the candy floss back. Turning, he scanned the crowd and spotted a young boy.

'Harry!' he yelled at a nearby youngster who was wandering across the road. Although the boy's clothes looked a bit old and dirty, he seemed happy enough, even more so when he noticed who was calling him. In fact, his face lit up as he ran towards them.

'Afternoon, Dec.'

'Afternoon, sonny boy. Do you like candy floss?'

Harry drooled and nodded, wiping his mouth with the back of his hand as Declan handed him the stick with the large fluffy pink stuff.

'Here you go then, enjoy it! And stay out of trouble, all right?'

The boy nodded, grinning before he ran away.

'Sorry about that,' said Emma, 'I don't really like sugar.'

'That's quite all right. You made Harry's day anyway,' he said with a warm smile. 'Here, come on, we're nearly there,' he said, directing them to follow him.

After they'd walked for another five minutes, Lana and Emma exchanged an odd look as they both realised they'd gone round in a circle. But before they had the chance to say anything, Declan turned to them and started laughing. His laughter was infectious, and soon, the girls were giggling alongside him as he walked back towards Westminster Pier.

'What are we doing?' giggled Lana.

'I just figured you'd need a bit of exercise after being on the ferry for so long. Plus, I knew you'd want to get a little look at London before you get settled in. Here we are, home sweet home.'

Lana looked around before standing, arms down, totally confused.

'Erm, where exactly is home sweet home?' she said as Emma just watched, waiting.

'Right here,' said a beautiful Asian woman who stepped off a large houseboat directly in front of them.

'Hey, Sweetheart. You miss me?' Declan said as he leaned forward, put their bags down, and gave the woman a long kiss and a gentle hug.

'Always,' she smiled before she turned to them with the kindest smile they'd ever seen.

'Girls, this is Saleena.'

Saleena was like no-one Lana or Emma had ever seen. Her beauty was breathtaking, with her long luscious dark chocolate coloured hair with caramel strands that seemed to bounce in the light breeze. Her eyes were the colour of jade, so crystal clear that you could almost see right into her soul. Perfectly formed pink full lips and high cheekbones finished off her look to utter perfection. Saleena looked just like an angel.

Smiling softly, she hugged each girl tenderly.

'It is such a pleasure to meet you both finally. I have heard a lot about you. I do hope you have surpassed your fear of the water, my dear Emma Jane?' she enquired.

'Just Emma,' she replied, almost shyly, 'and yes, I honestly think that I have.'

'I am delighted to hear of it,' she said as she turned to Declan who winked surreptitiously at her.

'Do come aboard. This is to be your home for the next couple of weeks. We had to keep it a secret, of course. Otherwise you might not have come had you known,' she said to Emma who giggled as they stepped onto the boat and followed Saleena indoors.

Lana was uncharacteristically quiet.

'Are you all right, my dear?' Saleena asked, 'I understand you are normally the chatty one?' she smiled.

Glancing around at her surroundings, Lana finally closed her mouth. 'Erm, yeah, yes I am,' she chuckled, 'I'm just so, so... you know, blown away by it all,' she said as she pointed to the boat's interior which wasn't what she had been expecting at all.

From the outside, the boat had been well hidden, and even when they'd stepped aboard, it didn't look too special, but the moment the door opened, and they saw inside, it was like stepping through the looking glass.

Brightly coloured fabrics of satins, silks and velvets adorned the space which was far bigger than the eye could have imagined. Golden Asian inspired paintings hung from the walls, while several large sofas covered in pretty intricately patterned scatter cushions sat around the room. It even smelled divine, both sweet and spicy notes caressed their noses and tempted their taste buds.

Saleena walked through the living area towards the kitchen space, where she removed the lid from a pan and very lovingly stirred it, causing more aromas to fill the air. Emma's stomach grumbled loudly, and she looked at Declan before her face began to colour.

Smiling, he picked up their bags and gestured for them to follow him. 'Come on, you can put all your stuff away, and then we can have something to eat. I'm starving too.'

Saleena smiled as they walked past, 'Give me fifteen minutes and the food will be ready.'

Pushing open the door to the back of the boat, Emma gasped at the size of the room that greeted them. 'How is it possible? This boat looks so small from the outside and then, this! It's like the Tardis,' she exclaimed at the room which contained two large single beds, a large wardrobe and a dressing table. One bed was covered in a brightly coloured funky bedspread while the other in a more sombre black and purple cover that had little skulls and crossbones on its edges.

Emma smiled, 'How did you know?' she asked as Declan laughed and shrugged his shoulders.

'Just make yourselves at home. We'll give you a shout when the food is ready,' he said as he slowly stepped back and closed the door behind him.

As soon as he'd gone, the girls looked at each other silently before leaping up and screeching loudly, jumping up and down happily.

Josiah sat quietly on the floor in the corner, watching and smiling.

$$\maltese \quad 15 \quad \maltese$$

After they'd eaten a meal of delicious Indian food, Declan gave the girls a map of London and let them go off and explore by themselves.

'I know you're probably dying to get out and have a good look around. Just be careful. Here's my number in case you get lost or if you need anything,' he said, handing them a card that Emma had tucked into her pocket without even glancing at it.

Saleena stepped off the boat with them and pointed out the general direction they should head.

'Please try not to go too far. Just stay safe,' she said as she hugged them both before disappearing back indoors.

'Right, where shall we go first?' asked Emma as she turned the map around and began inspecting it closely.

'Big Ben, I wanna see Big Ben,' giggled Lana as she hooked her arm into her sister's and pulled her away from the water's edge.

'But it's right there,' said Emma with a sigh. 'We're practically there already.'

'I know that,' she tutted, 'but I just wanna get right up close, c'mon.'

The girls exited the pier and headed across the road where the world-renowned clock stood magnificently in all its glory.

'I wanna hear it,' yelled Lana above the traffic noise.

'But, I don't think that's going to happen for another thirty-five minutes,' moaned Emma, 'I want to go for a walk. We'll still hear it wherever we are.'

'Okay. Let's just walk slowly and not go too far then. How about we cross the bridge to the Eye?'

'No, let's save that for another day and just wander around here, the Houses of Parliament are just there, look... and Westminster Abbey over there. There's plenty to keep us busy.'

Lana stopped abruptly and crossed her arms, almost dropping the map in her hand, looking at her sister as if she was mad, 'We come all the way to London, and you want to look at the boring Houses of Parliament? After Big Ben, I wanna see Trafalgar Square and then head down to the greatest shopping streets in the world,' she huffed.

Emma tried not to laugh. 'We come all the way to London, and all you want to do is go shopping?'

'Well... yeah. It's not like we ever had much choice back home, is it? Thank God for the Internet is all I can say.'

Shaking her head, Emma leaned back against the wall overlooking the Thames and chuckled, 'I guess so. But we've got a couple of weeks. I know we're doing work experience most days, but we'll have the evenings and weekends free. Can't we just take in some of the sights first? Please?'

Big Ben surprised them by chiming even earlier than they thought it would while they were wandering around the outskirts of the Palace of Westminster, the home of the Houses of Parliament and even Lana was stunned by its impressive architecture.

So deep in concentration were they, that when the bells did begin to chime (after just fifteen minutes), they both jumped and nervously giggled while they stood and looked across at it in admiration.

'Boo!' came a voice behind them, making them both jump again.

Turning, Lana and Emma were face-to-face with the ghost of Joe, who had disappeared during lunch.

'God... don't do that, Josiah Grimshaw' scolded Lana. 'Where have you been anyway?'

'Oh just wandering around the streets of London. I've seen almost all of it.'

'Already? But that's impossible.'

'Not when you're dead,' he added, smiling sadly. 'I did find something intriguing though.'

'What?' asked Emma.

'Erm, not sure how to explain. Why don't you just follow me and you'll see what I mean...' he said as he drifted off into the distance.

'Joe... wait for us,' they yelled as they ran after him, not noticing the strange glances they'd been receiving from a group of Japanese tourists who had witnessed them talking to nothing but space.

After fifteen minutes of running, Lana and Emma came to a standstill at a set of traffic lights. Joe stopped, waiting patiently in the middle of the road.

Forgetting that he was in fact, a spirit, Lana screamed when a double-decker bus slammed right into him.

'Oh My God, Oh My God. Joe... Josiah,' she mumbled to herself, her eyes wide open in shock.

On the other hand, Emma glanced around at the strangers who had stepped away from them, looking at Lana as if she were a one-eyed monster.

'He's already dead, Lana. Remember?' she whispered as she grabbed her arm and pulled her quickly across the road at the turn of the lights.

Lana pulled herself together pretty quickly after that, blushing and trying to hide her face from the onlookers.

Joe appeared by their side, a look of terror on his face, 'That was so strange,' he whispered, 'the scariest thing that's ever happened to me,' he mumbled.

'What? Worse than being washed up on the shore and then dying in the hospital?' asked Emma quietly as they continued walking through the streets at the same pace.

Joe nodded and then hovered on ahead, moving increasingly quicker and quicker until the girls had to sprint to keep up.

Lana had gone very quiet, not even mentioning the many shop fronts they'd passed, or Trafalgar Square which they'd since passed by ages ago.

'Where are we?' yelled Emma as she held firmly on to her sister's hand while copying Joe's slowing pace up in front.

'I... I don't know. Let me get the map out.'

Before she could even open it, Joe was beside them.

'Forget about the map, Lana. I think this is far more important,' he said as he pointed to a run-down old building across the street from where they stood.

'Yeah, so it's an old building... you dragged us all this way to show us an old building? This is crazy, Josiah Grimshaw. You know, I think maybe I should just call Declan, and he can come and find us. Give me the card, Emma...' said Lana as Emma put her hand in her pocket and pulled out the now creased business card.

As she passed it to her sister, Lana's breath caught in her throat.

'What? What is it?' asked Emma as she glanced down.

'Oh My God,' she exclaimed, covering her mouth with her hands.

The business card, which had the words Declan Alexander written on it, also contained something else, something familiar, something that shocked the girls into silence.

There on the silver and white card was the same emblem that they now had inked onto their bodies: the winged eye.

Even Joe gasped, 'But that's... that's.....'

'Yeah, we know Josiah, it's the same as our tattoos...' answered Lana.

'No, it's not that. I know that already. It's just that, that...'

'That what? Spit it out, Josiah,' said Emma uncharacteristically bossy.

Indicating that they should follow him, Joe held out his hand and pointed once again to the old building. As they got closer, they realised what this was all about. Why he'd brought them through Central London in the first place. He'd brought them to this decrepit old house because right there, below an intricate wrought iron door knocker was the very same symbol.

16

As they stood staring, mouths drooped, the door slowly opened in front of them.

Emma stepped backwards while Lana tripped over the steep step that led indoors.

'Lana? what on earth are you doing?' whispered Emma desperately as her sister pushed the door further ajar and peered inside.

'What does it look like I'm doing? I'm going in.'

'No... you can't. We can't, that's trespassing...' she added rather pathetically.

Lana turned to look at her sister, 'Really? Oh, come on. The door just opened for us. Whoever is here clearly wants us to come in. So come on, follow me...' she said as she disappeared inside.

Catching her breath in her throat, Emma turned to look at their surroundings. People went about their lives around them, walking in and out of an impressively large building just a little further down the street, but no-one seemed to be taking any notice of the two girls and the ghost. Not that they could see the ghost, of course.

Swallowing loudly, Emma stepped up onto the step, followed by Joe, and walked into the darkness that beckoned.

As her eyes adjusted to the lack of light, the door closed of its own accord behind them, making her heart feel like it was about to hop out of her chest.

'Sis? Lana? Where are you?' she said, outstretching her arms and finding her sister directly in front of her. 'What are you doing?' she whispered.

'Just waiting for my eyes to adjust,' she whispered back, 'Joe, can you see in the dark?'

'It's just an old disused room. There's nothing in here at all,' he said, 'But there's a door... follow my voice,' he said as the girls did just that until eventually, they came upon the door he'd mentioned. Holding Emma's hand tightly, Lana found the doorknob and turned, pushing it open slowly. They stepped forward into a room with a large window, daylight so bright that they had to shield their eyes for a moment until they re-adjusted once again.

Sparsely furnished, a rather elegant faded yellow chaise-longue stood just beneath a large bay window, covered in a thick layering of dust, giving the impression that the last time it was used was decades ago. Standing to its side was a short little round table, gathering just the same amount of dust, although a tall champagne glass stood on top of it. Lana stepped forward and picked the glass up, gently blowing much of the dust away, leaving a semi-clean circle on the wooden table.

Emma began to cough loudly as little particles of dust entered her throat.

'Oops,' said Lana as she patted her sister on the back. 'Look, there's another door,' she said, almost instantly forgetting about Emma's coughing fit as she walked across the room.

Opening the door, they saw a grand hallway, its centrepiece, a dramatic wrought iron spiral staircase, the railing caked in dust.

'Please don't touch the dust again, Sis,' wheezed Emma as she followed behind Lana and Joe as they cautiously began to climb the stairs, not wanting to be left behind.

When they reached the top, there were several doors off to each side, and a double door directly in front of them.

Lana looked across at Emma and smiled before she put both her hands on the two doorknobs and pushed them open dramatically, expecting something impressive beyond them. But there was nothing except a large empty room, bar an old oak wardrobe that looked like it was falling apart.

Stepping inside the room, the three of them wandered around, looking out the window, with its' little balcony overlooking a tiny courtyard below.

Joe disappeared momentarily.

Turning, Lana looked disappointed, 'So this is it? Not really what I was expecting.'

'But what were you expecting, Lana? It's not like we knew this place even existed.'

Shrugging her shoulders, Lana pouted, 'I don't know. I guess I was hoping to find the answers, you know?'

'Well, perhaps the answers lie with Declan. We should just ask him about it.'

'I guess you're right.'

'I just checked the rest of the building, and I can see nothing but dusty rooms that haven't seen the light of day for years,' said Joe.

'Well, I guess that's it, then. Thanks for bringing us though, Joe,' Lana said with a sad smile.

Standing beside the window, Emma turned abruptly towards them, 'Did you hear that?' she whispered.

'Hear what?' Lana replied as she rushed to her side.

'Listen... someone is... singing.'

The three of them stood silently, straining their necks out to hear.

Her eyes wide with excitement, Lana turned to Emma and grinned before she followed the sound, moving across the room until eventually, she stood in front of the rickety old wardrobe. Emma followed, her eyebrows knitted together, with Joe standing firmly behind them.

Lana carefully pulled open the wardrobe door, expecting to find a woman hiding in there, but instead, there was a whole other room. Emma and Joe followed as she stepped through until they were all standing in an old-fashioned clean and dust-free large airy living space. Shadows from the flickering flames of an open inglenook fire danced across the room, which looked like it was from the Victorian era. Lana and Emma only knew this because the only museum on Andilyse Island just happened to specialise in items from that time.

It was a beautiful room, and even though everything in it seemed to scream Antiques Roadshow, it was warm and inviting.

So taken by the grandeur of the room that they failed to notice the soft singing had halted. When a chair facing the fire creaked, Emma and Lana gasped. Fearing the unknown, they gulped and stood dead still for someone to make the first move.

Suddenly, a warm laugh filled the air, and an old lady leaned sideways from the chair, turning so she could see them.

'Don't be so frightened... come, come... let me have a good look at you.'

Lana grabbed Emma's hand, and they cautiously stepped towards the old woman, Joe hovering in the background behind them.

As they approached her, she removed her glasses and put down the book she was reading, placing it face down on a coffee table to her right. Emma glanced at it, expecting to find Jane Eyre or something similar. Instead, she was surprised to see the old lady had been reading The Hunger Games.

'Well, you've certainly grown up into beautiful creatures you two. Come, step closer, Lana, I won't bite. You too, Emma.'

So shocked that the woman knew their names, the sisters were unable to speak.

'You look a little like your fathers, both of you. They'd be so proud, they really would. Fine specimens, both of you. Now, did you find the place all right?' she asked as Lana and Emma shared a shocked glance, both swallowing loudly.

The old lady chuckled and shook her head. 'Now I'm pretty sure you're not normally this quiet. I understand you're confused, possibly even a bit scared but there's no need to be. You're quite safe here. I will fill you in, don't worry about that, but I am going to need you to be a bit more vocal. You're not going to get anywhere if you don't open your mouths and speak to me, you know?' she said, pointing to them both.

'S...s...sorry,' said Emma, 'We're just.... just... surprised that's all.'

'That's to be expected. So, did you find the place all right?'

Lana nodded, 'B...but how did you know that we would come?'

'Of course, I knew you would come. I sent for you.'

Exchanging glances once more, the girls were dumbstruck.

'All right, all right... why don't you both sit down over there,' she said, pointing to a narrow settee for two opposite her.

'My name is Eleanor Hayden-Jones and this....,' she said with her arms up in the air as she looked around the room, 'is the Fourth House of Praxos.'

17

The girls learned that the Fourth House of Praxos was one of many such houses around the world. This particular property was the base for the Praxos Foundation within south-east England.

'Oh thank you, dear,' said Eleanor to a middle-aged gentleman dressed in green and black who appeared out of nowhere carrying a tray with a teapot and three cups and saucers. Carefully placing it on the large coffee table in between them, he stole a glance at the girls and smiled a wide grin.

'Girls, this is Wilbur, he's a great help to me here at the house.'

He tipped his head, 'A pleasure to meet you,' he said before he continued to pour the tea. 'Milk and sugar?'

Emma shook her head while Lana nodded, 'Yes, please.'

'Perhaps a slice of lemon instead, Emma Jane?'

She caught his eye and nodded, intrigued to find out why these people seemed to know so much about them.

After preparing the tea, Wilbur took his leave with a nod of the head and a warm smile. Eleanor slowly stood and leaned back on the arm of the chair.

'As I was saying, the Praxos Foundation consists of a wide group and variety of persons who, shall we say, fight crime? We investigate wrong-doings and make things right,' she smiled, turning her head so that the light from the window highlighted the many deep lines and wrinkles that covered her face, which was quite beautiful, even in old age. Her silvery-white hair almost twinkled, just as her eyes did, when the light caught it.

'But how do you know who we are? And how do you know our, our... fathers? Why did you want to bring us here?' asked Emma.

Eleanor smiled, 'I'll get to your fathers in time, my dear. But you should know that you were always destined to join the Praxos Foundation. Both of you were.'

'But you didn't bring us here... Joe did,' Lana let slip before she'd even thought about what she was saying.

'Joe? You mean the young man standing at the back of the room right now?'

The girls gasped, and Joe moved quickly towards them.

'You can see me?' he croaked.

Chuckling, the old lady looked right at him, 'Yes. Of course I can see you, Josiah,' she said before turning back to Lana, 'Yes, Josiah led you here but only because we summoned him in the first place. We knew he was doing the rounds all over London and so we thought it only apt that we used him to lure you here, for want of a better word,' she chuckled.

'You lured us here?' whispered Emma, a little scared.

'Oh, I'm sorry, dear. There's no need for you to fear any of us here at Praxos. We are like a family, and you've just joined us.'

Looking up suddenly, Lana said, 'We have? But we've not agreed to join anything.'

Eleanor smiled, 'It's not something that you have to join as such, you don't have to sign anything. You were destined to be a part of us. You joined us the moment you grew your tattoos.'

'We...g..grew them?' said Lana, absentmindedly rubbing her lower back.

'But how do you know about our tattoos?' exclaimed Emma breathlessly.

Turning around so that she no longer faced them, Eleanor lifted her top to reveal the same kind of tattoo etched into her own lower back.

'Stamus Contra Malum - We stand against evil,' she said as she dropped her top and turned to face them. 'You are now part of the Praxos family. It is simply meant to be,' she said, returning to her chair and lowering herself into it like the very old lady she was.

'So let me get this right. We were born into the Praxos Foundation, and we have to be a part of it, whether we like it or not, because we 'grew' a tattoo?' asked Lana as she stood up to return her cup and saucer to the table.

'Exactly.'

'But what are we meant to do, Eleanor?' asked Emma.

'You will use your special skills to fight evil in whatever form it may arise.'

'Special skills?' asked Joe quietly.

'Yes, I believe the girls have already experienced some of them?' she asked as the sisters looked at each other in pure bewilderment.

Letting her head fall back gracefully as a gentle chuckle erupted from her lips, Eleanor shook her head before continuing, 'Being able to jump from great heights and swim beneath icy cold waters are something you've been able to do throughout your lives, is it?'

Comprehension dawned on the girls as the old lady carried on, 'We all have them here at Praxos, special skills, that is. As you begin your initiation and training, they will develop, you'll see.'

'Initiation?' Lana and Emma said at the same time as Emma's hand shot out to hold her sisters tightly.

'Of course. You didn't think we'd let you loose on the world without one, did you?'

'B... but... what kind of initiation?' asked Emma as she tightened her grip.

Laughing, Eleanor lifted herself from her chair again and stepped towards them, 'Oh, don't worry about that. It's nothing too gruesome,' she winked as she walked past them towards the door through which Wilbur had earlier disappeared.

'Come on, it's time I showed you around,' she said as the girls tentatively stood and followed slowly behind the old woman, with Joe hovering behind.

As they approached the door, Eleanor had barely touched it when it opened wide, revealing a darkened passageway beyond. As they walked along, candles seemingly came to life, flickering pockets of fire dancing in the shadows.

Emma, still clutching tightly onto her sister's hand, swallowed hard as they reached the end of the corridor. She had no idea where they were going or what they were doing. Her thoughts began to race, finding herself recalling her earlier adventure in the Thames. She remembered the adrenaline pulsing through her body and the feeling of extraordinary ecstasy that enveloped her soon after she'd jumped into the water.

The memory was enough to give her newfound confidence, and she released Lana's hand and smiled.

A closed, wrought-iron gate was in front of them. Eleanor reached forward and slid it across sideways, revealing a stainless steel door beneath it. Pressing a hidden button, it instantly opened. Lana gasped as Eleanor smiled and stepped into the modern elevator.

'Well, come on then,' she said, waiting for them to climb in. 'It's only a lift; it's not going to bite you.'

The three of them followed, noticing there was room enough for about another ten people. As the door quietly closed behind them, Eleanor pressed a button, and they stood silently waiting to see where they were going. Before they'd even noticed any movement, the door slid open, and Wilbur stood grinning on the other side.

'Have the others arrived yet, Wilbur?' Eleanor asked as he slid the wrought iron gate across to let them out.

'Yes, they're waiting for you in the White Room.'

She nodded as Wilbur walked away, turning left and out into another room beyond.

The girls and Joe stood staring ahead at the vast room that surrounded them, awe-inspired by the sheer size of it. It was like a giant tunnel, built in old red brick, with massive arches above them. They'd never seen anything like it.

Eleanor stood watching as they took it in. 'It's beautiful, isn't it?' she asked as they nodded.

'Where are we?' asked Lana.

'This is our HQ. We're beneath the city,' she replied, gesturing for them to follow her.

Strolling along, Eleanor pointed out tunnels that seemed to head off in different directions, 'We're actually underneath The British Museum at the moment, and if you wandered off in that general direction, you'd be standing beneath The Great Ormond Street Hospital. That tunnel leads to Westminster, this one to Hackney Marshes (which is a long way away), oh and over there, if you walked for quite a while, you'd walk under Greenwich and underneath the Thames Barrier...'

'But why, Eleanor? Why are we here? What are the tunnels for?' asked Lana.

'It's easy to access for us, we are well hidden beneath the city, and we're protected down here.'

'Protected from what?' whispered Emma.

'We'll get to all that in time, my dear. For now, I want you to meet others like you; others who also have no idea why they are here. You're all in the same boat. But it's a safe boat, don't worry,' she said with a smile, pushing open a large white door, into another room painted entirely in white where a group of about ten teenagers sat drinking from cans, reading books and playing on their phones.

As they entered the room, their faces lit up, and they all stopped what they were doing.

'Well, everybody is here now. We can begin,' smiled Eleanor. 'Would you girls like a cold drink before we start?'

Both nodded as a boy with cropped blond hair stood up and handed them both a coke. Lana took it immediately, opened it and began to gulp the cold liquid before she eventually stopped to say thanks, while Emma shook her head with a shy smile. 'Is there any water?' she asked him. Grinning, he nodded and bent backwards, putting the can back on the table and grabbing a small bottle of mineral water.

She took it gratefully, drinking it all while Eleanor stood patiently waiting for her to finish.

'Right then, hello everyone. I believe Wilbur has already given you a quick explanation of where you are?' she asked as the others nodded. 'Good, no doubt he has told you about me? I am Eleanor Hayden-Jones, and I'm the Guardian of the Fourth House of Praxos. Why don't you follow me, guys and gals...'

Breaking the silence of the room, everyone stood up, grabbed their belongings and walked out, some chatting to others, some just walking alone, a little too embarrassed to engage in conversation.

Lana left Emma alone to go and chat up a cute dark haired boy she'd had her eye on since walking in.

'Hi,' said a voice to her side as they strolled along behind Eleanor.

Turning, Emma saw that it was the boy with the cropped blond hair who'd kindly given her a drink.

'Hi,' she answered shyly, her cheeks turning a little shade of pink.

Holding out his hand, he said, 'I'm Diarmuid'.

Taking it and shaking gently, Emma smiled, 'Emma Jane. Well, just Emma really,' she said, the pink tinge of her cheeks darkening into more of a red hue.

'It's great to meet you, Just Emma,' he laughed. 'So...'

'So...' she replied, feeling more and more at ease with him.

'Where are you from?' he asked as she pushed strands of her hair behind her ear before remembering she wasn't keen on her ears, so she pulled the strands back down again.

'Andilyse Island. You?'

'Andilyse Island? Where's that?' he asked.

'You've never heard of it?'

He shook his head, 'I never was much good at geography,' he smiled, the brightness of his near perfectly formed teeth almost enticing her in.

'It's just off the English coast, east of here. I guess it's not the most popular of the British Isles,' she giggled before realising she sounded like a love-struck moron and shut up.

'It's not? How come?'

'People are put off by all the fog we get there, I guess... and the rain. And they're not too keen on all the wind turbines. We have tonnes of them on the island, but they don't bother us. We kinda like them, actually. I find them quite soothing, and it's nice to know that our electricity has all been generated by nature if you know what I mean.' Oh My God, I'm mumbling like a moron, she thought to herself just as she tripped up, almost falling to the ground. As Diarmuid caught her, she practically swooned as he very carefully pulled her upwards, looking down into her eyes. Her heart fluttered, and she could have sworn her stomach did its very own triple salchow.

As he eased her back up into position, he grinned at her again as she bit down on her lip, completely embarrassed.

'Thanks,' she muttered.

'Your island sounds nice. I like wind turbines.'

This time her stomach did a backwards somersault.

'Hmm,' she muttered, 'You never told me where you're from?'

'Ireland.'

'You're a long way from home.'

'Well, I grew up in Ireland, but I live in Oxfordshire now with my mum, well, she's not my real mum. I found that out just last week. Came as a bit of a shock.'

'Oh... I'm sorry.'

'That's okay. Did you know about, you know?'

'That I'm adopted? Yes. It was always pretty obvious when you look at the rest of the family. They're all blue-eyed blondes, yet there's me with my dark hair and green eyes and my sister Lana with her afro hair and amber eyes. Not exactly a secret they could keep from us,' she smiled. 'But we only just found out about th... this.......'

'Okay, everyone. Gather around please,' announced Eleanor from the front of the group. The teenagers began shuffling forwards, so they almost surrounded her. Behind her was a massive statue of an angel with enormous wings that cloaked a small child. At the foot of the statue was a plaque with an inscription that included The Praxos Foundation's emblem: the winged eye.

'This statue is thousands of years old, created by those who started Praxos. Each house across the country, and actually around the world, has a similar statue in their HQ. It signifies everything that we stand for. If you look closely at the plaque, it has the words Stamus Contra Malum.'

'What's that mean?' asked a girl wearing glasses and her hair in a high ponytail.

'We Stand Against Evil. Simply put, it signifies that we promise to defend the innocents of this world, whoever they may be. Praxos is all about fighting evil, in whatever form it may present itself.'

'But how are we going to fight evil? We're just teenagers,' said Lana from the other side of the group.

'You might be teenagers, Lana, but you are all exceptional teenagers. One of your parents was very special, indeed. One of your parents was an angel.'

Pausing for a moment as gasps flooded through the small group while they all looked around at each other in shock, Eleanor continued, 'You are what we fondly call the Watchers.'

'The Watchers,' everyone whispered.

'Yes, that's right. It's a kind of nickname we use for all those who have an angel as a parent. All those like you.'

'Do you know our parents? Do you know where they are?' asked Emma.

Turning to look at her, Eleanor smiled sadly. 'Your parents no longer walk among us. The angels were here for a brief time and then they had to re-join the upper societies. Your other parent, I'm very sad to say, also no longer walks among us simply because they perished. But I did have the opportunity to meet some of them, yes. But that I will tell you about, individually, another time.'

With tears welling up in her eyes, Emma didn't know where to look. She didn't want to wipe her eyes either, for fear that the others would see she wanted to cry, so she looked down towards the ground as Eleanor continued speaking.

A soft, firm hand reached out to her, gently squeezing her shoulder. She glanced up as Diarmuid smiled sadly.

She didn't do anything. She just let the warm glow flow all over her body. He had such a soothing effect on her, and she soon almost forgot about her birth parents.

'On your 16th birthday (your actual 16th birthday, not the day your adopted parents celebrated) each of you became one of us. Something huge happened to every one of you and resulted in what looks like a tattoo growing into your skin. You each have a few words etched beneath it. These words are words you will live by. It has been known for the words to change over time, so if this happens to you, fear not.'

'But why do we have them? How did we get them?' asked Lana.

'Every Watcher grows them. It is simply a part of who you are, something you must accept. I have one, Wilbur has one, every one of you has one. In fact, why don't we share each other's so we can all understand. Seeing one another's artwork will help you all to accept them. Emma, let's start with you.'

Eleanor reached out and gently pulled her to the front of the group, Emma turned around and lifted her top, revealing the now-familiar winged eye with the words, Lux in Tenebris Lucet. Gathering around, the group had a good look before Eleanor continued, 'Actually, this is probably a good time to introduce yourselves, tell everyone your name and your words. Go ahead, Emma.'

Blushing brightly, Emma put her top back down and turned around. Attempting a smile, she said, 'Hi. I'm Emma Jane Morgan. Lux in Tenebris Lucet. It means light shines in the darkness.'

Eleanor pointed to Lana next, who stepped forward with a wide grin on her lips.

'Hi, all! I'm Lana Beth Morgan, Emma's sister, and my tattoo,' she said, lifting her top slightly to show everyone, 'says Provehito In Altum. It means launch forward into the deep. It's also 30 Seconds to Mars' pretty cool motto,' she said, holding up her hand like she was at a rock concert. The others laughed. Lana had broken the ice.

'Hi, girls and boys. My name is Liam Hawkes, and my tattoo says Citius Altius Fortius, faster higher stronger. Check it out,' said the cool shaggy brown-haired guy to which Lana had been chatting.

Next up was a girl who wore glasses and her mousy brown hair was fixed in a high ponytail.

'Hello,' she said shyly with a wave, 'I'm Moira Lynn. My motto is In Somnias Veritas, in dreams there is truth,' she said before stepping down, having flashed her lower back just briefly.

'Diarmuid O'Connor. Crescente Luce, light ever-increasing,' he said with a smile as he turned and lifted his shirt to reveal a nicely toned torso before revealing his tattoo. Emma's knees slightly buckled as he beamed at her when he returned.

His motto is like mine. It's connected to the light, she thought, squealing inside like a child.

'Hi, everyone. My name is Ava Burton, and my words are Audi Vide Tace, meaning hear, see, be silent,' said the most exquisite looking petite girl with very fine features, slightly dark skin and piercing blue eyes. After she'd revealed the words inked on her back, she dropped her top and flicked her shoulder-length mocha coloured hair back over her shoulder with a friendly smile.

'Opera et Veritate are my words... Oh, I forgot my name. It's Penny Vega,' she said, laughing before continuing. My words mean in action and truth. Nice to meet you all.'

'Hello everybody. I'm very pleased to meet you. My name is Nisha Singh and on my back are the words Mortui Vivos Docent, which means the dead teach the living. A little morbid, I know,' she said, shyly smiling as she stepped back into the group.

'I'm Rupert Henson, and I'm a chocoholic... oh, is this not the chocolate addicts group? Oh sorry, must dash,' he said as he jumped back into the group and pretended to run away before Eleanor, laughing, pulled him back by the collar.

'Woah there miss Hayden-Jones,' he joked. 'Right then, seriously now. My name is Rupert the bear. Okay, maybe not. It's Henson, Rupert Henson, but you can call me oo8,' he said in a terrible Scottish accent as the group laughed out loud at his silliness.

'Get on with it, Rupert,' said Eleanor with a smile.

'In Omnia Paratus...which means hot sexy guy,' he said as he pouted momentarily before glancing across at Eleanor and straightening himself up. 'No, really, it means prepared for all things,' he said with a wink as he turned around and pretended to do a striptease.

Somebody wolf-whistled loudly, and the group all cracked up as Rupert finally dropped his shirt, took a bow and stepped back as the Watchers gave him a round of applause.

'I'm afraid I can't match that,' said a tall, pretty girl with curly blonde hair, 'Hi fellow Watchers, I'm Cassie Stanton, and my motto is Esto Quodes, be what you are. I'm looking forward to working with you all,' she said, grinning as she showed off her tattoo.

'Hello! It's wonderful to meet you. I'm Imran Chaudri, and on my back, I have the words Tempus Edax Rerum, time devourer of all things. Thank you,' said the young Asian man with a baseball cap on backwards.

The last person to step forward had a body like a rugby player with muscular arms, sturdy legs and a stocky torso. As he turned to face them, he ran a large hand through his short brown hair and smiled a little nervously. 'It's a pleasure to meet you all,' he said as he blushed slightly, 'My name is Elliott Drake, and my motto is Lux Veritas Virtus, light truth courage,' he said with a nod of his head, a quick flash of his back and that was it. That was all the Watchers.

18

Eleanor showed the group around some of the other rooms and tunnels that led off of the main hall, including a large dining area complete with several tables and chairs positioned around the room giving it an almost restaurant-like appearance. There was a small cosy room filled with over-sized beanbags for them to chill out in, a few well-hidden bedrooms and bathrooms, and a large living room complete with a massive library to one side of it. There was a strange fusion of contemporary style with old fashioned Victorian and Edwardian aged furniture and décor. But it was comforting, and the group of Watchers soon felt at home. But they still had so many questions that needed answering.

But before they had the chance, something remarkable happened.

A beautiful oak grandfather clock that stood in one corner of the living room began to chime loudly. On its first chime, Eleanor looked startled and rushed over to a big golden yellow chaise-longue beside an ornate coffee table in dark hardwood.

As the others looked at each other, wondering what was going on, Eleanor said quickly, 'After the fifth chime, I will cry out in pain. Do not worry. It happens to me every day. Just bear with me for a moment while I change,' she said with a smile.

With no clue as to what was going on, the group stayed where they were; some sat on chairs around the room, others stood facing each other, chatting. But true to form, as the clock chimed its fifth chime, Eleanor let out a deep throaty cry that seemed to echo from the deepest depths of her body.

Emma was about to rush to her side, but Wilbur stepped forward and shook his head with a smile. 'No need,' he whispered before he stepped back into the dark corner from where he'd appeared.

Her cries of pain went on for what seemed like ages. In truth, though, it was merely a few seconds. As they watched her writhe on the chaise-longue alone, shocked gasps could be heard throughout the room as Eleanor physically changed right in front of their eyes.

Emma's hand was being gripped tightly by Lana.

After a few more moments, Eleanor turned to face them and stood up with a huge grin plastered across her face. A face that was no longer that of an elderly lady, but of a beautiful, youthful person more akin to that of a 20-year-old. Eleanor was young again.

'There, that's better,' she exclaimed to the group of shocked faces. 'Oh, don't worry, I'm fine. In fact, I'm better than fine. I always feel so much better at this time of day. It's good to be young again.'

'What? Why? But, how?' asked Lana, unable to put together a full sentence.

Eleanor laughed as Wilbur stepped forward with a handful of clothes.

As she took them gratefully, Eleanor stepped behind a large dressing screen that stood in the corner of the room, speaking as she changed out of her old clothes.

'I am a little different from all of you. I was once a fully-fledged angel, but I made a decision that they didn't like upstairs, and so they banished me to this strange life, half young, half old yet never really ageing, if you know what I mean,' she said as she finally stepped out from the screen wearing skinny jeans, black knee-high boots and a tight, bright pink T-shirt.

'That's better,' she smiled as Wilbur took away the other clothes.

'So how old are you, exactly?' asked Cassie.

'Quite old,' she smiled.

'Aww come on, Miss Hayden-Jones. Do tell us,' asked Elliott shyly.

'Let's just say I've been around a long, long, long, long time.'

'What, like hundreds and hundreds of years?' asked Nisha.

'That, and more,' she answered, 'But that's enough about my age,' she laughed as she took the brush being handed to her by Wilbur and brushed through her long thick mane of wavy blonde hair.

'Why did they banish you, Eleanor? What did you do?' asked Emma.

Turning to face the young girl, the look on Eleanor's face changed slightly, and the happiness disappeared from her eyes. 'I fell in love, choosing him over my work as an angel. I told them I didn't want to return there, that I was staying with him and they weren't happy, so this is what they did to me.'

'What happened to the man you fell in love with?' Lana asked curiously.

Again, her eyes seemed to glaze over as she continued, 'His name was Tarquin. We stayed together, and I watched as he aged and eventually died. It broke my heart.'

'I'm so sorry, Eleanor,' whispered Emma, 'That must have been horrendous.'

The smile returned to Eleanor's face as she looked at the group with warmth, 'Thank you, but it was an awfully long time ago. I let him go many centuries ago. My only wish is that I had a photograph of him, but such things weren't in existence back then,' she chuckled as she walked across the room towards the door.

'Come on, everyone. People are waiting for us,' she said with a twinkle in her eyes.

As they walked out of the large living room and back into the grand hall, a whole host of people waited to greet them, including Declan and Saleena.

'Declan!' exclaimed Emma as she rushed towards him. 'Why didn't you tell us?' she asked as Lana joined her.

Saleena smiled and walked away as Declan began to speak, 'It wasn't up to me to tell you. Ellie is the guardian, and she must tell you the truth. It's the way it's always been. How are you taking it? Are you okay?' he asked

'We're great, thanks,' said Lana, 'It's all kinda cool, actually. Quite a lot to take in, but cool. So are you, you know... one of us?' she asked cheekily.

Nodding, Declan lifted his shirt, revealing the tattoo in all its glory. Lana and Emma both leaned forward at the same time to check it out, 'Resurgam' was written across his back.

'What does it mean?' asked Emma curiously.

'I shall arise,' he answered as he put his top back down and turned to face them.

'Do you know what it means though, what it really means?' Lana said, twisting her hair around her finger.

'Yes I do, but that's not something you need to know. Not yet, anyway.'

'Spoilsport.'

'Do our parents know, Declan?'

He shook his head. 'No, they believe you are here for work experience.'

'But what do they think we're doing? How can we keep this a secret?' Lana said.

'You'll be amazed how easy it is to keep this a secret, girls. When your lives depend on it, believe me, you will keep the secret. I told Patrick that you were both going to work as assistants/secretaries for me, for my private investigation business.'

'Dad thinks we're working for a private investigator?' exclaimed Emma, 'No way, he would never allow that.'

Smiling and shaking his head, he said, 'Your dad trusts me. Let's just put it that way. He knows I would die for his children and in his eyes that makes wherever I am, the safest place in the world for his daughters.'

'Wow, that's awesome,' said Lana, 'But why does he trust you so much?'

'Because when he and your father worked together in the police force, Declan took a bullet for him on more than one occasion. They were like brothers,' said Saleena, who had crept upon them quietly.

'Wow,' whispered Emma, 'I mean really, like wow.'

Before he explained anything more, Eleanor retook centre stage to speak.

'It's such a pleasure to have everyone together again. Thank you for offering to be this year's Mentors and for coming down to collect your Watchers. The initiation will begin shortly. I'll see you all back here again in the morning. You know what to do,' she said with a cheeky smile. 'Ciao!' she exclaimed, and before the Watchers knew what had happened, Eleanor had disappeared.

'What? Where did she go?' whispered the youngsters as they looked around in astonishment.

The so-called Mentors rounded up their Watchers and started heading out of the main hall. Declan and Saleena led Lana and Emma down a tunnel they'd not been before.

'What was all that about?' asked Lana as they followed behind them.

Taking no notice of her sister, Emma was walking backwards trying to spot Diarmuid, but it seemed he'd already left. She sighed heavily and turned back around, just as Declan chuckled in front of her, 'Don't worry, Emma, he'll be here tomorrow. You'll see him then,' he said.

Lana giggled too, as did Saleena. And Emma blushed from head to toe.

'He seems like a charming young man,' said Saleena quietly over her shoulder and Emma grinned broadly, nodding.

'So what's going on now, Declan? What is this initiation? And where are we going?' Lana asked as they continued to walk down the darkly lit tunnel.

'Where's Joe?' Emma suddenly said, noticing that he was no longer with them.

'Don't worry about Josiah. He's been asked to stay away during the initiation. You'll see him afterwards. He's fine.'

They continued walking in silence, Emma thinking about what the initiation would entail. Lana was thinking about Liam, the sexy rocker type Watcher she'd been chatting to most of the afternoon.

'Is it going to... hurt, Declan?' whispered Emma as her musings began to go into overload.

He smiled and shook his head. 'Don't worry. It's nothing like those horrible rituals they do to students at some of those scary college fraternities in America. You'll be able to do it easily enough. Just remember that you mustn't be seen using your special skills by the general public. That's all you need to know. Everything else will come naturally.'

'Here we are, Declan,' said Saleena as they stopped beside an archway that led up an old crumbling flight of stairs.

'Right girls, take this. Once you get to the top and out into the open, the door will close firmly behind you, and you won't be able to get back in. You'll know what to do. Don't look so scared, Emma. It'll be a piece of cake. Good luck,' he said, handing them an expensive-looking envelope sealed with wax.

Saleena put her hands on Emma's shoulders and kissed her on both cheeks before doing the same to Lana. 'Good luck,' she said as the girls turned away nervously climbing the stairs. As they faced the old heavy door, they both took a deep breath before Lana leaned forward and unlocked it, pulling it open to reveal another dark tunnel up ahead.

As the door slammed behind them, they realised they couldn't see a thing. The two girls stood in complete pitch darkness.

❦ 19 ❦

'**N**ow, what do we do? There's no point in opening the envelope either, coz we can't see it!' said Lana, who was starting to get a little annoyed.

'There's no point in getting irritated, Lana. We're in this situation, now we have to deal with it,' reassured Emma.

'Yeah, I know that, but how?'

'Let's just think... I don't suppose you've got any matches on you?' she joked. 'Okay, maybe not.'

The two stood for a moment in silence.

'This is part of it, isn't it?' asked Lana.

'What? Do you mean part of the initiation? Probably. I guess we should try and walk down the tunnel until we see daylight,' suggested Emma.

'The only problem with that is we don't know how long that will take. It must be nearly seven 'o'clock now. It'll be getting dark around ten-ish, won't it?'

'Well, I hope we're not down here for that long. Let's just try it.'

So the girls tentatively began taking steps in the darkness, one foot carefully in front of the other. But when Lana stepped on something a bit squishy she let out a startled shriek that bounced off the walls around them, echoing off into the darkness.

'No... I can't do this. What WAS that? Ewwww. It could have

been anything. We could be walking in the sewers. That could have been a dead rat or worse. It could have been someone's poo...' she wailed.

Emma tried not to laugh and steadied her sister.

'There must be something we can d...' Lana said, suddenly stopping. 'Oh My God, I just realised. Duh! Our special skills, Emma. It's you.. You can light the way.'

'I can?'

'Yes, of course. What does your tattoo say?'

'Lux in Tenebris Lucet,' replied Emma with a grin, adding, 'Light shines in the darkness, of course!' she giggled.

'Okay then, so go ahead,' prompted Lana.

'Erm, I don't know how.'

'Well, just concentrate.'

Standing dead still and closing her eyes in the darkness, Emma concentrated hard on creating light, but nothing happened.

'Well?'

'Nothing's happening,' said Emma with a sigh. 'I just don't know how to do it.'

Lana sighed as she tried to think of something that would work.

'Think about what happened before; concentrate on what happened when you were in the water. Maybe that'll work,' she suggested as Emma closed her eyes once again and took herself back to that morning when she'd thrown herself into the Thames. As she fell beneath the surface of the water, she recalled the feeling that filled her body. It was like adrenaline pumping through her veins, and she'd felt so completely alive.

Suddenly, Lana began laughing and clapping her hands together like a child.

'You're doing it, you're doing it,' she shouted, her words echoing throughout the tunnel around them.

Sure enough, Emma opened her eyes to find light emanating from every pore of her body. She was like a human light bulb. The feeling warmed her as Lana hugged her tightly before they both investigated their surroundings. A thin tunnel led ahead for quite some distance, with several built-in ladders positioned at various locations along it.

'What do you reckon? asked Emma.

Shrugging her shoulders, Lana glanced around, avoiding looking down, she really didn't want to see what the squishy thing was that she'd stepped on. 'Let's open the envelope. It might give us a clue.'

Emma removed it from the back pocket of her jeans and unfolded it before she popped open the red wax seal. Inside was a blank piece of paper.

'Great, now what?' she said as she showed it to Lana who tutted angrily.

'How the hell are we supposed to know what to do now?' she said.

'Let's just walk down the tunnel and maybe climb some of the ladders until we find our way out. At least we can see now,' Emma suggested.

Half an hour later, the girls felt like they'd walked miles. Every ladder they'd climbed had led to a locked hatch, and they were getting increasingly irritated.

'I need a drink.'

'Here, I've got some water in my bag,' said Emma as she pulled out the bottle and handed it to her sister.

In the meantime, Emma was looking more closely at the blank piece of paper, hoping for some sort of clue to appear, but it was just blank, plain and simple.

A loud noise in the distance made Lana spit out the majority of the water in her mouth, drenching Emma's face.

'Great, Lana, thanks!' she said, wiping her face with the sleeve of her cardigan. As she did so, she noticed something on the paper. A couple of letters had appeared.

'Lana... look.'

'Huh? Didn't you hear that? It's freaking me out... what if that... oh,' she said as Emma waved the piece of paper in front of her face.

'It's the water. The paper needs water to reveal what's on it.'

Lana carefully flicked little spots of water onto it, and they watched as words began to unravel before them.

Excitedly, they waited to see what it revealed.

'Stamus Contra Malum'

'Is that it?' Lana reeled. 'We already know what that means... jeese...'

'Wait, it's not finished yet. The words are still forming.'

And sure enough, the paper revealed more for the girls to try and figure out.

Have you found your way yet? London is a big place for two small girls in the dark.
But fear not, for losing yourselves is the best way to find yourselves and become who you are truly meant to be.
Fear not of the dark, for you have light
Fear not of the water, for you can swim
Fear not of the heights, for you can jump
Fear not of the evil, for you are Watchers
The Guardian and the Mentors await your return with newfound courage, newfound strength and a newfound passion for the work of Praxos.

'WELL, WHAT'S ALL THAT MEANT TO MEAN?' SIGHED LANA, feeling as though the paper did nothing to help them.

But Emma smiled, 'It means that we shouldn't be afraid of anything. Whatever comes our way, we can rise above it all. Come on, let's go.'

'But go where? We don't even know that. We don't know how to get out.'

'Sure we do, we just have to keep going until the exit reveals itself, Lana.'

'I'm glad you've got the point of all this,' sighed Lana, following the light in front of her.

Two ladders later, Emma laughed as she pushed against the hatch and found it opened quickly in her hands.

'See?' she said, 'I told you so,' she chuckled as Lana scrambled up the ladder after her.

'Wait,' she said, 'Don't step out yet... your light. You need to switch it off.'

'I'm not a light switch, Lana,' laughed Emma.

'You know what I mean.'

Extinguishing the bright light just as she pushed the hatch

open, Emma let out a low groan as she realised they were going from one to tunnel to another.

'What? What is it?' asked Lana as they both emerged into the darkness once again.

'Switch it back on please, Emma,' she sighed.

About two hours later, the girls had followed five different tunnels and had climbed nearly 30 different ladders until eventually, they came out into fresh air.

Laughing out loud as they emerged, the two had barely climbed out before realising they weren't at street level but were far higher than they'd imagined. Somehow they were standing on the rooftop of a particularly tall building in the centre of the city, with no obvious way down.

'Right, I guess it's over to you now Sis,' said Emma as she sat down to catch her breath back as she took a swig of the water from her bag.

Handing it to Lana, she looked around, mesmerised by the view. Lights were beginning to switch on throughout the city as dusk started to settle in.

'It's impressive, isn't it?' asked Lana as she joined her sister on the floor. 'Look, there's Big Ben, the wheel, the Gherkin. You can see for miles up here.'

'Yeah, but don't you think it's a bit weird how we got here? I mean, we were in tunnels under London all this time. At no point in our walk did it look like we were in a building, yet here we are, climbing out on the top of one?'

Emma nodded, 'It is bizarre, but the past few weeks have been bizarre, haven't they? We're children of angels, for goodness sake. Our birth parents are either dead or upstairs - whatever that means. We've got special powers; we're doing some weird initiation thing for a weird foundation that we were destined to belong to. It's all got weird written all over it,' she sighed.

'We met some cute guys, though,' laughed Lana.

Emma laughed loudly and nodded, 'They are super cute, aren't they?'

'And I noticed you already seem to have bonded with that Diarmuid guy. Cute.'

Emma playfully punched her sister on the shoulder. 'You'd make a cute couple. I'm serious,' she said as they giggled.

'So do you and Liam. With him, you'd be like a rocker chick or something, and that's right up your alley,' Emma laughed.

'Yeah well maybe, we'll see.'

The girls sat quietly for a while, still taking in their surroundings when they heard Big Ben chime in the distance. It was 10pm already and almost dark.

'Have you decided how we're going to do this, Lana?'

Biting her lip, Lana shrugged, 'I guess we have to take a leap of faith, literally. I just hope I'm strong enough to hold both of us,' she said swallowing hard.

'You will be, don't worry,' reassured Emma.

❧ 2 0 ☙

They waited until the city was as dark as it was going to get, which wasn't that dark considering all the millions of little lights that twinkled from all around. Luckily for the girls though, their building had no lights on it at all, and the area where they were going to jump looked almost pitch black.

'Are you ready?' asked Lana as she held tightly on to Emma's hand.

Nodding in response, Emma grabbed on to her sister's back while she swallowed hard.

'You can do this, Lana. It's up to you now. Fear not of heights, for you can jump.'

Listening to her words, Lana took a deep breath and leapt from the side of the building.

With the wind rushing through the girls' hair, their eyes began to water as Emma gripped tightly on to her sister's back. She caught her breath when she realised they didn't seem to be slowing down.

'Fear not of heights, for you can jump,' she shouted again when all of a sudden, they seemed to appear weightless. Emma let out a deep sigh of relief as Lana laughed out loud, the two floating the last few metres until they landed softly on the ground.

'I knew you could do it, Sis,' said Emma as she hugged Lana tightly and wiped her eyes with the back of her hand.

'For a split second there I didn't think we were going to make it. Thanks for having faith in me, Em. Right, where are we?' she said as they looked around in the darkness. 'Can you give us a little light please?'

Emma responded by letting her body very gently light up the area surrounding them. They'd landed within an inner courtyard, surrounded by tall brick walls and just one heavy-looking wooden door in front of them.

Approaching the door, Lana turned the handle, and it opened easily. With a grin she turned backwards, 'After you,' she said as Emma walked into the darkness. Her glow lit up what looked like an empty warehouse. Walking through it, they could hear the gentle trickle of water. That's when they noticed the curve of the floor. It wasn't flat; it seemed to be at an angle.

'I bet I know what's coming next,' whispered Emma as they continued walking. Turning the corner, they saw where the sound was coming from: a huge hole in the ground.

'Are we going to have to go down there?' breathed Lana as she screwed up her face. 'But I don't have the skills you have,' she said panicking.

'I'm sure we'll be fine,' reassured Emma as she peered down the hole, lying on the floor. 'Its pretty dark, it's an underground river or stream or something. It does look like the only way out, though.'

'Great, just what I wanted, to get freezing cold and my hair all wet. It's gonna go all frizzy.'

'We don't have a choice, and your hair will be fine. Come on, let's get it over with.'

Sighing heavily, Lana watched as Emma carefully lowered herself into the water, her handbag slowly soaking it up. When she disappeared, Lana followed, screeching at the water temperature. Within moments her teeth were chattering.

'Hold on to me. If you start to struggle and we can't get any air, tug at me. I know I can breathe for us both. I don't know how. I just know.'

Lana nodded with her eyes wide open, but she tried not to panic.

Taking a deep breath, they both ducked down under the water and began to swim, Emma lighting the way ahead. They followed the course of the river as it delved deeper and deeper below ground.

But after just a couple of minutes, Lana tugged on Emma's arm, and she pointed upwards. It appeared that she wouldn't have to breathe for her sister after all. Swimming upwards towards a light, the girls eventually pulled themselves out of the freezing water into a large bright room.

Shivering, the two girls stood and shook off as much water as possible. With her teeth chattering, Lana looked pale, as if she might pass out.

'I have an idea,' said Emma as she gently placed her arms around her sister. Closing her eyes tightly, she began to concentrate.

'Close your eyes, Lana. It might get a bit bright.'

The sound of her teeth chattering together began to ease as Emma's light began to shine brighter and brighter, bringing with it an intense heat which warmed them both, lightly drying their clothes. Emma's light began to fade, and they both opened their eyes after ten minutes.

'Are you okay?' Lana asked as Emma stumbled backwards slightly.

'Just a little weak, that's all,' she smiled. 'I'll be fine.'

A worried crease indented Lana's brow as she helped her sister sit down. 'Let's take a break. It looks like you need a rest.'

'I'm fine... honestly. Well, okay then, but just for ten minutes and then we should get moving.'

Leaning against the smooth plastered wall with their legs outstretched in front of them, Emma tipped her head backwards and closed her eyes temporarily while Lana looked around the room.

But it wasn't an ordinary room. It was more like a dilapidated hall with plaster peeling from the walls all around them. It was easy to see that it was once probably a grand hall, perhaps where the wealthy would dance and entertain themselves. Looking upwards, Lana noticed the fading grandeur of intricately sculpted plaster-work, cherubs with missing wings and beautiful ladies with only one arm or leg. Further down the hall were several large archways, partitioned off with huge pieces of board, clumsily nailed to the walls. Only one arch remained open, a once-elegant large wooden door beneath it.

That's our way out; she thought as she too closed her eyes, just for a moment.

An eerie drifting sound made its way across the floor. The soft, gentle strum of classical instruments pervaded her ears, and she sighed, letting her head drop to one side in her slumber, Emma quietly slept beside her.

The sound continued and violins, harpsichords and harps struck up the music of a bygone era. Then the gentle chatter of conversation, the sound of feet moving across the floor, dancing to the rhythm of the music. Laughter permeated the room and inter-mingling odours of tobacco, sweat and perfume tickled her nostrils when suddenly she woke up. Eyes wide open, she looked around the hall expecting to see a scene from a party, one from long ago. But there were no sounds, no smells, nothing.

It was just a dream; she thought as she gently tugged at Emma's arm.

'Emma? Emma?'

'Hm?' she mumbled as she came out of her snooze, pulling her knees up to her chest and sighing before she opened her eyes.

'Emma, it's time to go.'

Slowly opening her eyes, the sudden realisation of where she was hit her, and she shivered.

'I thought I was asleep in bed, all cosy and warm. Bluh,' she said as Lana smiled.

'I know, I fell asleep too. You okay?'

She nodded as the two slowly stood up, stretched and dusted off their jeans.

'How long was I out?'

'I dunno, maybe twenty minutes or so?' Lana shrugged. 'Come on, let's find our way out of here. I noticed a door down here.'

Walking past the boarded-up archways, Lana couldn't help but feel sad for the building.

As if reading her mind, Emma sighed, 'I bet it was quite beau-tiful once.'

'I know, I dreamed about it when I nodded off. It was full of colour, deep azure blues and pinks covered these walls. Well, I dreamed they did anyway. It was used for balls with music played by harpists, violinists and harpsichordists, harpsichord players, whatever you call them,' she said.

'You've got one hell of an imagination, Lana,' laughed Emma as they reached the door.

Clearly, it hadn't been used for a while. As they pushed against it, the door creaked and groaned, eventually opening just enough to let them pass through. On the other side was a massive curved staircase, opposite what appeared to be the main door to the building.

Choosing between the two, they decided to try and get outside, but the door was locked.

'Damn it,' tutted Lana as she leaned against a particularly dusty set of velvet curtains that hung on either side. 'Ew,' she shrieked when she realised it was covered in cobwebs.

'Get em off, get em off me,' she said, dancing around trying to free herself from the sticky webs as Emma shook her head and tried not to laugh.

'Oh, Lana look out!'

But it was too late, Lana had bumped into a slender vase, knocking it to the floor with a smash.

'Eek, I hope that wasn't a family heirloom or something,' she said guiltily as she suddenly forgot all about the cobwebs in her hair, spotting something shiny lying among the broken pieces of porcelain.

Picking it up, she turned to Lana with a grin, brandishing a key in front of her.

Breathing in the fresh air as they stood outside, closing the door behind them, the girls looked around. Neither of them knew the city and had no idea where they were.

Hopping down the steps, they turned to look at the building they'd just left. It was impressive, with towering columns on either side of the door. But why was it so neglected? Surely a building like that in the middle of the city should have been restored to its former glory.

Shrugging her shoulders, Lana turned to face the road in front of them. 'Which way?' she asked.

'Down there,' Emma pointed.

'Any reason?'

'A few more taxis seem to be heading in that direction. I think maybe that leads back towards the centre? Maybe we can try and find our way back to Westminster from there, you know, back to the boat?'

Lana tried to smile as they began walking, hoping that they were headed the right way. She was getting tired of this initiation business. She just wanted to get back, have a shower to get rid of those horrible cobwebs and have something to eat before bed.

But it wasn't going to happen quite like that, because, before they'd even gotten to the bottom of the road, the sound of footsteps closing in on them startled them both.

As Lana turned to see who it was, she felt something sharp on her neck and Emma gasped loudly beside her.

'If you just do as I say, you won't get hurt,' said a man's voice as they were dragged down a dark alleyway to their right.

'Who are you? What do you want?' said Lana, her voice quivering.

Cruel laughter erupted from behind her as she realised there were two large men. Both had knives, and both were holding them to their throats.

'Who are we? We're your new boyfriends, my love, that's who we are. And you're going to give us what we want.'

'And what's that?' cried Emma, but she already knew, and she wasn't about to let that happen.

Both girls felt it at the same time. Something cracked within them. Glancing at each other, they smiled. They had no idea why they smiled, it just came naturally, and before they knew it, they'd each grabbed the hand of their attackers and swung them around, so they were facing them.

Now Emma and Lana stood, holding the knives in their own hands. Flinging them to the floor, the girls both kicked out at the thugs, doubling them over, before landing elbows first into their backs.

The two men fell to the ground, shocked expressions filling their eyes before a final blow was placed firmly across their cheeks, rendering them both unconscious.

Emma and Lana high fived each other and laughed loudly. 'Now that's what I'm talking about,' yelled Lana as they giggled to themselves.

Their laughter soon fizzled out when the reality of what just happened began to sink in.

'What just happened?' whispered Emma.

'I...I don't know. I think we... I think we kicked ass, Em,' she said seriously, holding her hand over her mouth.

'We kicked ass all right,' said Emma. 'Oh My God,' she said. 'We kicked ass,' she shrieked, turning to look at her sister, grinning.

'What should we do with them?' Lana asked.

'Tie them up, leave a note for the police and then let's get out of here,' she suggested. 'I can't believe I just suggested that but I meant it,' she laughed. An unusual feeling was fighting in her stomach, trying to get out.

'I love it. Let's do it,' said Lana as the same feeling twisted in her gut.

Scrambling around the alleyway, they looked for something to tie the men up with, but there was nothing remotely useful.

The sound of something dropping from above startled them but when they spotted a load of rope just metres from their feet, they shrugged at each other and continued.

Fifteen minutes later they walked away, leaving two thugs tied up to an iron railing. On their foreheads in dark purple lipstick were the words, 'Please arrest me. I attack girls.'

❦ 21 ❦

The feeling that was making its way from the pits of their stomachs was one of pure elation. Once they'd walked away, it finally erupted as the girls began to walk quicker and quicker, laughing and dancing.

'Hey, I recognise that building over there. It's that theatre. Theatre Royal. This is Drury Lane! There's a cool show on there at the moment. I saw it advertised on TV the other week,' announced Lana as she rushed over to it with a grin. Do we still have the map?'

'Yeah but I don't know whether it survived the river or not,' Emma answered as she pulled it out of her slightly wet bag. The map, although damp, was still intact. Holding it beneath the street lamp outside the theatre, they eventually figured out exactly where they were in comparison to Westminster.

'That way,' pointed Lana as Emma folded the piece of paper and kept it in her hand as they walked down Drury Lane, with the pretty theatre behind them.

'If we head towards the Thames and then walk along the embankment, it shouldn't take us too long to reach the pier,' said Lana, hooking her arm through her sisters.

'Why do you think that happened back there?' Emma asked a little while later.

'Because those guys were just pure evil and wanted to take

something precious from us. Something I'm keeping for the guy I love,' sighed Lana.

Chuckling, Emma shook her head, 'I didn't mean that! I meant us. Why could we fight like some kind of super ninjas? I never knew I had that in me. I mean, it just came so naturally. I just don't understand why.'

'Oh that,' Lana replied, her cheeks pinking slightly. 'I guess it's just something to do with us being Watchers, I guess.'

'Yeah I guess so, but why didn't they tell us we could do that?'

'Maybe they don't know. Maybe they don't know what we're all capable of until we've gone through the initiation. That's probably why we have to do it.'

'Hm, I suppose. But sending in horrible men to attack us? That's a bit much. What if we couldn't fight? What if we were completely helpless? Those guys would have... would have...'

'No, they wouldn't. I reckon it was just a test. We would have been okay,' Lana reassured.

After a couple more minutes of walking in silence, Emma said, 'For the record... I'm keeping that precious thing for the guy I eventually love too.'

Lana smiled and squeezed her sister's arm as they walked the rest of the way in silence, watching the city around them.

As they finally spotted Westminster, they loosened their grip on each other and began to run towards the pier. On arrival, though, they were greeted with something they weren't quite expecting.

'I should have known,' said Lana as she kicked the pavement.

'It's not here, the boat's not here,' whispered Emma. 'Where do you think it is?'

'Honestly? I have no idea. Now, what do we do?'

Both of them sat down on the pavement in a huff.

'Maybe we need to get back to the Praxos house?' suggested Emma.

'Maybe... but do you have any idea where it is?'

Emma shook her head.

'Thought so. Me neither. Although...'

'What?' questioned Emma.

'Nah, it's nothing.'

'What, it might not be anything.'

'When we were underground with Eleanor, didn't she say something about not being far from the British Museum?'

'Yeah she did,' Emma said as her face brightened.

'You're not meant to go back there just yet,' said a voice from behind them, making them jump up in fright.

'Josiah Grimshaw! You've got to stop creeping up on people like that,' scolded Lana. 'What are you doing here, anyway? I thought you were supposed to stay away during the initiation?'

'I am, but I just figured I'd come and give you a clue. It won't hurt,' he said innocently.

'Well?' Lana said, standing and tapping her foot impatiently on the pavement.

'Well, what?' he said as she tutted. 'Oh, the clue,' he chuckled. When he looked at her face, he shut up immediately. 'Sorry,' he muttered, 'It's the boat. You're meant to find your way to the boat.'

'But how Joe? How are we meant to do that?' Emma said as she, too, stood up and faced him.

A couple of people walked past, eyeing the girls as if they were mad.

'Did you see them, Jim? Those girls, they looked like they were talking to someone who wasn't there,' said the woman with curly purple rinsed hair.

'Just keep walking woman,' said her husband as they hurried away. The girls just heard him say, 'This city is full of weirdos.'

Emma turned to Lana, and they both cracked up laughing, but when they turned back, Joe was gone.

'Great,' Lana huffed, 'Now what?'

Emma smiled, 'We do what he says. We find the boat.'

'But how?'

'I don't know, Sis. All I know is that we can and we will. If they believe that we can find it, then we should believe in ourselves too.'

'Okay,' sighed Lana as they turned to face the water. 'Which way was it facing earlier?'

'Left,' said Emma.

'Then left we shall go,' Lana said as she hooked her arm into Emma's once more and they began walking along the embankment, hoping that Declan and Saleena would appear.

But the further from Westminster Pier they went, the more they realised it wasn't going to be that easy.

'This is crazy,' Lana sulked, 'We have absolutely no idea where to go. Do you remember anything being said earlier? Anything about where they might have gone?'

'I would have told you if I had, Lana. Nobody said anything about it.'

Emma stopped suddenly in her tracks, deep in thought.

'What? What is it?'

'I just had a thought... remember when Eleanor was pointing out where some of the tunnels went off to?'

'Hm-hm.'

'Well, she did say that one of them went underneath the Thames Barrier and Greenwich. I guess Declan might have taken the boat down there. All other directions were on land within the city. What do you reckon?'

Rubbing her chin, Lana nodded briefly. 'That's a good point. And it's the only idea we've had so far. Let's do it. Let's head in that direction. It's going to be a long walk, though. It'll probably take us all night.'

'Not necessarily,' added Emma. 'Why don't we swim?'

'You're joking. I nearly froze to death earlier.'

'But look how quickly I was able to de-freeze you,' smiled Emma. 'If you hold on to my back, I can swim really fast. We'll be there in no time at all.'

'I don't like it,' sighed Lana, 'But I can see that you won't take no for an answer. So okay, then. But we need to find a hidden spot to get into the water. We don't want anyone to see us.'

Ten minutes later, the girls were swimming beneath the cold waters of the Thames. Coming up for air as often as possible so Lana could breathe comfortably. Soon afterwards, the girls had reached the Barrier.

Climbing out of the water, they found a hidden spot so Emma could warm them both up and dry them off a little. When they were comfortable enough to carry on, they turned back to face the water.

'There!' yelled Lana as she spotted a familiar boat moored just a little further downriver. Grinning, they ran towards it and climbed aboard happily.

'I can't believe it! We've found it,' sighed Emma as they looked for signs of their Mentors. But Declan and Saleena were nowhere to be found.

'Let's just have a quick shower and put some warm clothes on,' shrugged Lana as they walked down towards the back of the boat into their room.

'Where do you think they are?' Emma asked as she began to take off her shoes.

'Dunno. Does it matter?'

'Well, it's just a bit weird that the boat is here and they're not.'

'Can we worry about that after we've got cleaned up? I'll shower first. I think I'm colder than you.'

While Lana showered, Emma had a proper look around the boat, not having the chance to do so before. A door further down from their room led to Declan's bedroom, so she quickly shut it and turned around and faced another, smaller entrance. Opening it, she saw lots of shelves holding fluffy towels and a few dressing gowns. As she was closing it, she accidentally knocked one of the towels onto the floor. Picking it up and folding it neatly, she was about to put it back on the shelf when something caught her eye. Turning her head sideways, she bent her knees to lower herself a little and spotted something familiar behind the shelf. It was a small handle in the shape of an eye with wings.

'What are you doing?' asked Lana who had just stepped out of the bathroom and was towel drying her hair.

'Look,' pointed Emma.

'What is it?'

'Looks like a handle.'

'Pull it,' Lana suggested.

'What if it does something weird?'

'Whatever. I'm going to get dressed. Are you having a shower?'

But Emma was too intrigued to really take any notice of what Lana had said and so she put her hand out and gently tugged at the handle.

It was another door. A hidden door.

'Lana, come and check this out,' she said as her sister appeared fully dressed in clean, warm clothes.

'Oh wow,' she said, almost pushing Emma aside so she could step inside.

'Don't mind me.'

'Sorry Sis. It leads down to somewhere. You coming?'

Emma followed as they both stepped into the tiny room which contained a thin ladder leading downwards. Emma closed the door behind them, and they walked down to the bottom where they were faced with a hatch.

'Well, we can't open it. It'll flood the boat,' Emma said with a sigh.

'Not necessarily. It looks like one of those submarine hatch things that you see in the movies. It's got something to do with air pressure or something like that.'

'So you want to open a hatch on a boat on the river based on old movies you've seen? Lana, we're not even on a submarine. We're on a boat that doesn't belong to us. We can't sink Declan's boat on a hunch.'

But it was too late, Lana had taken it on herself to open it.

'Lana, you're insane,' yelled Emma as she started running back up the steps.

When she heard chuckling, she turned back and peered down.

'See,' said Lana with her hands on her hips. 'It's a hatch that leads to another tunnel. This Praxos Foundation has certainly got everything covered. Come on, let's go.'

'But I never got to shower or get cleaned up,' complained Emma as Lana left her behind.

With her hands on her hips, Emma dropped her head backwards. Looking upwards, she let out a deep sigh before following her sister into yet another tunnel.

❧ 2 2 ❧

The tunnel seemed cleaner, more modern like it was built relatively recently. There were a few lights overhead, some that flickered off and on every few minutes. They slowly walked through it, both wondering where it would lead them.

Emma let out a deep yawn.

'I know, me too,' answered Lana as she couldn't stop herself from doing the same thing. 'It must be pretty late. It's certainly been a long day. Hey, what was that?' she said as she stopped suddenly, putting out an arm to prevent Emma from moving further.

She pulled them both to one side of the tunnel.

'What?' whispered Emma.

'There's something down there.'

'Maybe it's just Declan.'

Shaking her head, Lana put a finger over her mouth to quieten her.

'No, it definitely wasn't Declan. I'm sure I saw glowing red eyes in the darkness down there. It didn't look human, Em...' she breathed.

'That's crazy, Lana. What else could it be?'

'I don't know. All I know is what I saw.'

'It is dark in here; there are creepy shadows everywhere. Maybe it was just your imagination. Let's walk a bit further and see,' said Emma.

But as they tentatively began taking steps further down the tunnel, a deep roar echoed down towards them.

They stopped, eyes wide open and looked at each other.

'What now?' mouthed Emma.

'Let's get out of here,' whispered Lana.

The girls were about to make a run for it when a high pitched scream pierced the air around them.

'Oh God... someone's in trouble down there. We've got to go and help,' shouted Lana as they both turned back again and began to run towards the frightening sounds ahead.

As they rounded a corner, they saw something that stopped them dead in their tracks. Lana was right, whatever it was certainly didn't look human. Well, not really. He was probably at least seven feet tall with large, broad wings that scraped the top of the tunnel. Deep-set fiery red eyes turned towards them, and he scowled, snarling.

A woman lay unconscious at its feet.

The sisters turned to look at each other as the same euphoric sensation began to bubble in their stomachs. With adrenaline pumping, they ran towards the beast. Just before they reached it, they literally ran up the sides of the tunnel and threw themselves on top of it.

But moments before they could do any damage, a bright light was shone directly onto them, and the beast began to laugh. Not an evil laugh like they would have expected, but a familiar gentle chuckle.

Sounds of laughter and applause began to fill the tunnel all around them as the beast opened his mouth and began to speak, much to Lana and Emma's confusion.

'It's okay now, girls. You can stop beating me. I'm not the enemy,' he said softly as the girls stopped what they were doing, shielding their eyes from the light.

Looking down, Emma noticed that the woman was no longer lying on the ground. She stood smiling up at them, clapping her hands.

'Emma, Lana, initiation is over,' said a familiar voice from behind the light. 'You can let Wilbur go now.'

'Wilbur?' said Emma.

As the beast gently placed the girls back on the ground, they watched in utter shock as he transformed back into the man who they'd met earlier at the Praxos House.

'Well done, you've passed with flying colours,' said Eleanor who stood with Declan, Saleena and the rest of the Watchers who all looked exhausted.

'This was fake? This was part of the initiation? And Wilbur? What is he?' asked Lana as Emma let herself plop down on the ground as she got her breath back.

'We'll update you tomorrow. For now, you can head back to the boat with Dec and Sal and get some sleep. I bet you're both exhausted,' she added as everyone began talking among themselves.

Lana quickly disappeared to chat to Liam who stood at the back of the crowd, leaning against the wall, grinning.

'Hey, Emma, how are you doing? Did you get on okay?' asked a lovely voice that made her grin and made her feel all warm inside.

'Hey,' she said as Diarmuid helped her up off the floor. 'I'm okay. Seriously ready for a good night's sleep though. How did you get on with your initiation?'

He smiled, warmly at her. 'It was good. I know what you mean about being tired, though. It's been a long night. It's good to see you,' he added as the group began to gather together.

'The initiations went remarkably well, everybody. I just wanted to let you all know that it's over now. You can all go home and get some food and rest. We'll reconvene tomorrow at Praxos House. Thank you for all your efforts. You should all be very proud of yourselves,' announced Eleanor. 'Now go. See you tomorrow,' she added.

'Look, we'll catch up tomorrow, okay?' Diarmuid said as he casually leaned forward and kissed Emma's cheek before he smiled down at her and then turned and walked away.

Standing with her hand over her cheek, which had turned a distinct shade of pink, Emma sighed happily and she squealed inside. He kissed me!

'Come on, girls, let's head back,' said Declan as he ushered them away from the group.

'Congratulations,' said Saleena as they walked back towards the hatch. But they were far too tired to answer back, and Emma was far too entranced by that gentle kiss to even think about anything else.

❧ 23 ❧

Sitting on her unmade bed, Lana was humming along to her phone, painting her nails a bright shade of orange, while Emma lay sprawled across her immaculate bed reading a book when Declan appeared at the door.

'We'll be leaving in ten minutes girls,' he said with a smile before disappearing again.

'Okay, thanks,' Emma yelled after him as she placed a magnetic skull and crossbones bookmark inside the book and closed it, carefully placing it on the bedside table.

'Lana,' said Emma, but she ignored her.

'Lana,' she repeated, louder.

When she still didn't hear her, Emma stood up and pulled the earphone out of her ear with a quick tug.

'Ow, what did you do that for?' she complained.

'We're leaving in ten minutes.'

'Oh, okay,' Lana said, carefully placing the brush back in the bottle and screwing the top on. With her fingers flared out, she shook her hands and blew on her wet nails while she sat and watched Emma put on her shoes.

'I wonder what's in store for us today.'

Emma raised her eyebrows, 'Whatever it is, I'm sure it's nowhere near as bad as yesterday. I hope not anyway.'

'Yeah, I know. I'm just looking forward to hearing about some of the others' initiations.'

'You mean Liam's,' Emma said with a smile.

'Maybe. I bet you can't wait to see Diarmuid again. Young love,' she said with a sarcastic sigh, 'and first kisses...' she said as Emma laughed, standing.

'Come on, let's go,' she said, playfully punching her on the shoulder as she walked past.

'Are you coming, Saleena?' asked Lana as they stood on deck waiting for Declan as he put on a light jacket and basketball cap.

'No, I'm staying here this morning, girls. I'm going to prepare a nice dinner for this evening. I might pop over this afternoon though, but I don't know yet. Have a good time,' she said, smiling as they headed off while Declan busied himself by taking his girlfriend in a long hug and a kiss.

'See you later, Sal,' he shouted as he joined the girls.

'Oh,' Emma suddenly said, 'When did this happen?' as she realised they were no longer moored by the Thames Barrier.

With a cheeky grin, Declan told them he'd stayed up later and moved the boat to another location.

'Where are we now?' Lana asked as they followed behind him, matching his fast stride.

'We're in Camden,' he said, barely taking a breath.

'Is that the same Camden with the cool shops and stuff?' Lana asked.

'Hm-hm,' he replied.

'Cool.'

'But we're not here to shop, Lana. We're heading down to Praxos House.'

'Are we close?' Emma asked.

'So so,' he said, pointing straight down the road. 'Just a few miles or so in that general direction. Not far from the British Museum, UCL, the Royal Academy of Dramatic Art....'

'UCL? What's that?' asked Emma.

'University College London.'

'Are we using the same entrance as yesterday? You know, in through the house and the weird wardrobe thing?'

'There's a different entrance we prefer to use. Less conspicuous,' he said with a grin as the girls noticed a group of young women smiling at him.

'Looks like you've got plenty of admirers down here, Declan,' Lana said cheekily.

He just turned and smiled, saying nothing.

Continuing to walk in silence for a while, Emma was taking notice of all the street names they'd walked down. They were now on Gower Street.

Just a little further down the road was a beautiful red brick building on their right. Declan, who noticed Emma's admiring glances, piped up, 'That's the UCL Cruciform Building.'

'Oh, right. It's impressive.'

As they walked by a couple of red telephone boxes, Emma's eyes suddenly widened, and she cursed to herself.

'What?' asked Lana.

'We forgot to ring Mum.'

'Uh oh... we'll be in trouble,' said Lana as she grabbed her purple leather handbag, delving inside it to the find the mobile phone Audrey had given her before they'd left Andilyse.

'Oh, God... it's broken. I guess water got into it last night.'

'Don't worry, girls. Sal and I both spoke to your Mum and Dad last night. They know you've got lots going on and they're fine that you haven't spoken to them. In fact, they said for you just to ring them at the end of the week. I reassured them that all is well and you're having a great time.'

'Aww thanks, Declan. That's a relief. She'll kill us though when she hears we've broken my phone.'

'Mine's broken too,' added Emma as she pulled out her mobile and found water sloshing about inside it.

'Here, give them to me, and I'll get them fixed before the end of the day. Don't worry about it,' said Declan as they handed him the phones with a grin.

'Grant Museum of Zoology... sounds like a blast,' said Lana sarcastically as they walked past a sign pointing down to the right.

'I bet it's great,' said Emma.

'Yeah, if you're a total geek,' replied Lana, sticking out her tongue in jest.

'Ooh look there's a Waterstones!' Emma said, almost jumping

up and down. 'Must remember that for when we have some free time. I could use some new books.'

Lana rolled her eyes as they carried on walking.

'Eleanor's got tonnes of books if you need some more reading material,' smiled Declan.

'I doubt she shares the same tastes as Emma,' joked Lana.

'Actually, I think she does. When we first saw her yesterday, she was reading The Hunger Games.'

'Really?' said Lana, 'Cool.'

After walking a little further, the trio turned left down Great Russell Street, where there seemed to be a lot more going on. Little cafés, restaurants and shops scattered the right-hand side of the road and on the left was a vast, very grand building which, as they walked farther along, eventually revealed itself to be the British Museum.

'Impressive, isn't it?' Declan remarked as they stopped for a moment to admire the grandeur of the architecture.

It's incredible,' sighed Emma. 'I wish we could go in.'

'We will, just not today. Don't worry; you will get a chance,' he said with a smirk.

'How old is this building? It's not like anything I've ever seen. It's more like something from a movie, isn't it?' Emma said in awe.

'Yeah, like Night at the Museum or something.'

'Not quite what I was thinking,' laughed Emma, 'but I guess you catch my drift.'

'It was established in 1753,' Declan piped up, 'and was added to substantially over the next 200 hundred years or so. It's believed to be one of the finest museums in the world, you know?' he said proudly as the girls looked at him and smiled.

'I wouldn't have thought you'd be the history buff type,' said Lana.

'You'd be surprised. There are lots about me that you don't know about,' he said, tapping the side of his nose and smirking again. 'Come on, if we don't get moving, we're going to be late.'

Continuing past the museum, they stopped by a small square of greenery, Bloomsbury Square, where Declan turned to face an old white building with a couple of pillars by the front door. Expecting to walk up the stairs to the house, the girls were surprised when he turned slightly to the right of the building and walked around some old iron railings, disappearing down a few well-hidden steps into what looked like a basement flat.

Turning to look at each other, the girls shrugged their shoulders and followed down the dingy steps, slightly slippery, and moss-covered, with Lana trying very hard not to touch the slightly grimy looking handrail. 'Ew,' she muttered to herself.

After they'd stepped inside the old wooden door, Declan closed and locked it behind them. They were inside what looked like an ordinary spacious basement flat, decorated pleasantly enough with modern furniture. Stepping through the open plan living and dining room, they walked through a long galley kitchen complete with all mod cons. Stopping while Declan opened another door, Lana wondered what it would be like to live there; so close to all that London has to offer. She sighed, remembering that in a few short weeks they'd be returning to the middle of nowhere, at least that's what she often called Andilyse Island. She yearned for the hustle and bustle of city life. One day, she thought. One day I'll come and live here.

Turning to face them, Declan said, 'After you. But be careful of the steps.'

The door he'd opened led down some more steep steps.

'I thought we were already in the basement?' she piped up.

'You should know better than to assume anything like that after yesterday,' answered Emma as the two carefully headed downwards, one steep step at a time.

Once they'd reached the bottom, Declan called down from upstairs, 'You okay?'

'Yeah,' they yelled back.

'I'm closing the door behind me and its a bit dark so don't get spooked.'

The moment he stopped speaking, they stood in complete darkness.

But as Declan turned to begin walking downwards, he was faced with a bright light leading the way. He laughed and thanked Emma as he reached the bottom before turning left through a low archway that led to a series of arches - all sloping downwards, leading them further and further away from the flat.

'Where are we?' asked Lana.

'Nearly there.'

And through just a few more archways, they were faced with what appeared to be a brick wall.

'Oh,' said Emma, 'Did we take a wrong turn?'

Declan's mouth twitched as if he was trying not to smile as he pushed one of the bricks inwards and the faux wall slid to one side, revealing a familiar site: the grand hallway of the Praxos Foundation.

'Brilliant!' Emma said as they walked through, spotting Eleanor on the other side talking to Nisha, Imran and Cassie.

'Good Morning, girls. Morning Dec,' she said with a smile before returning her attention to the others.

Declan disappeared into another room, leaving the girls alone. The moment Lana spotted Liam, she grinned at her sister and walked towards him.

Emma, feeling a little silly just standing alone, decided to have a look around until Eleanor was ready for them.

Peering upwards, she admired the beautiful brickwork of the archways high above her head. It reminded her of the intricate designs found in many of England's old cathedrals. Not that she'd ever visited any of them, but she'd seen plenty of pictures in history class, and they'd always intrigued her.

As she looked upwards, she continued to stroll backwards, walking straight into someone.

'Oops, sorry,' she said as she turned to find a handsome face looking down at her with a huge grin.

'Diarmuid,' she exclaimed, turning pink as he immediately took her hand in his.

'Good morning beautiful,' he said, bending down to kiss her on the cheek, cheeks which then darkened to a much deeper shade of pink.

'Good morning,' she breathed, barely able to speak.

'Did you sleep well?' he asked.

She nodded, 'Really well. It was a long day yesterday, though. I was exhausted. How about you?'

'Yeah, me too. Where are you staying?' he asked.

'On a boat. Declan's boat. Have you met him? He's like an uncle to us. Declan saved my dad's life, like on numerous occasions, so they're great friends. They worked in the police force together before I was born...' when she realised she was babbling, she shut up.

Diarmuid's smile lit up his face. 'I met him yesterday after I finished my initiation. He seems like a pretty cool guy.'

Emma just smiled.

'Hey, so how was your initiation?' he asked as they continued strolling around the edge of the hallway.

'Scary, invigorating, euphoric, terrifying, weird... shall I go on,' she laughed, 'How about yours?'

'About the same as yours. I teamed up with Liam. He's crazy that guy, but cool. I think we passed,' he grinned.

'So what's your... your... erm....'

'Special ability?' he asked her.

Laughing, she nodded.

'I can light up from the inside and...'

'Really,' she coughed, her eyes wide in astonishment. 'So can I.'

'Awesome!'

'Sorry, what else?'

Smiling, he added, 'I can also control electricity.'

'Really? That sounds painful,' she said, pulling a funny face, making him laugh aloud before he shook his head.

'It's not painful, well, it hasn't been painful yet anyway.'

'That's pretty impressive, Diarmuid.'

'So what about you? Other than being able to light up? I'm assuming there is more to your hidden talents?'

'Well, I can swim really, really fast and when I'm underwater, it seems like I don't really need to breathe... oh and last night, last night Lana and I were able to fight like some kind of ass-kicking ninja chicks,' she giggled excitedly.

'Ass kicking ninja chicks?' he repeated with a massive grin, making Emma's face blush yet again as she almost melted into him.

'I assume you're talking about me,' said a voice approaching them.

'Yeah, Emma was just telling me about you two being able to fight like... ass-kicking ninja chicks,' he repeated, laughing.

'It's true. We don't know where it came from. It was when those scary thugs attacked us in the alley.'

'Excuse me,' said Eleanor, who had overheard the conversation, 'What thugs?'

'The Praxos thugs you set on us as part of the initiation,' Lana replied, but Eleanor was shaking her head.

'We didn't set anybody on you, Lana.'

Emma and Lana looked at each other in shock.

'Can you tell me exactly what happened?'

'We'd just managed to get outside, and we were deciding which way to go when two big guys stuck knives at our throats and pulled us into an alleyway. We were terrified at first, thinking we were done for,' the girls looked at each other again before Lana continued, 'But something kicked in and we just started fighting. We ended up knocking them both out before we tied them up with rope. We wrote on their foreheads with lipstick and left them there,' she laughed.

'What did you write?' asked Moira, who had been standing at the back listening.

'Please arrest us, we attack young girls,' Lana said proudly.

Some of the other kids laughed and Liam high fived Lana as Eleanor's eyebrows raised before she spoke, 'These men had nothing to do with Praxos, Lana. They were seriously dangerous attackers. I'll check with the local police to ensure they've been apprehended. Why did you think it was part of the initiation?'.

Sharing a glance, both girls shrugged their shoulders, 'I guess we just assumed it was. Especially after you threw the rope down to us,' Emma said quietly.

'Rope?'

'Yeah, after we'd knocked them out we were looking all over for something to tie them up with but couldn't find anything. And then some rope was thrown down from the top of one of the buildings. We figured it was you,' Lana responded.

Eleanor, Declan, Wilbur and a few of the other Mentors looked alarmed.

'No, it wasn't any of us. There was clearly someone else out there who gave you a helping hand,' she said slowly, a worried look in her eyes. 'But we'll worry about that later. Today we will assess your initiations. But don't worry, you all passed,' she said with a smile, 'with flying colours. I was most impressed. Now come, let's go into the white room to begin.'

☙ 24 ❧

'The purpose of this assessment is not to criticise anything that you may have done wrong. It is simply to demonstrate to each other what you went through, how you did it, and what your special skills are. This is about working together; something of utmost importance at Praxos,' said Eleanor once they were all settled, sitting scattered around the room, with all the Mentors sitting around them.

'However, before we start, I'd just like to introduce you to the other Mentors in our group,' Eleanor said as she pointed to a small group of adults who sat waiting. 'Declan Alexander lives on a houseboat on the Thames. He is currently looking after Lana and Emma. His girlfriend, Saleena Bennett also lives on the boat, but she's not with us today,' Declan smiled and nodded his head as she continued, 'Zane and Marian Chambers live on Gower Street not far from here. They are currently looking after Liam and Diarmuid.'

A young couple holding hands, both with shoulder-length brown hair, stepped forward and waved with their free hands, grinning.

'Bryn Cooper has recently joined us from the States where he worked with the Seventh House of Praxos in New York. He is now looking after Cassie and Elliott where they are staying in a converted loft in Kings Cross.'

A tall, muscular man with a crew cut stepped forward and backwards with a brief salute to the group.

'Habika Buhari has worked with Praxos for many years. She originally came from Africa, as you might imagine,' Eleanor said with a smile to a woman wearing traditional African garb whose smile lit up the room. 'Penny and Nisha are under her care. Habika also lives on a houseboat on the Thames. Oksana is mentoring Moira and Imran from Ukraine and her Scottish husband, Brody McGregor.'

A very tall and beautiful blonde-haired woman nodded with a smile, as did the fair-haired even taller man next to her. 'Oksana and Brody have a penthouse apartment in Camden Town. And finally, Ava and Rupert are staying with Megan and Rhydian Llewellyn, originally from Wales but have been living in Waterloo, in the capital for the past ten years.' Megan and Rhydian both had beautiful faces, he with short red hair and she with cropped black hair. They both grinned at the group and said hi.

'Now that we all know each other let's continue. Right, we just heard about Lana and Emma's experience that turned out to be something quite alarming. An attack on two innocent young girls by two evil thugs isn't something we take lightly. This is exactly the kind of thing we want to help prevent from happening on the streets of London, and elsewhere. It turns out that Lana and Emma did exactly the right thing by subduing the men. In ordinary circumstances, the victims should have immediately contacted the police. At Praxos, however, we cannot always do that because of our secrecy code. Yes, Moira?' said Eleanor as Moira's hand shot upwards.

'Secrecy code?'

'Yes, because of our unique characteristics, and the true nature of who we are, we cannot let the general public know of our existence. However, we do work in conjunction with certain authorities...'

'So not all police know about us? Then who does?' asked Ava.

'We often work with the British Secret Service...'

'Cool,' added Liam and Rupert who looked across at each other with a laugh.

Raising her eyebrows, Eleanor continued, 'the Prime Minister is well aware of our existence, of course. So, in the event of something like this ever happening again, you are to contact me, or your Mentors, immediately so that we can alert the necessary authorities. Due to last night's initiations, it is perfectly understandable that you, Lana and Emma, assumed that it was our doing. You did the right thing. In fact, you worked so well together; I think you deserve a round of applause,' she said with a cheeky smile, small dimples appearing in her wrinkled cheeks.

Both girls blushed and laughed as the room exploded with clapping and cries of 'well done'.

'Now, while we're on the subject of Lana and Emma, let's talk about their initiation. Girls, talk us through it. Why don't you start, Emma?'

'Well, it started with being trapped in the tunnels that were, like, seriously dark. All we had was a sealed letter from Praxos, and we couldn't even read it, it was so dark. And then we remembered what happened to me when the tattoo appeared and when I fell in the Thames...'

'You didn't fall, Sis. You threw yourself in,' laughed Lana.

'Oh, yeah, I guess. Whatever. When I was in there, and it was dark and cold and wet...' she laughed nervously, 'I realised my body kind of glowed, giving me a sort of light, letting me see all around. Well, in the tunnels, we decided I should try and make that happen again. Thankfully it worked, and we could see!' she said as the rest of the group clapped.

'Unfortunately, when we opened the letter, it was completely blank...'

'Yeah, that happened to us too,' said Diarmuid.

'And us,' Moira added along with Elliott, Rupert and Nisha.

'So I'm guessing you figured out the water then?' she asked as the others all nodded enthusiastically.

'Anyway, we then...' Emma continued to explain what had happened to them until they arrived at the dilapidated hall where they'd fallen asleep.

'Something weird happened to me in there,' Lana said, recalling her dream-like state.

'It did? You never mentioned it,' Emma whispered.

'Yeah, I did. I told you about it. You know, I thought it was a dream...?'

'You should always question these things during the initiation, and afterwards of course,' interrupted Eleanor, 'Because it is often another skill, or ability whatever you want to call it, revealing itself to you. Tell us what happened, Lana.'

'Well, we were sitting having a break in this dilapidated old hall. It was easy to see that it was once a beautiful and grand place where wealthy people would have dances and stuff. Anyway, Emma had fallen asleep, and I began to hear things, music and voices, feet tapping on the floor as if people were dancing. I could even sense the scents of mingling tobacco, perfume and sweat...'

'Sounds lovely,' cringed Moira with a giggle.

Lana smiled, 'Yeah, I know. But it began to feel real, you know? An image popped into my head of all these people having fun. It was kind of surreal, which was why I just figured it was a dream.'

'Can you describe what the music was like, Lana? What the people were wearing?'

Nodding, Lana said 'Hm-hm,' before continuing, 'There were sounds from a harp, a violin and erm, oh yeah, a harpsichord,' she closed her eyes for a moment, remembering the images in front of her eyes. 'There was a woman in front of me, her skin was all white, and she had a black beauty spot just above her lip. Decorated with feathers, her hair was piled high on her head and looked like it had been powdered white. She wore a long azure blue silk dress which pulled her waist in so much it must have been difficult to breathe, and then it fanned outwards at the sides and back. It was cut so low that her cleavage was well on display, with a bundle of little pink roses pinned to one side of her top. She was flirting with two men who sat beside her...'

Lana seemed to have zoned out and was talking, barely taking a breath while the others sat silently listening in fascination.

She could hear the same music, chattering and people dancing. As she watched the scene unfold before her, she continued to describe all that she saw in real-time.

'The woman is standing up. She's walking to the nearest window. It's a door. She pushes it open and walks outside to get some air. She's fanning herself with a pretty pink fan made of feathers. She's leaning over a railing; there's a staircase below her. A man walks up to her. He's not someone I noticed before. She turns to him and smiles. She's kissing him passionately and, oh,' Lana stopped abruptly, her eyes shooting open in absolute shock.

'What happened?' asked those surrounding her, 'Lana, what happened?'

'It's quite all right, Lana. I'll finish for you. The man pushed her down the stairs, didn't he?'

Lana sat bolt upright and nodded, 'H... how do you know?' she breathed while Wilbur suddenly appeared by her side with a cup of tea. 'It will make you feel better. It's sweet, for the shock,' he added. She took it gratefully as Eleanor continued.

'What you've just described is the murder of Countess Dolly Van der Bergen in 1754. Unfortunately, there were no witnesses to the actual event, and so it was deemed to be an accident. I had my doubts, of course. I always suspected it was her husband who pushed her.'

'Did you know her, Eleanor?' asked a suitably impressed Nisha.

'No, not personally, but I knew of her. She was quite well known in London at that time. It was very sad. Her husband was killed in an accident some years later; a horse-riding accident, I believe. But that's by the by.'

'But how come Lana was able to describe the event?' asked Emma.

'I do believe that the initiation helped establish one of her other abilities. Lana can visualise things that have happened in the past, whether it be yesterday, a year ago, ten years ago or a hundred years ago. Certain things will trigger images, sounds, smells all to overcome her, allowing her to see the whole event, almost in a movie-like sense, I believe. Is that right, Lana? Did you see it as if you were watching a movie?'

Lana nodded, 'It started that way but then it was like I was actually there. I could see everything around me. It was weird.'

'Carry on Lana, continue with what happened during the rest of your initiation.'

As she spoke of what they experienced for the rest of the evening, the group listened intently until she'd finished.

'Thank you. Does anyone have any questions? Anything they'd like to add?' asked Eleanor.

Penny's hand shot up into the air.

'Yes, Penny?'

'Earlier on, Lana and Emma said that something kicked in and they turned into ass-kicking ninja chicks...'

The group laughed.

'Well, how come that didn't happen to Nisha or me? I want to be able to do that.'

Eleanor smiled. 'Unfortunately, not everyone will develop the same skills...' an audible sigh filled the room before she continued, 'however, we will train you so that you can fight. But I'll get on to that bit later. If there are no other questions for Lana or Emma, we can move on to the next group?'

'When you were swimming in the Thames... didn't you get covered in sewage?' asked Rupert, who kept his face completely serious.

'That's enough Rupert,' Eleanor scolded as she tried not to laugh. Emma shook her head while Rupert pinched his nose and pretended there was a bad smell in the room.

Declan stepped forward and gave him a gentle slap on the back of the head as the group giggled.

'Right then Rupert, seen as you seemed to have gotten every-one's attention, let's hear about yours and Ava's initiation.'

'Oh, okay then Miss...'

'Please don't call me that, Rupert. My name is Eleanor, not Miss. Well, it's Eleanor when I'm like this, but you can call me Ellie when I'm young if you like,' she smiled with her eyebrows raised. 'Continue.'

'Okay Eleanor,' he said, sounding her name out slowly for added effect. 'Well, Ava and I began our initiation in the centre of the Thames, on a little boat. Like you, we just had the blank letter for information....' and he continued to tell the group about how his and Ava's ability led them slowly and inevitably back to Praxos, where they were greeted by the same thing the girls had been confronted with: Wilbur in his more unusual state.

Rupert's special abilities not only include him being able to see through solid walls, but he can also walk through them whereas

Ava can hear things from miles around and can focus on specific sounds far in the distance. She can also make herself be heard in people's minds who are miles away.

After a few questions, it was Cassie and Elliott's turn. Cassie confidently stood up and explained how they'd been plunged into darkness in the tunnels beneath the city. Elliott was able to use his fingers like a lighter, making small amounts of fire from his fingertips, which helped to light the way, while she could move at the speed of light. With Elliott holding on to her, they were able to move beneath the city quicker than anybody else. But when they were faced with a massive wall of ice which they couldn't break through, Elliott's gift was accentuated so that he could create a constant source of fire to melt it.

Imran shyly stood up when it was his turn to speak.

'I can play with time,' he smiled cheekily, 'and I was able to stop, rewind or fast forward time, giving us an added advantage of extra time to fulfil our duties. As long as Moira held on to me, she came along for the ride.'

'Which we needed because my gift happens when I sleep. Through dreams, I can see what I must do next...' she continued, telling everyone what they had done, finally summing up, 'So once we were at the bottom of Big Ben, I simply went to sleep for a while, which led us to our next clue, which we kept doing until we eventually found Wilbur,' she smiled.

'Awesome, can you imagine that? Being able to manipulate time, that's seriously impressive, Dude,' said Liam with a high five.

'Nisha, tell us what you got up to last night.'

As she stood up, Nisha looked around at her colleagues and smiled, a little embarrassed, 'You could say that my ability is kind of creepy. Basically, I can see dead people.'

'Oh, that sucks man,' Liam said with a grimace.

'It is not too bad. Most of the dead people I have seen and spoken to so far have been nice enough. And the ones I saw last night were very helpful. Our initiation began in the cemetery, where we followed clues on some of the headstones until eventually, we reached a group of dead people who were waiting for us.'

Penny continued the story, 'Which totally freaked us out, of course. I couldn't see them at first, but once Nisha began communicating with them, their spirits appeared to me too. But only while she was speaking to them. And then it was over to me. You see, I can make people speak the truth, which certainly comes in handy sometimes. Well, I had to speak to the spirits last night to find out our next clue. They wouldn't tell Nisha, but they told me,' she smiled. 'And then we went on to...', and she continued talking until she eventually finished where they met Wilbur.

'Thank you, girls. Now there's just one group left to tell us about their initiation, and that's Liam and Diarmuid.'

Diarmuid suggested Liam go first, who grinned at Lana as he stood up proudly, leaning against the wall casually.

'We were given the letter the same as you guys, and then left in that tunnel under the Thames Barrier where we saw you all last night. It was completely dark. Although Diarmuid can light himself up from the inside, he wanted to use his other talent instead, which is to manipulate electricity. It was totally sick as he managed to switch on most of the lights down there... with his mind. Sick yeah? Anyway, as we moved along the tunnel, we soon realised we were completely locked in. A huge boulder was in our way. I mean it was like, massive. It wouldn't budge, we tried pushing it, but there was nowhere for it to go, so I started punching it, and sure enough, I eventually managed to make a hole big enough for us to get through...'

'You punched a hole in a massive boulder? Dude, that's epic,' said Rupert, nodding his head in respect.

'I know man. But once we got to the other side, we were faced with a wall of electricity. I didn't realise it until it was too late. I got a shock like never before, man... it threw me back about ten metres, knocked me out for a couple of seconds. When I came to, Diarmuid was standing with his arms outstretched, pulling the electricity into him. It was unbelievable,' Liam said, still trying to understand how it was done.

'Wow,' said a few of the group.

'I know, wow, yeah?'

Diarmuid interrupted him then, and Liam sat back down. 'All in a day's work,' he said with a smile which melted Emma as she sighed quietly to herself.

'But it wasn't over yet. Once we'd got through and out of the tunnel, we had to make our way back upriver to Praxos. We found a small rowing boat and Liam literally rowed us there in just a few minutes. The speed was something else. It was like being in a speed boat. That guy has got some serious muscle,' he chuckled as Lana grinned at Liam who winked back. It didn't take us long to figure out the way back to the Foundation, and that was pretty much it, I think?' he said, looking over at Liam who nodded.

'Well, I think everybody here deserves a round of applause,' Eleanor announced as she and the Mentors stood up while the room exploded with clapping and cheers.

When it had quietened down, she smiled and began again, 'Relatively simple initiations to bring out your true skills. That was the purpose of last night's challenges. We already had a pretty good idea of what you were capable of, but we needed to know your strengths and weaknesses before we could continue on this journey with you. Now that is over with; I'd like to discuss something essential with you. Your education,' she said, as she strolled from one side of the room to the other.

'As you have all recently completed your GCSE exams, we would like to invite you to attend an extraordinary academy run by the Praxos Foundation... here in London,' she added with a smile.

Lana was practically hyperventilating as Emma put her hand upwards.

'Yes, Emma?'

'You mean, we can come to London to do our A-Levels? Actually live here in London while we do them?'

Eleanor nodded, 'Yes, we have special facilities for you to continue your education here, but not just A-Levels, this is also your opportunity to learn more about your true skills, to develop them, to learn about the history of the angels, about your parents, how to fight, how to investigate and also...' she stopped momentarily for effect, '... to learn about the Paranormals, the Supernaturals and the Elementals.'

As Lana continued to hyperventilate with absolute delight, Emma asked, 'Elementals?'

'Yes, just another kind of paranormal beings.'

Suddenly the room was full of noise as the twelve students began chattering loudly, all asking questions at once.

'Quiet please,' said Declan loudly, and the room became immediately silent.

'It should be no surprise to you that supernatural beings exist because you already know of your existence,' Eleanor chuckled before continuing, '... and you are half-human, half angels which makes you a paranormal being. Here at Praxos, we tend to call those that are not human or are part human, Paranormals and there are rather a lot of them in our world. You've already met one other kind,' she said, pointing towards Wilbur who took a bow.

'What kind is he? Sorry, what are you, Wilbur?' asked Penny.

'Go ahead, Wilbur,' Eleanor encouraged.

Taking a few steps toward the front of the room, Wilbur turned to face the teenagers. 'I am a Mothman,' he said gravely. 'Well, I am part Mothman. I can change from human form into that which you all saw last night.'

'I've seen that movie,' said Rupert, 'Aren't you supposed to foretell death or something?'

Wilbur's mouth twitched to one side, and he chuckled, along with Eleanor and the other Mentors who stood listening, from around the room.

He nodded, 'Old wives tales,' he said, tutting and shaking his head, as he turned to walk back to the edge of the room.

'Over the millennia, humans have associated so much death and destruction with the Paranormals that they now believe it, for the most part anyway. But we're digressing. I was talking about the Academy. It is, of course, entirely up to you whether you choose to continue your education at the Academy but, considering who and what you are, I would highly recommend it. You will reach your potential here. But, as I said, we are not forcing you to study here. We would just be delighted should you choose to,' she said with a smile.

'Where is the Academy, Eleanor?' asked Nisha.

'We have a building over on Gower Street, next to the UCL. However, our more unusual classes are underground.'

'The UCL?' Imran asked.

'The University College London,' piped up Lana who had recalled what Declan had told them earlier that morning.

'That's right, Lana.'

'I don't remember seeing any entrance to another Academy just there,' Emma said as she tried to remember the street.

'That's because our entrance is a little more discreet, that's all. But it is there,' smiled Declan.

'We all give classes at the Academy, but there are other professors too.'

'Our group is a little small to warrant a whole Academy, isn't it though?' asked Elliott curiously.

The Mentors all smiled as Eleanor answered, holding her hand over her mouth for a moment as she tried not to laugh, 'The Academy teaches students from all over the country, Elliott. We also have some that travel from abroad.'

'Oh, cool,' he said.

'But what about our parents? What do we tell them?' asked Emma as she suddenly realised her Mum and Dad didn't know about anything that was happening.

'Don't worry about that. We've got it covered,' Declan answered with a grin.

＊ 25 ＊

Later that day after the group had eaten lunch and talked more about their skills and their future, Eleanor and the Mentors were having a private meeting while the teenagers chilled out and talked among themselves, lounging on many of the oversized beanbags in the room.

Lana leaned across Liam as they chatted quietly, while Emma, Diarmuid, Ava and Rupert discussed what they had learned so far.

They were all in such deep conversation that they barely even noticed when the door was flung open, and Wilbur appeared.

'Lana and Emma, Eleanor would like to see you both in her chambers,' he said, making them jump.

The girls immediately climbed off their beanbags and followed him through the main hall and down an unknown corridor, until they reached Eleanor's office, a room they hadn't yet visited.

As Wilbur tapped on the door and pushed it open, they were surprised to find a very contemporary looking office suite, with one wall almost covered entirely by a projector screen showing what appeared to be Westminster in real-time. Inviting and spacious, the room's walls were painted in a light aquamarine blue with a white horizontal stripe. In the centre stood a solid oak desk with a thick glass top, covered in a bundle of black and white files and a neat stainless steel covered laptop. Several sizeable white filing cabinets stood along the opposite wall to the screen, the top drawer of one was wide open, where Eleanor leaned reading a piece of paper.

'Come in, girls,' she said just as the screen changed to show Times Square.

'What is that, Eleanor?' asked Lana as they all looked across at the big screen.

'That's my view of London. Seeing as we're so far underground, I do miss having windows, and Praxos has numerous cameras around the city where I can see what's going on. Here, I'll show you,' she said as she picked up a sleek remote control and pressed one of the buttons, changing the image so that it showed Notting Hill (Emma and Lana both recognised it from the movie), Gower Street, 'There's the entrance to the Academy,' Eleanor said before continuing to flick, showing the entrance to the British Museum, Tower Bridge, the Thames Barrier, Buckingham Palace and more.

'That's pretty cool,' Lana said as the screen was then flicked to feature London Zoo, where she left it for the time being.

'Not only is it beautiful, but it's a handy tool for our work. But that's not why I called you in. I wanted to have a chance to talk to all of you to answer any questions you might have about us, the foundation, the academy and of course, your parents. Your birth parents, that is,' she said, walking around to her chair behind the desk.

'Please, sit down,' she suggested as the girls wandered forward and sat in the two swivel chairs opposite Eleanor.

'I know it must have been a very peculiar and perhaps challenging few weeks for you both. Ever since your 16th birthdays, everything has changed. How are you feeling?' she asked with genuine concern, leaning forward so that her chin rested on her hand.

Lana glanced across at her sister before speaking first, 'Honestly, I've never felt better. This is all like a dream come true for me. And now to have the opportunity to come and study in London. I feel like I'm on cloud nine. I'm so happy. I'm just so grateful.'

With a smile, Eleanor put down her hand, 'And we're grateful to have you with us, Lana. This is your destiny. However, it's not all fun and games as I'm sure you will understand. You must work hard to achieve your best. It will be a struggle, but I do believe in you.'

'Thank you,' Lana grinned.

'And Emma. How about you?'

Looking down at the floor, Emma felt her cheeks turn a little pink before she opened her mouth to speak, 'I'm good, I guess. I mean, it's been life-changing and, erm, I don't know. I think I'm confused if you know what I mean? So much has happened so quickly that I feel like my head hasn't really caught up yet...'

Eleanor leaned right across the desk and put her hand on top of Emma's for a moment, 'I know exactly what you mean, Emma. Nobody expects you to be able to accept all of this in a matter of days. It takes time to come to terms with it. But you've already proven yourself, you've shown yourself how strong you are. You too, Lana. I've never seen Watchers with the strength you both have, both physical and mental, at this stage in your development. It usually takes a few years to get to where you both are now. When you were attacked last night, you both mentioned a feeling you got in the pits of your stomachs, a euphoric kick? Many Watchers never get that at all. And yet here you are, both experiencing the same thing after just a few short weeks. It's quite remarkable. This takes me to the next thing I wanted to talk to you about. Because you share the same quality of internal strength, it is proof that you share a parent. Watchers usually stem from a human mother and an angel father. However, your mother was the angel, not the other way around.'

Emma and Lana both sat with their mouths open, listening intently, not knowing what to think.

'What about our fathers?' Lana asked, finally closing her mouth.

'Clearly, you have different fathers,' Eleanor smiled. 'Sadly, both died shortly after your births.'

'But how? And how is it possible for an angel to give birth?' Emma whispered while a few tears drifted down her cheek.

Leaning back, Eleanor opened the top drawer of her desk and pulled out a packet of tissues, handing them to Emma.

'Well, as I told you before, I was an angel who came to earth and fell in love. I too, had a child,' she said as the girls gasped, but let her continue, 'My child was taken from me the same time they banished me to live in this form, neither young nor old. So, it can happen; it's just usually the other way round, that's all.'

'But what happened to our fathers? How did they die? And what happened to your child?' Lana blurted.

'Lana, your father was a man called Baraka. Originally from Africa, he came to London to join Praxos thirty years ago. He died just over sixteen years ago.'

'Baraka...' Lana whispered, as she tried to discreetly take a tissue before wiping at her eyes, careful not to smudge her mascara.

'Yes, he was a very gentle man, Lana. Fiercely loyal and protective.'

'How did he die?'

Eleanor pushed her chair backwards and slowly stood up, walking towards the screen where she watched the lions sleeping in their enclosure. With a deep sigh, she turned, 'There is something we haven't spoken about yet. I wanted to wait until you were all more prepared, but I guess you have a right to know. You have a right to know who killed your father. Not all Watchers are good like we are. Some fight for another cause. They fight for evil, not against it. Baraka was killed by one of those, who we call, The Skulls. I'm sorry, Lana.'

Lana's shoulders shuddered slightly as she blew into the tissue and wiped at her eyes as Emma leaned over and hugged her lightly.

'And what about Emma's father?' she sniffed.

Turning to look at the pale dark-haired girl, Eleanor nodded, 'I'm afraid he too was killed by the same group.'

'What was his name?' Emma asked, sadly.

'Abraham. He was American, from somewhere near Boston, I believe. I'm truly sorry, girls.'

As they sobbed the loss of fathers they had never known, Eleanor sat back down behind the desk and gave them a few moments before she spoke again.

'I know it's not easy to talk about all of this, girls, and I'm so sorry, but there is something truly remarkable here that you have failed to pick up on,' she said before adding, 'You are sisters. Twin sisters, in fact. Well, kind of twin sisters. As an angel, your mother was able to carry you both at the same time, although you Lana were born a few days earlier than Emma. I know it sounds unbelievable, but angels have many special powers, and she wanted to carry you together. She wanted you to develop a special bond, which you have, of course.'

As the truth dawned on them both, they turned to look at each other, the tears soon turning to smiles and they stood up and held on to each other for a minute before returning to their seats and looking toward Eleanor.

'I have always known the truth, of course, but I couldn't divulge it until you were of age. I was there when your fathers were killed; they saved a lot of people that night. Your mother, however, was so distraught that she couldn't continue to live with the humans and so she took steps to find the right family for you to grow up with. She chose the Morgans.'

'That's just so... so incredible. It's unbelievable. But how did we get there? Mum and Dad always told us that we were found on the island as babies?' asked Emma as she continued to wipe the tears from her cheeks.

'Before Baraka and Abraham died, Della was...'

'Della?'

'That was your mother's name,' smiled Eleanor kindly before carrying on, 'She was fun-loving, a little eccentric, and she loved to do the unexpected. So she first sent you, Lana, in a little hot air balloon across the water so that you landed almost on your parents doorstep.'

Lana's eyes widened in disbelief, 'She put me in a hot air balloon? I could have died!' she blurted out.

'Shaking her head, Eleanor continued, 'That was impossible. You see as I said before, the angels have many special abilities, some might call it magic. You were safer on that balloon than anywhere else on earth, Lana, she made sure of that....'

'Hang on a minute,' Lana suddenly blurted out, standing up and pacing up and down the room, 'I dreamed it, I did, I dreamed about it fairly recently. I remember it so clearly now, the balloon drifting through the night sky and eventually landing in the back garden. Oh My God, that was me, that was real,' she shrieked.

'Yes, Lana, that was you. It was real. And as I was saying, a few days later, she sent you, Emma, in a miniature boat down the

Thames and out into the North Sea. You were bound for Andilyse Island, for the Morgans. You too were incredibly safe. Della was determined about that.'

'What happened to her?' Emma asked as Lana finally sat back down.

'You must remember that she was heartbroken. She'd lost the two men that meant the world to her. She needed to mourn her way, and she couldn't do that with two babies. She knew that your lives would be so much better with the Morgans and so she had to let you go. Once she knew you'd arrived safely, she returned home,' Eleanor said, pointing upwards.

'But how is that possible?' Lana asked.

'What do you mean?' Eleanor replied.

'When you chose love over your work as an angel, they - whoever they are - cast you aside and cursed you. Why didn't they do that to our mother?'

Eleanor looked sadly at both the girls before sighing loudly, 'When the angels come down to earth, they are given a limited amount of time to spend here among the humans. To learn, to love and some to reproduce, but they must eventually return home. They are usually given between five and ten years. Della was here for two years before she returned.'

'You mean... she was going to leave us anyway?' Emma said distraught.

'I'm afraid so.'

'But that sucks,' Lana muttered.

'Yes, well. That's the way it's always been. And if you try and do something about it, you end up like me,' sighed Eleanor as she re-arranged some papers on her desk before Lana spoke again.

'Is she still alive?' breathed Lana.

'I believe so. But once the angels have come and gone, I don't think they can return. I'm sorry. But you've had wonderful upbring-ings, haven't you? I know that Audrey and Patrick Morgan were chosen for a reason.'

'If Della really is our mother, how come we have different birthdays?' asked Emma pouting.

'As I said before, Della was capable of powerful magic. Lana came first, and you Emma, weren't ready to come into the world for another few days. She had a long labour,' Eleanor smiled. 'I know this all sounds like fiction but their world,' she said, pointing upwards, 'is very different to the world we live down here.'

'But what about you? Did you lose all of your abilities when you chose to stay here?'

Eleanor nodded, leaning back in her chair, 'Most of them. They left me with a few, but I can only use them in my younger state. But enough about me, it's almost five o'clock. I should prepare myself for the change. Do you have any more questions?'

The girls stood, shaking their heads.

'I know you will have more once you've had time to take it all in. Just know that my door is always open for you, for both of you, okay?' she said as the girls reached the door.

Just as they were about to close it behind them, Lana turned back and asked, 'What about your child, Eleanor? What happened?'

Eleanor shook her head, 'My daughter was taken from me. I never knew what happened to her,' she said sadly, turning away from them, indicating they should go.

Lana quietly closed the door behind her, just as the clock struck five o'clock. A long deep groan could be heard as they walked away.

❧ 26 ☙

The following day, the group was given a 'pass' day, where they could do whatever they wanted, so the girls decided to go shopping. Before they left the boat, Declan handed them an envelope, 'Your Mum and Dad asked me to give this to you for when you had some free time. Have fun today, but remember, don't use your abilities in front of anyone. See you later,' he said before disappearing back indoors.

As they stepped off the boat, which was moored at Westminster Pier again, they avidly opened the envelope to find a card from their parents and a rather large stash of 50-pound notes.

Lana gasped, jumping up and down, while Emma giggled along with her before reading the card:

'We hope you're both enjoying your work experience in the city, girls. We know that shopping on the island isn't much fun for you both (especially you Lana!). So here's some spending money to buy whatever you want in London. Don't spend it all at once! We love you lots, see you soon. Love Mum & Dad xxx.'

'Come on, let's hit the shops,' giggled Lana as she dragged Emma along beside her.

'Would you mind if I came along,' said a voice out of nowhere.

'Joe!' squealed Lana, 'Where have you been? We didn't see you at all yesterday? Of course, you can come with us.'

Grinning shyly, Joe floated alongside them, 'I was with some of my own kind.'

'What? Like other ghosts, you mean?'

Josiah nodded as they stopped at traffic lights waiting for them to turn green.

'Yes. I found a cemetery where there are quite a few of us.'

Once the lights had changed, and the three of them had continued across the road, Emma made sure no-one was watching when she turned to look at him, 'Do you know why you're still here, Joe? Do all those others know too?'

But he looked at the floor and shook his head, 'I wish I knew.'

'Hey, let's not dwell on that now, we're here to have fun today!' squealed Lana again, as she practically ran down the road, as if she could hear the shops calling to her.

'Wait up!' shouted Emma as she sped up to catch up to her.

'No can do... Oxford Street awaits,' she giggled as she stopped just for a moment to check the map.

'This way,' she laughed, pointing over to the left, leaving Trafalgar Square to their right.

After they'd taken a few wrong turns, and Emma had taken over the map reading, the girls, along with Josiah, eventually found themselves on Oxford Street. Once they'd arrived, Lana erupted in a fit of giggles.

'I can't believe it. I'm actually here. I'm finally here on Oxford Street in London,' she said, dancing around in a little circle.

Emma looked at her, embarrassed, glancing at the shoppers who were giving her sister a bit of a wide berth.

'Erm, Sis. People are staring.'

'So?'

Emma shook her head and smiled before she left Lana and carried on walking down the street with Joe beside her. After about a minute, Lana was with them, grinning from ear to ear.

'Where shall we go first?' she asked, excitement bubbling from her every pore.

'Wherever takes your fancy,' Emma replied as they glanced from one shop to another.

'Is that... Zara?' squealed Lana as her feet moved faster than the rest of her, to get to the fashion store. Emma rolled her eyes as Joe whispered in her ear, 'Your sister is quite crazy, isn't she?'

Laughing, Emma nodded.

'Why is she going so insane over clothes shops?' he asked as they stepped inside the giant shop, watching as Lana stood still for a second and took a deep breath as she took it all in.

'Because Andilyse Island doesn't have anything like this. You must remember what shopping is like at home, Joe? There's not much choice, not for a fashion victim, anyway.'

'I... I don't remember,' he stuttered.

'Didn't you ever go shopping?' she asked him discreetly as a couple of young girls walked by giving her a funny look.

'I... I don't know. I can't seem to remember anything about the island.'

'Nothing at all?' she asked, alarmed.

When he shook his head, she turned to face him, 'Maybe it happens to all, you know... ghosts?'

'OMG,' shouted Lana from across the shop floor, 'Emma, you have GOT to come and see this...'

When Emma turned back to Joe, he had disappeared.

Shrugging her shoulders, she went to see what all the fuss was about. As she approached her sister, Lana was already bogged down with countless items of clothing and pairs of shoes.

Emma couldn't help but burst out laughing at the sight.

'Lana, you don't have to get the first things you see, you know!'

'I know, I just want to try all these on,' she said almost stumbling over the heap of clothes as she rushed towards the changing rooms.

'Here, let me give you a hand,' Emma offered, taking some of the items of clothing out of her grasp.

An hour later, Emma was still sitting in the changing rooms, watching as Lana paraded the clothes she'd chosen.

'Is this the last one?' she asked, sighing.

'Yeah, this is it, and then I promise we can go.'

'You said that twenty minutes ago.'

As Lana swept back the curtain, she stepped out like a model on a catwalk, wearing a cute little white crochet dress, brown knee-high boots and a brown hat that wouldn't stay put on her unruly hair. She bent forward, blew a kiss and continued to strut around the changing rooms.

Emma shook her head and laughed out loud. 'Okay, it is cute. I like that better than anything else you've tried on. I think you should get it, although I don't think much to that hat.'

With a huge smile that scrunched up her cheeks, Lana twisted her shoulder, turned her head and cracked up laughing. 'Yeah, my hair is just too big! Okay, I'll go take it all off, spend some money and we can get out of here.'

As the girls walked out of the store back onto Oxford Street, Emma took in a breath of fresh air, 'It's nice to be outside again,' she said thoughtfully.

Lana swung the carrier bag and hit her with it, 'Hey, we weren't in there that long,' she laughed. 'Where's Joe?' she asked, suddenly realising he was no longer with them.

'He disappeared when we walked into the shop. It was weird; actually, he told me he couldn't remember anything about Andilyse.'

'That is weird... and kinda sudden? I wonder where he went?'

'Anywhere away from two girls clothes shopping, I expect,' Emma answered as Lana tucked her arm into hers and they walked down the street, occasionally stopping to peer into shop windows, or for Lana to rush indoors to take a closer look at things that took her fancy.

'It's a shame you haven't seen anything for you, Em?' Lana said a little while later, as they walked back down another street.

'Apparently, my kind of shops are back in Camden?'

'How do you know that?'

'Because I googled them before we left Andilyse,' she said with a smile.

'Why didn't you say anything?'

'Because I knew how desperate you were to come down here.'

Lana grinned, 'Well now it's your turn. We're on the hunt for goth shops!'

'Are you sure? Have you had enough of these chain stores?'

'A girl can never have enough of these shops, Em, but for you, I'm happy to take a break. Besides, you desperately need some new clothes, and I can be your personal shopper,' she beamed while Emma wondered what on earth she'd let herself in for.

After getting off the tube at Camden Town, the girls looked around until they found what they were looking for. Emma certainly wasn't disappointed. Spotting one particular shop from a distance, Emma turned to Lana with a smile, 'Now that is more me,' she laughed as Lana cringed as they walked inside.

The shop was full of black, deep reds and purple items in velvet and lace. Beautiful Victoriana and gothic black chokers covered in beads, lace and silk. Cameo brooches with pictures of Victorian women, cats and moons. Emma swooned as she inspected item after item before eventually moving along to the clothes section where she picked up a red and black gothic tutu dress.

'Now this is gorgeous,' she sighed as Lana promptly removed it from her hands and put it back on the rail.

'Where on earth would you wear something like that? There must be something a little more, you know, sensible? Subtle? Classy? Stylish? Cool?'

Emma laughed at her as she continued to rifle through the lush fabrics she so loved. 'How about this?' she said as she pulled out a lime green rockabilly vest top.

She put it back when she saw Lana's face.

'Here, now this is cute,' Lana said as she handed her a black and white polka dot halter top. Agreeing, Emma took it out of her hands and held on to it.

'How about this?' she said as she held up a black and white gingham bodice top.

'Yep, I like that. It'd look gorgeous with a pencil skirt...'

Emma screwed up her face, 'Okay then, with a pair of skinny jeans?' she continued, handing Emma the top.

'This is beautiful. Very me,' Emma said as she inspected a black organza blouson top.

Lana, dropping her head to one side with a finger in her mouth, nodded. 'Yes, it is actually. In a good way,' she smiled. 'How about a dress? You never wear dresses. Oh come on, don't look at me like that. At least try some on, please? For me?' she pouted.

'I'll try on a dress but only if you try some of them on too?'

Lana's eyes flew wide open before she laughed, 'If that's what it takes to get you to put on a dress, then you've got a deal,' she said as she held out her hand so Emma could shake it.

'Oh, and the other thing... I get to choose them,' Emma said before she quickly disappeared to another section of the shop where more dresses were hanging on rails.

Stepping out of the changing room at the same time, the girls laughed as they swirled in front of a huge mirror, showing off the mini tutu dresses that Emma had chosen. They wore the same style of dress, in organza and velvet; the only difference was that Emma wore a red one and Lana a green one. Although Lana felt ridiculous, she was having fun, even more fun than on Oxford Street, in fact.

Stepping back into their respective changing room cubicles, they changed into medieval-looking gothic dresses, Emma's in purple and Lana's in red.

'Wow, I love this,' said Emma as she turned around in front of the mirror as Lana just shook her head and laughed.

'Seriously though sis, where on earth would you wear it? I feel like I've stepped off of a movie set, a horror movie,' laughed Lana.

Pretending to sulk, Emma stepped back behind her curtain and soon exited again wearing an extravagant long black gothic mermaid dress. She stood outside, waiting for Lana to appear in the same dress.

'OMG, how the hell do you walk in this?' she uttered as she almost fell out of the cubicle, trying hard not to laugh.

'Oh, I look absolutely ridiculous!' she squeaked. 'And you... well, you look like Morticia Addams!'

'I do? Cool!' Emma said as she twirled in front of the mirror. 'I've always wanted to look like I belong to the Addams Family,' she said, her face deadly serious.

Lana shook her head and waddled back into the changing room. Her sister soon followed.

When Lana had eventually managed to get out of the mermaid dress, she stepped back outside and stood waiting for Emma. She knew there was one dress left.

'Well? Have you got it on yet?'

'Almost,' Emma said quietly.

'Let's see.'

As Emma pulled the curtain back, Lana took a deep breath and nodded her head in approval. 'OMG, Emma... you look amazing. Come out, come out and see,' she said as Emma stepped forward and looked in the mirror.

A smile appeared on her lips as she admired the pretty dress, a knee-length halter-neck frock covered in red roses and skulls that cinched in at the waist and then flared out in true 50s style.

'Here, look,' said Lana as she stepped behind her and took her loose hair and held it upwards, 'Wow, Emma. Who knew you could look so beautiful,' Lana said with a smirk.

'Well, thank you very much, Sis,' Emma said, rolling her eyes.

'You realise you've got to buy it, you know?'

'When would I ever wear it though?' she said sensibly.

'It doesn't matter. This dress was made for you. It should be yours. How much is it?' she said as she searched for the label. 'Oh wow, it's only £36! That's a bargain, Sis!' she squealed.

As they exited the shop later, Emma carried a bag containing not only the rose and skull dress but also several pairs of black tights, of varying thickness and patterns, a couple of tops and two chokers. Lana didn't buy a thing.

'And now for shoes,' Lana said as they headed down the road, with Emma shaking her head, laughing.

They were mid-way into their so-called 'work experience' fortnight in London when they realised Joe had never returned after their shopping trip. Something was niggling Emma.

Just before he'd vanished, he'd said that he couldn't remember much about the island, yet earlier on hadn't had any trouble in recalling where he had come from.

Voicing her thoughts to Lana, the girls decided to talk to Eleanor about it, hoping she would be able to tell them what had happened. Much to their dismay, however, she didn't have a clue either.

'It's unusual for ghosts to just disappear like that unless of course, he was finally able to cross over,' she suggested as she took a sip of her lemon tea.

'But the fact that you mentioned his memory loss is a concern. That is highly unusual. And I don't think he'd leave without saying goodbye. He was so drawn to you, especially you, Emma. Do you have any idea why?' She asked just as Wilbur appeared carrying a large plate of biscuits. Emma politely shook her head as he passed them around.

'Mmmm, Jaffa Cakes, my favourite,' said Lana as she took three from the plate.

'I think it's because of the way he died. Oh, of course, we never told you about that...' and so Emma began recalling how the bodies of both the old and the young man were found. How they appeared to be the same man and how they had both died in front of her in the hospital. The younger version later returning as a ghost to his home. Lana interrupted to tell Eleanor about the photographs of the young woman who looked a little like Emma.

Standing to move across the room, Eleanor lay down on the yellow chaise longue just as the clock began to strike five o'clock.

'Excuse me for a moment, girls. Hold that thought...' she said as, just like clockwork, a deep groan escaped her lips before she turned to face them a few moments later looking decidedly younger.

'Oh that's better,' she said, stretching her lithe limbs before disappearing to change into more suitable clothes. From behind the screen, she asked questions about Joe while the girls waited for her to step out.

'He was a very lonely old man,' answered Emma. 'He had few friends; he never married or had children. After seeing his home, we realised that he only ever lived for that woman who disappeared back in the 50s.'

'That must have something to do with his coming back as a young man. He yearns for her so badly that he never really lived after she disappeared. I'm curious as to his memory loss though and to his disappearance, of course.'

Wilbur returned to the room carrying a bowl of fruit which he offered to Emma with a smile, 'Perhaps an apple, banana or a pear?' he suggested, 'Considering you turned down the biscuits,' he said with a wink.

Leaning forward, Emma picked out a large pink pear and took a big bite out of it, juice dribbling down her chin. 'Thank you,' she said, shyly wiping at her mouth with her hand, 'It's delicious.'

'Well, I have made up my mind,' blurted Eleanor after she'd sat quietly for a few moments with her head in her hands.

Looking up at her, Emma and Lana waited curiously, wondering what she'd made her mind up about.

'Every Watcher must complete their first task before acceptance into the Academy in September. I do believe that your first task has just presented itself to you both.'

'It has?' asked Lana, confused.

'Yes, you must track down the ghost of Josiah Grimshaw and then you must uncover what is keeping him from crossing over. Once you've worked that out, you must help him pass over to the other side,' she said, smiling.

'You are authorised to use any of the facilities at Praxos, and you may ask any or all of the other Watchers for assistance. However, as is always the case with the foundation, you must not reveal your skills to anyone out of our circles, other than paranormals. Do you understand?' she asked firmly.

The girls nodded avidly.

'Very well then,' she smiled. 'Good luck. You have until you return home.'

'Can I ask a question?'

'Of course you can, Emma. What is it?'

'Have all the other Watchers been given their first tasks?'

'Some have yes, but a few will be told today or tomorrow what they must do. Don't worry about them, unless they ask for assistance, of course. Now you must concentrate on Josiah.'

Standing to leave the room, the girls looked at each other unsurely.

'Don't worry so much,' Eleanor added, 'I'm sure you'll find this to be a piece of cake,' she chuckled.

❧

'JOE? JOSIAH ARE YOU THERE?' EMMA ASKED A LITTLE LATER. BUT there was no reply. No matter how long she tried calling out his name, or how loud, Joe refused to appear.

'Josiah Grimshaw, I demand that you show yourself at once!' shouted Lana after they'd been trying uselessly for over an hour.

'This is crazy, why won't he come to us?' she added with her hands on her hips.

'I don't know,' sighed Emma as she flopped down on the beanbag.

'Hey girls,' said a familiar voice as Liam opened the door and waltzed in, leaving Lana beaming at the sight of him.

'Hey,' she said as she draped herself across him as he got comfortable in one of the other giant beanbags.

'Whaddya doin?' he asked.

'Getting more and more irritated by the minute,' she replied as she looked into his eyes with a grin.

'You don't look too irritated to me,' he said, laughing.

Sighing, she leaned forward and kissed him.

Emma, feeling a little uncomfortable, cleared her throat.

'I'm not irritated any more,' Lana muttered as she leaned her head on his shoulder.

'Don't mind me,' Emma said quietly as they completely ignored her. 'Right, I'll go then...'

With no response from Lana or Liam, Emma rolled her eyes and quietly stood up, walking out of the room on her own. 'I guess the task can wait then,' she muttered to herself.

'What's that?' said a voice that practically welded her knees together. Turning, Emma stood face to face with Diarmuid who had just stepped out of Eleanor's office.

'Hiya,' she said as he took her hand. 'You okay?' she asked.

'Yeah, I'm good now you're here,' he said, leaning in to kiss her gently on the cheek.

That's it, Emma's knees were permanently locked together while her stomach did more of those triple salchows. Just the sight of him had that effect on her.

'I've just been given my first task,' he said. 'How about you? You got yours yet?'

Nodding, Emma tried to extricate herself from the spot as Diarmuid gently guided her across the hall towards the dining area where he pulled out a chair for her to sit down before sitting down beside her.

'We have to find Josiah and help him cross over, basically,' she whispered as he casually moved one of her stray hairs from her face so that it was back behind her ear. 'Wh...wh...what about you?' she asked, her voice all a quiver.

'Liam and I have some puzzle to solve... something about electricity, light and strength. I dunno. We're going to start working on it tomorrow. What are you doing later?'

Emma shrugged her shoulders.

'How about coming out with us tonight. We could go on a double date?' he suggested.

'A date? That would be great,' she smiled. 'I'd love to.'

❧ 28 ☙

'Wow... you can see for miles from up here,' breathed Lana from the London Eye later that evening. The four of them stood in one of the pods, along with about ten other people, admiring the view and the slowly setting sun. It truly was spectacular.

Liam stood with his arm draped over Lana's shoulder, while Diarmuid and Emma were sitting down, holding each other's hands as they tried to identify many of the sights in front of them.

'No prizes for guessing what that is,' he said as they looked towards the cylindrical, pointed glass building over to their right. 'The Gherkin?' she asked with a giggle. 'What about that one over there...'

'That's St. Pauls. And there, that's Canary Wharf. And if you look just over in that direction, you can see Buckingham Palace.'

'Really? Wow, that's so cool.'

Liam and Lana came and sat beside them for a moment as Lana whispered, 'You know, just over a few weeks ago, I'd never have been able to do this.'

'How come?' asked Diarmuid and Liam at the same time.

'I grew up with a serious phobia of heights. I was terrified.'

'What changed?' asked Liam as he pushed his hair off his face.

'My 16th birthday?' she said with a smile.

'Oh right, I get you,' he laughed. 'Everything changes on your 16th birthday.'

'It's funny though that you had that phobia, coz I had one too,' Diarmuid said.

'You did?' Emma asked, surprised.

'I know it sounds insane, but I was afraid of electricity.'

'Oh, that is weird. I had a fear of water. What about you, Liam, did you have any phobias?'

'This is freaking me out a bit,' he laughed, 'To be honest, I had a thing against speed. I couldn't travel in a car if we were going over 50mph and, and this sounds so lame, I'd never been on a plane because they travel so fast. But, like you,' he said, dropping his voice to a low whisper, 'that changed with the tattoo... on my 16th birthday earlier this year.'

'Cool,' said the others in tandem before they all went quiet, watching the sights unfold in front of them.

'Hey look,' said Lana, as she stood up, pulling Liam away with her. 'Isn't that the....' she said to him, her voice trailing off as they walked away from her sister.

'Whereabouts are you staying, Diarmuid?' asked Emma.

'On Gower Street. It's kind of in that direction over there,' he pointed slightly over to the left. 'You see that green dome over there? Well, that's part of the British Museum, and we're just around the corner from there.'

'Cool,' whispered Emma.

'You're staying on Declan's boat, aren't you?'

'Hm-hm.'

'Is it on the river now? Or is it in one of the canals?'

'When we left this morning, it was moored at Camden, but we never know. We've had to phone him a couple of times to find out,' she laughed.

'It must be great staying with Declan and Saleena. He's a cool guy, isn't he?'

'Totally,' said Emma, whispering in his ear, 'He won't tell us what his skills are though. I keep guessing, wrongly. He finds it funny.'

'I'm sure he'll reveal all when he wants you to know.'

'Yeah, I guess. What about Zane and Marian? What are they like?'

'Pretty cool. They've lived in London all their lives, like Declan. Their house is amazing. I bet you'd love it there. It's a Georgian terraced house with huge rooms and high ceilings which they've decorated in a contemporary style. It's exactly the kind of house I'd like to own at some stage,' he said shyly.

Emma watched him as he spoke. It was clear that he had a love for property or architecture or both. She smiled when he stopped talking, noticing that he had blushed a little.

'Why are you smiling?' he asked.

'I just think it's cute.'

'What's cute?'

'That... passion you have about houses. I'm guessing architecture is something you're into?' she asked while he nodded.

'That obvious, huh?' he laughed as they finally reached the end of their ride on the Eye.

'It's cool,' she said as they hopped off while it continued to turn slowly and steadily with Liam and Lana following behind.

It was a beautiful evening, not a cloud in the sky, as the sun finally began to descend beyond the horizon, leaving hues of pink and purple in the evening sky.

Hand in hand, both couples were oblivious to the other, as they chatted and walked down towards the bridge that would take them back over the River Thames.

As they crossed over, they looked back towards the Eye, admiring it from the distance when the sound of a police siren could be heard getting closer. The siren multiplied and soon, three vehicles sped over the bridge at such speed that it made them all jump.

'I wonder what's going on?' said Lana as they watched them disappear around the corner.

'Why don't we go and check it out?' Liam answered.

Before Diarmuid or Emma could say a word, the two of them were running across the road, following the sounds of the sirens.

Glancing at Diarmuid, Emma rolled her eyes and shook her head, 'I guess we ought to go, make sure they don't get up to mischief,' she smiled as he took hold of her hand and the two followed suit.

'Hey, wait up!' she yelled to Lana from the other side of the road.

'Keep up, Em!'

Eventually rounding a corner, Lana and Liam spotted the three vehicles parked, blocking the road. Three police officers stood, stopping the general public from getting through.

'What's going on, Officer?' asked Liam.

'None of your business, young man. Just keep away,' one of them said with a curt nod of his head.

'It's better not to bug them, Liam. My Dad's the chief of police on Andilyse, and I know they're not keen for the public to get involved,' Emma said, a little embarrassed.

'She's right, especially if it's something serious. Dad would hate to be distracted,' Lana said, backing her up. Emma smiled at her.

'Look over there,' said Diarmuid, pointing to a large jewellery shop ahead of them. 'They're in there. Someone's broken in. Look at the smashed windows.'

'Do you think we should help out?' Liam asked over his shoulder.

'Absolutely not. I'm sure there's enough police here to sort them out. Let's just get out of here,' Emma said.

Suddenly, there was a massive crash, and two masked men were thrown through what remained of the jeweller's window. They were tied up.

'What the hell?' shouted one of the police officers.

'What's going on?' asked Diarmuid as the police ran forwards and cuffed the robbers.

'Look,' said Emma, 'Look in the store... there's a woman there. Oh... she's gone.'

'I didn't see anyone,' Lana said, a bit miffed.

'Emma's right, there was a young woman there. I wonder who she was,' Liam said, adding, 'Actually, I wonder what she was. I reckon that was another Watcher we don't know about.'

'Come on; there's nothing we can do now. If she was one of us, she could be miles away by now. Maybe we ought to just let Eleanor know?' Lana suggested.

'I'm on it,' Liam replied as he pulled out a mobile phone and rang through to Praxos. But when he was put through to Eleanor, she was already aware of what was going on.

'I saw what happened, although I didn't see the woman you mentioned. Thanks for letting me know. We'll look into it. Oh and by the way... well done for not getting involved. I hope you enjoyed the Eye,' she chuckled before putting the phone down.

'Oh man...' Liam laughed as he put his phone back in his pocket.

'What?' asked Lana as he casually draped his arm over her shoulder.

'Eleanor... that woman doesn't miss a thing. She knew we went on the Eye. She could probably see us.'

'Yeah, have you seen her office? She's got a giant screen that shows images from all over London...' Lana said as they began to walk away from the commotion.

$ 29 $

After deciding their best bet to find Joe was to visit cemeteries in and around the city, they didn't realise quite what they'd gotten themselves into. The next morning, borrowing Declan's computer, they found out that London had a whole host of places where the dead were laid to rest.

'Oh no,' cried Lana, 'where on earth are we going to start?' she sighed.

'The nearest one?' suggested Emma as she stood looking over her shoulder with a mug of tea in her hand.

'Good Morning,' said a cheery voice behind them as Saleena appeared from the bathroom, towel drying her long brown hair.

'Morning Saleena,' they smiled.

'What's the matter? I can see something is bothering you,' she asked as she approached, the whiff of fresh shampoo filling the air.

'We need to find Joe, but there are, like, so many cemeteries in London. We don't know where to start,' sighed Lana as she sat back in the chair, letting her head fall backwards.

'The St Pancras and Islington Cemetery is the largest cemetery actually in London. But if you think he may be at the largest over-all, then you'd need to visit Surrey, the Brookwood Cemetery,' she said matter of factly.

'How do you know all this, Saleena?' asked Emma in amazement.

She just shrugged and walked into her bedroom with a smile, closing the door behind her.

'What do you think?' Emma asked.

'Let's try the St Pancras one first,' she said to Emma as they turned off the computer and went back into their room to put on their shoes.

'We'll see you guys tonight,' they called out as they hopped off the boat a little while later, finding themselves still moored at Camden Town.

'That's useful. According to this map, the cemetery isn't that far from here,' said Lana as she glanced down at the piece of paper and up at their surroundings. 'We just need to hop on the Tube, get the Northern Line and get off at East Finchey. It takes us right there.'

'Cool, come on then,' Emma said as they headed down to the Tube station.

When they eventually found the shady spot where the cemetery was hidden, the girls walked through the gates and down towards Islington Chapel, where they stood outside, waiting for the occasional stranger to pass them by before calling out Joe's name. They went inside the chapel, called out to him and then walked along the numerous gravestones, all the time, saying his name, hoping that he would hear and come to them. But it wasn't going to happen, not at the St. Pancras cemetery nor at the Brookwood Cemetery where they had spent almost two hours to get there.

'I'm beginning to get irritated now,' cursed Lana after spending two further hours wandering around Brookwood trying to track the ghost down. 'Why the hell won't he come to us?'

'I really don't know. Let's call it a day. Let's head back, we can think about our next move later on,' said Emma sadly as they began to stroll out of the calm peacefulness of the cemetery.

Sitting on the train a little while later, Emma suddenly had a light bulb moment. Smacking her forehead with the palm of her hand, she said, 'I don't believe it.'

'What?' asked Lana as she sat flicking through the pages of a gossip magazine she'd bought while waiting for the train.

'Remember Eleanor said we could ask the others for help?'

'Hm-hm,' she said with a long yawn.

'Well... awwww,' Emma said, yawning herself, 'the answer is Nisha!' she giggled.

Lana looked at her as if she was mad before glancing back down to her magazine, 'Why?'

'Because duh... Nisha can...' lowering her voice, she continued, 'speak to dead people.'

'Of course!' Lana said, nodding her head. 'Why didn't we think of that before. We've wasted all this time.'

Once they'd gotten off the train and the Tube, the girls headed straight for Praxos. Still unsure which entrance was for Watchers, they chose the main front door, climbing the stairs and crouching through the old wardrobe. Wilbur stood waiting for them with a smile.

'How did you know we were coming?' Lana asked bewildered.

'I have my ways,' he said with a chuckle as he led them out of the large lounge, through the long candlelit hallway until they reached the modern elevator.

They followed him in, he pressed a few buttons, and they were soon stepping out into the grand hall of the Praxos Foundation.

'Thanks, Wilbur,' Emma said as he left them to their devices. He merely nodded and stepped back into the lift and closed the door behind him.

Spotting Imran and Moira on a computer sitting on the floor just below the old Praxos Statue, Lana walked over.

'Hey!' she said as Moira looked up with a smile. Imran was too deep in concentration to notice.

'Hey, honey. How're things?' Moira asked as she took an elastic out of her pocket and began to put her hair into a messy ponytail before standing up.

'Yeah, okay. We're looking for Nisha. We could use her help with our task. Have you seen her?'

'Cool. She went out with Penny and Habika a couple of hours ago. I don't suppose it's anything I can help with?' she offered kindly.

'Only if you can talk to dead people,' laughed Lana.

'Babe, that's one skill I'm seriously glad not to have to contend with,' she laughed. 'I thought you could talk to the dead, anyway?'

Lana shook her head as Emma walked over, 'Hey Moira.'

'Hi, honey. Lana was just saying you need Nisha to talk to the dead?'

Emma nodded, 'Yeah, for our task.'

'I figured you could talk to ghosts. Didn't you guys have a ghost with you when you first came?'

'That's the task... he seems to have disappeared. We're supposed to track him down and help him cross over.'

'Oh, right. Maybe he already has. Maybe that's why he's disappeared?' she suggested.

'It's not that easy,' Lana shrugged, 'Eleanor says he's still with us if you know what I mean.'

Moira nodded, 'Well, good luck.'

'Thanks,' said Emma. 'What are you up to? Are you working on your task?'

Imran finally broke his concentration and looked up, 'Oh hi,' he said, surprised as if he had no idea they had company. The girls smiled.

'Imran and I must unravel some age-old mystery about time travel. It's all very complicated, but I think we're getting there. I dreamed about it last night, which helped.'

Lana nodded, 'Cool.'

'We'd better see if we can find Nisha. Good luck guys,' said Emma as they turned away and headed to the dining room for a quick cup of tea first.

As they opened the door, the aroma of strong coffee filled their nostrils. Rupert sat lounging on one of the long black leather sofas that perched against the far wall, while Ava and Eleanor stood facing him chatting.

'Hi girls,' Eleanor said, barely turning to see who it was.

'Hi Eleanor, Rupert, Ava,' they said practically in unison which made them giggle as they walked over to the kettle.

'It's only just boiled,' Ava smiled.

'Thanks.'

With mugs of tea in their hands, they turned and walked towards the other sofa, sitting down and relaxing for a brief break.

'... and then Ava heard them say it was in Greenwich. When we got there, I was able to walk straight in without being spotted, taking the photo you wanted and getting out before the security guards could notice anything strange had happened,' Rupert continued.

Eleanor's face lit up with a huge grin, 'Well then, congratulations. You are the first Watchers here to complete your task. Well done. I'm rather impressed.'

Ava beamed at Rupert who stood up and high-fived her.

'Excellent!' he yelled.

'Already?' asked Lana, 'You've completed your task already? We've barely even started!'

'There's no hurry, Lana. All I ask is that the tasks are completed. It doesn't matter how long it takes. Well, within reason of course. As long as you've done it before you return home,' she smiled.

Lana dramatically sighed as Emma stood up, 'Well, let's not waste any more time then. Eleanor, do you know where Nisha is?'

'Yes, Habika took her and Penny to the National Archives in Kew. They won't be back for a while yet. Anything I can do?'

Emma shook her head, 'No thanks, Eleanor. We could use Nisha's skills.'

'Oh I understand,' she winked before adding, 'I shall leave you to it. I've got lots of work to do myself.'

Eleanor smiled at them before turning and walking out of the dining room, leaving the Watchers alone.

'So, why do you need Nisha's skills?' asked Rupert who had plonked himself back on the sofa like he owned the place.

'It's just for our task, that's all.'

'Which is?' he asked.

'Rupert, maybe they don't want to tell us,' Ava scolded.

'Of course they do. It's written all over their faces. See...' he said, sitting up and pointing at Lana's forehead, 'I want to tell Rupert and Ava about our task. It's right there in black ink,' he laughed at his own joke.

Shaking her head but smiling, Lana took the final gulp of tea before leaning back. Finally giving in to his questions, she began to tell them what they had been entrusted to do.

'... but he disappeared when we were shopping...'

'No surprise there. I would have done the same,' Rupert interrupted.

Lana glared at him before Emma continued, 'I noticed that he seemed to have been forgetting things before he disappeared though. It was weird.'

'And you think he's hiding at a cemetery?' Ava asked, intrigued.

'Possibly, although after this morning, we're not so sure. We looked all over for him in two of the largest cemeteries around, but there was no sign of him,' Emma sighed.

'But if he is losing his memory, perhaps he doesn't know who you are? Maybe that's why he won't reveal himself to you?' Ava suggested as she rubbed her dimpled chin.

'That's a possibility, I guess. We're hoping Nisha can help,' Lana replied.

'Good idea,' Rupert interjected. 'Well, we're here with nothing to do if you need any help,' he smirked.

'Thanks for rubbing it in, Rupert,' Lana said as she pulled the small cushion out from behind her back and threw it at him.

'Thanks though,' she added with a cheeky grin.

❧ 30 ❧

It was two minutes to midnight. Emma and Lana stood shivering, not with cold but with apprehension. Standing amid a multitude of gravestones, they waited for Nisha to arrive. When she'd finally returned from the National Archives earlier that afternoon, she'd been delighted to have been asked for assistance and had suggested they meet at midnight at another local churchyard, Abney Park.

The call of a hooting owl, followed by a deep creaking sound made Lana practically jump into her sister's arms, making Emma chuckle nervously.

The girls stood looking around, imagining eerie shadows dancing in the moonlight when it was just the trees swaying in the breeze.

When a deep throaty laugh made them bolt from where they stood, Lana soon came to a standstill when the laughter changed to one that was much more recognisable.

'Liam Hawkes, that is so not funny,' she shouted with her arms crossed, stamping her foot.

'Aw man, that was so funny,' he said from behind the tree where he'd been hiding. Stepping out from the shadows, Liam appeared, grinning widely. Lana couldn't be angry for long though, and she rushed into his arms, kissing him and hitting him at the same time.

'Okay, okay, I'm sorry, I'm sorry,' he laughed.

Stepping out gingerly from behind him was Diarmuid, who grinned sheepishly as Emma laid her eyes on him.

'You too?' she laughed. 'That was cruel,' she said as he walked over to her, apologising before he enveloped her in a big hug and planted a kiss firmly on her lips — their first real kiss. Emma melted into his arms, thoroughly enjoying the moment, forgetting about where they were and what they were about to do. But the sound of footsteps and someone clearing their throat broke them out of their loved up trance.

The four of them turned to face Nisha and Penny, Moira, Imran, Cassie, Elliott, Ava and Rupert.

'Oh wow, we weren't expecting the whole group to turn up,' smiled Emma, who felt herself blush from head to foot.

'There was no way we were going to miss out on a midnight trip to a churchyard,' said Rupert with a grin. 'Besides, considering we already finished our task...' he stopped, smiling, for added effect before continuing, 'We figured we had nothing better to do.'

'Oh grow up already,' Lana said, punching him softly on his shoulder as he came closer.

'Sorry guys, but they overheard me telling Penny about tonight, and I guess the word spread...' Nisha apologised.

'Although this is totally creepy, I think it's cool that we're all out together for a change,' Emma said happily, quickly getting over her embarrassment at being caught mid-kiss with Diarmuid.

'Absolutely. This should be fun,' Diarmuid said, a little unsure, causing the rest of them to laugh.

'Shall we go and find somewhere to sit down so we can make a start?' suggested Nisha as they walked towards the old chapel and further into the woodland area, where it grew steadily darker.

'A little light would be nice,' said Lana to Emma, who instantly began glowing ever so slightly, before Diarmuid did the same as they walked hand in hand.

'Oh I forgot you could do that too,' squealed Lana, clapping her hands like a delighted child.

'We mustn't light the place up too much. We don't want to attract any attention,' said Cassie, as Emma and Diarmuid both dimmed themselves a little. The group began to walk past the old decaying chapel and down a long windy pathway, covered on either side by overgrown ivy, which spread across the ground and over gravestones like protective wiry fingers.

Eventually, they came to a clearing. Nisha stopped and looked across to her right. 'Over there, let's head over there,' she said a little spookily.

Lana glanced at Emma, who in turn glanced up at Diarmuid. Nobody said a word; they just stopped behind the Indian girl, waited for a moment and then followed closely behind. They continued walking until they came upon a monument of an angel, one of many within the old abandoned cemetery. Nisha plonked herself down beneath it and leaned back to get more comfortable.

'Sit down,' she told everyone quietly before she closed her eyes for a moment. 'Can you dim the lights a bit more, please? I'm not sure if they'll come through if it's too bright.'

Diarmuid and Emma did as they were told. The fact that Nisha had said 'they' instead of 'him' preoccupied Emma a little. How many ghosts would there be? Diarmuid, noticing Emma shiver to his side, put his arm across her shoulders protectively, making her feel much better.

'We have come to speak to the spirit of the young man who goes by the name of Josiah Grimshaw. Josiah, show yourself,' Nisha said firmly.

The rest of the group bent their heads down and listened for the approach of well, anything really. But nothing happened. The owls continued to hoot, and the trees continued to sway as the breeze made them shiver in the semi-darkness.

'Josiah Grimshaw, we just want to talk. Are you there?'

Suddenly, a bright light flashed beside the angel monument, making Diarmuid and Emma lose concentration. Their light went out in an instant.

'Emma!' scolded Lana who sat between her and Liam.

'What the hell was that?' screeched Penny.

'Shhhh,' muttered Nisha, as she asked Josiah to show himself.

Again there was a momentarily flash of light.

'Who wishes to speak to Josiah Grimshaw?' asked a deep, unfamiliar voice in the darkness.

Nisha gulped before speaking, 'My name is Nisha Singh.'

'And who are you, Nisha Singh? And who are your followers?' asked the voice which seemed to move around them, causing a temporary wave of fear to flow through them all.

Nisha smiled before she continued, 'They are not my followers, they are my friends, and we are here to speak to Josiah. His friends are among us.'

'His friends?' said the voice.

'Yes, Emma Jane and Lana Beth Morgan. Josiah came to London with them, from his birthplace of Andilyse Island. They wish to talk to him, that's all. And who are you?' she asked confidently. 'Might you consider showing yourself?'

'You are a brave soul, Nisha Singh.'

A flash of light temporarily blinded them all. When their sight returned to normal, Penny shrieked at a deathly pale middle-aged man with a hole in his head, standing in between Nisha and herself.

'Wh....wh....who are you?' Penny gulped, unable to move.

'I am Granville Houston, who are you?' he asked back.

'P..P...P...Penny Vega.'

'A pleasure to meet you, Penny Vega,' he said with a curt nod of his head. 'And who might you be?' he asked as he looked over towards Imran.

'Imran, Sir, Imran Chaudri,' he whispered.

'Hi,' Rupert interrupted, 'I'm Rupert Henson. I'd shake your hand but, I guess that would be impossible,' he said with a broad smile, as if talking to dead people happened all the time.

'Rupert, eh? A good old fashioned name. And you?'

'Elliott Drake.'

'Elliot Drake,' said Granville, stroking his chin and looking towards the heavens. 'I knew me an Elliot Drake once. Evil man, evil,' he tutted. 'I hope you're not related. And who might you be?' he said, pointing towards Ava.

Gulping loudly, Ava had difficulty opening her mouth to speak.

'That's Ava Burton and Moira Lynn; this is Cassie Stanton, over there is Liam Hawkes and Diarmuid O'Connor. This is my sister Emma Jane, and I'm Lana Beth Morgan,' said Lana, getting bored of all the introductions. 'We'd like to speak to Josiah, please. Can you help us or not Mr Houston?' she said in a firm tone.

The ghost burst out laughing. 'Why I never,' he chuckled,

'That's the first time a good lady has spoken to me so curtly in over a hundred years. What a breath of fresh air. It's a pleasure to meet you Lana Beth and your sister and the rest of you. But I'm sorry to say that I don't know any Josiah Grimshaw, did you say?' he asked as Lana nodded. 'Nah, no Josiah passed through here lately. Unless....' he said, stopping for a moment to rub his chin again.

'Unless what Mr Houston?' asked Nisha.

'There was an odd chap here the other day. Didn't know where he was going or where he'd been. Couldn't remember his name at all. First ghost I ever met who couldn't remember his own name. Strange that was.'

'That must have been him,' said Emma breathlessly. 'Do you know what happened to him? Do you know where he went?'

Granville shrugged his shoulders. 'I got bored with him after a while and left him to it. He's probably still wandering around here somewhere.'

'Could you try and find him for us?' asked Elliott.

'I could try, but what's in it for me?' he replied.

The group suddenly went quiet, as they all looked across at each other, unsure what to say.

'Perhaps we can help you cross over, Mr Houston,' offered Ava.

'Cross over? I ain't ever been able to cross over. Been like this in this here state for, well, a couple of hundred years, probably. How are you going to help me cross over?' he asked dubiously.

'We have our ways,' said Lana. 'If you help us, we'll try and help you,' she said.

'Oh, all right then. You seem like a good bunch, and you're certainly the first to offer to help me, and I appreciate that. I'll go and see if any of my fellow spirits have seen him around. Don't go nowhere, mind. Although, you can do as you please. I'll find you,' he said before disappearing into thin air.

'Wow,' sighed Ava. 'I erm... how come...erm, why...'

'What Ava?' laughed Nisha.

'I thought you were going to speak to the ghosts. I didn't think we would be able to see and speak to them too,' she said, visibly shaken.

'Once I've got through to them, it's up to them who they make themselves visible to,' Nisha answered, pleased with herself.

'I hope he finds him,' Emma said, 'Because at this rate we'll never be able to complete our task. If Josiah can't even remember his own name, how will we ever help him cross over?' she sighed, holding tightly on to Diarmuid's hand and leaning her head on his shoulder.

'Don't worry, you'll do it,' he said, gently kissing the top of her head.

'Well, shall we have a look round while we're waiting? He did say he'd find us?' suggested Liam as he stood up and shook his legs to get rid of any loose leaves.

'What? You want to go poking around the graveyard, by choice?' asked Cassie.

'Yeah, come on. It'll be a laugh,' Lana encouraged.

In the little moonlight, there was, the trees continued to cast ominous shadows across their path as they walked, stopping now and then to get up close to some of the more unusual gravestones and statues. One that had particular appeal was a beautiful stone lion that perched with its eyes closed on top of a tomb of a man who had died in 1912. So lifelike, it was almost like Medusa herself had cast her eyes upon it.

Sauntering along, whispering among one another, the group, led by Lana and Liam, came to an abrupt standstill when the sound of something falling to the ground alerted them to the fact that they were not alone in the vast cemetery.

'Shhhh,' said Lana as she turned to the others with her finger over her mouth. 'There's someone here... it sounds like they're trashing the place.'

In a matter of seconds, Liam had left them behind, moving at the speed of light towards the noise. When he returned moments later, he said, 'It's just a drunk. He fell over and knocked his glass bottle into a gravestone. He's out cold.'

'Should we do something?' asked Ava.

'Yeah, let's at least move him, so he's undercover and safe,' suggested Penny as they headed towards the man. But when they arrived, he was nowhere to be seen.

'What the...?' said Liam. 'He was right there, out stone cold. There's no way he would have woken up and walked away, not in the state he was in. He reeked of alcohol.'

'Maybe someone else took him away?' said Emma, unsure.

'What, like one of the ghosts?' Rupert said, bending down and picking up the remnants of the bottle. 'What?' he said when the others looked at him. 'This is someone's grave; there's a body buried beneath this headstone. How would you like it if your grave was covered in glass from a bottle of booze? It's disrespectful.'

Nisha stepped forward and helped him pick up the pieces of broken glass with a smile before the others all pitched in to help. When the last few bits were casually brushed away, Rupert stepped back. 'That's better. Rest in peace old chap,' he said, touching the headstone momentarily before turning away to look for a bin to drop the glass into.

'You never cease to amaze me,' said Lana as she smiled at the comedian fondly.

'I found a rubbish bin over here,' shouted Imran from a distance. After they'd got rid of the old bits of glass, the group were just about to carry on walking when the soothing sounds of singing drifted to their ears. Ava heard it first.

'Do you hear that?' she asked.

'Nope. What is it?' asked Elliott, straining to hear.

'Someone's singing,' she whispered.

'Yes, but with your special abilities, it could be someone singing over at Hyde Park,' he chuckled.

'No, it's a girl, and she's here, here at Abney Park. Listen, her voice is extraordinary. I've never heard anything like it.'

The lingering sounds began to hover over the group, making them all stand perfectly still and captivating them, pulling them in.

'It's this way,' Ava said as they followed her, trying to move silently. Something that proved somewhat tricky considering the number of dead leaves and twigs beneath their feet.

'Look, over there,' she pointed.

Sitting alone beneath a statue of a headless angel sat a pretty young girl, about their age, singing quietly to herself, completely lost in her thoughts. Beside her was the drunk man, who lay sleeping by her feet.

'How the hell did she move him?' asked Liam in shock.

'Shhhh,' whispered Emma as they watched the girl with the tumbling red curls sit singing like an angel.

The sudden return of Granville the ghost made Rupert jump so much that he yelped out loud. The girl's singing stopped instantly, and within a second, she'd disappeared. And so had the unconscious man with her.

'Hey!' said Elliott loudly, 'Where did she go?'

'Who? What? When?' said Granville as he stood in the centre of the group spinning around.

'Tsk tsk,' tutted Cassie. 'You frightened her off, Rupert. What the hell?'

'Sorry,' he muttered, 'Granville here frightened the living daylights outta me,' he whimpered.

'Oh believe me young chap, you'd know if the living daylights were gone, I can tell you that from experience. Now, who are you talking about? Who was frightened off?' asked the ghost curiously.

'The girl with the red hair,' answered Imran.

'The girl with the red hair?'

'Hm-hm. She was just there singing, with the drunk man sleeping at her feet,' Lana explained.

'Oh, that girl with the red hair. She spends a lot of time here at Abney Park. And I do believe the drunk man is her father.'

'Really?' asked Ava, shocked.

'Yes,' nodded the ghost, 'The name's erm, let me think for a moment. Oh yes, the family name's Madigan, and the young girl is called, erm. Daisy, yes that's it, Daisy,' he said, quite proud of himself for remembering.

'But what is she doing here?' asked Emma with genuine concern in her voice. 'She's probably the same age as us. She shouldn't be here on her own.'

'Well, she's not really on her own, is she? Her father is here with her.'

'Not much of a father, is he?' said Elliott. 'He's a drunk. She's looking after him rather than the other way round.'

'I think we're all forgetting something rather crucial here guys and gals,' said Penny. 'There's something special about that girl... she's the one that moved her father, remember? How can a regular teenage girl move a fully grown unconscious man so fast that we never even saw her? And where did she go? I don't think Liam can move that fast. What's going on?'

The group looked at each other in dismay.

'Well, whoever she is, she doesn't want to be bothered. That's clear as day, don't you think?' said Lana. 'As much as I'd love to help her, we're here for Josiah. Granville, do you have any news for us?'

'The boy you described has been here, on and off, for the past few days. I've spoken to some of the others over at the crypt, and they've seen him, some have spoken to him, but he hasn't made much sense, I'm afraid. He doesn't seem to be here at the moment, though. Sorry, I'm not able to offer much assistance in the matter,' elaborated Granville.

'That's helpful, though, thank you,' said Nisha. 'Who are the others, Granville? And what is the crypt?'

'There are several crypts here in the park, but we generally meet at one, further down that way,' he said pointing. 'The others are just like me, I suppose. Spirits lost in time. Stuck here,' he said sadly.

'How many are there?' she asked just as a flash of light blinded them for a few seconds.

When they could see again, the group found themselves surrounded by about fifty ghosts.

'Holy cr....' said Rupert as Ava placed her hand over his mouth.

'Language, Rupert,' she scolded, smiling.

'Oh, hello,' said Nisha with genuine surprise written all over her face.

'Hello my love,' said an elderly woman with a stoop. 'We don't get many of your kind around here these days, not the friendly kind anyhoo' she said.

'Erm, my kind?' asked Nisha.

'Yes, my love. The kind that can freely see us and communicate with us like this. Granted, many people can see us and hear us but only if we want them to. You can see us regardless; it's nice that you want to see and talk to us. It certainly makes a change, I tell you,' she cackled. 'Been here a long time, and we don't often get to talk to anyone other than this ghostly lot,' she smiled, revealing several missing front teeth.

'I seen that boy you're looking for. He seems very frightened and lonely. Best you find him as soon as you can and lead him down the right path 'fore those others lead him the wrong way,' she said.

'Others?' asked Nisha.

'Yes, my love. The others, those evil ones. They often have their eye on the newcomers. If you don't get him soon, it'll be too late.'

'But who are they?' asked Penny.

Before she could get an answer, though, the ghosts had vanished right before their eyes. Even Granville was no longer with them.

'Something's wrong,' said Nisha, looking around. 'I felt it. They got spooked. We need to get out of here.'

'What is it? What's wrong, Nisha?' asked Emma. 'Ava, can you hear anything?'

Ava closed her eyes and concentrated hard. 'Someone is coming. It's a group; they're moving quickly. They're coming towards us,' she whispered shakily.

'Rupert? Can you see anything?' she asked as he focussed hard into the distance. 'There's about eight... no, nine. There's nine of them. They look mean, guys. We need to get out of here. Get to the old chapel, as fast as you can, now' he said.

'But we're Watchers. We can take them,' growled Liam with clenched fists.

'No,' said Emma, 'We don't even know who they are. We mustn't get involved. Let's just get out of their way. Please, Liam, come on.'

Liam reluctantly nodded at her before they all rushed away and headed toward the old chapel from where Rupert kept a lookout.

His exceptional vision skills allowed him to see through the trees, the crypts and anything else that stood in their way.

'What's going on, Rupert?' whispered Imran as they all huddled behind him.

'They're looking for something,' he replied. 'But I can only see, I can't hear. Ava, what are they saying?'

Ava closed her eyes and stood silently listening.

'They're after someone. They're laughing. Wait, he's saying, we're gonna get her this time. It's about time we showed her who's boss around here...'

'They've stopped,' added Rupert, 'One of them seems to be... sniffing the air. He's looking in our direction. Shhhh everyone,' he whispered as they all stood as silently as they possibly could.

'They're on the move again. They're coming this way. Oh God,' he said.

'What is it, Rupert?' whispered Lana.

'A couple of them... they're not... human.'

Lana gasped as Liam grabbed hold of her hand.

'What do we do?'

'Just stay quiet, hold still,' Ava whispered. 'They're still looking for someone.'

'They've changed course,' said Rupert, 'They're heading away. I think they're goin...' but before he could even finish his sentence, something appeared at the door to the chapel, making them all jump backwards.

The four-legged creature snarled as it stood watching them, its black eyes flicking from one side of the nave to the other. Slowly stepping inside, the moonlight shining in from the holes in the roof glistened on its glossy black fur.

Lana began to step backwards, catching her foot on a broken stone tile in the floor. She stumbled. Before she hit the ground, Liam caught her just as the beast leapt forward. At the same time, Elliott held out his hands and shook them until flames appeared dancing before his eyes. Flicking his fingers, the hot flames grew larger until the smell of burnt hair filled the air.

The creature yelped and dropped back as it continued to snarl at the group, standing in the broken doorway. Elliott concentrated, keeping the flames coming, just in case.

'They're coming,' said Rupert, 'They heard it yelp.'

'Now what? We're trapped in here,' Penny said as they all stood waiting while the beast continued its terrifying snarling.

'Not much we can do now. Let's just see what they want,' Diarmuid said as the figures burst through the chapel's entrance.

There were four men and three women, all dressed in black, and another large wolf-like beast.

Bending down, a woman with long straw-coloured dreadlocks stroked the creature who had thrown itself at the group. When she realised his fur had been singed, she stood, her eyes glowing yellow in the darkness. Stepping towards them, she let out a deep hiss.

One of the men, presumably their leader, held out his arm as a barrier to stop her.

'Wait,' he said, his voice slightly muffled. 'Who are you?' he asked them.

Liam stepped forward slightly, 'Nobody. Just kids,' he answered bravely.

The man started to laugh, which rippled through to the others in his gang.

'Just kids? I don't think so. What are you doing here?'

'It was a dare,' lied Lana from behind her boyfriend. 'We dared each other to come to the cemetery at midnight, that's all.'

'That's very brave of you,' he said, stepping forward so that his face was illuminated by the little moonlight from above the broken roof. He would have been very handsome, were it not for the deathly pale, gaunt skin. He was about nineteen or twenty, with black shoulder-length hair and light blue eyes. He pushed his hair away from his face, revealing a deep scar across his cheek towards his ear.

'You never know what's lurking in the shadows of a graveyard, especially one like Abney Park,' he laughed.

'We were just leaving,' squeaked Cassie from the back of the group.

'I'll tell you when you can leave,' he growled, curling his lip. 'But first, you must pay for the damage you've done to Grycan,' he said, glancing down at the slightly singed wolf.

Elliott stepped backwards nervously, brushing against the stone altar.

'Who did this to you, Grycan,' the leader asked.

The wolf let out a deep howl, followed by what sounded like a bark.

'Him,' said the woman with dread-locks, 'The stocky one in the rugby shirt,' she pointed to Elliott.

'You will pay.'

'No!' Liam interjected. 'Your mutt tried to attack us; we were defending ourselves.'

'A pathetic excuse for injuring one of us. Now you will all pay,' the leader growled before leaping forward towards Liam.

Liam responded by dipping his head down and throwing himself at his opponent, pinning him to the far wall of the church.

'I don't think so,' he snapped as the rest of the Watchers reacted, preparing to defend themselves.

The wolves howled loudly as the four men in the other group jumped into action, attacking Elliott, Rupert and Diarmuid.

The three boys immediately retaliated, while the others all threw themselves into the fight causing the church to rumble and rocks to tumble all around them.

Lana and Emma worked together, the very same way they had done in the alleyway the week before, moving too fast for the women in the gang to get hold of them, eventually beating them down. But whenever they were thrown to the floor, the women were right back up again with their yellow eyes narrowing into slits, and their sharp teeth poking out from behind their red lips.

Cries of pain, punches and kicks echoed around the chapel as Elliott managed to dodge a sloppy attack from one of his enemies. Stepping backwards, he held out his hands and allowed huge flames to erupt from his fingertips towards the wolves who yelped the moment the heat grew too much. But they kept coming back for more.

Liam, who had so far managed to dodge the leader's attacks, was growing weaker.

'Get beside me,' shouted Diarmuid suddenly,' I can create a shield,' he said as the others waited for a break to rush to his side. Closing his eyes just for a moment, he let out a deep breath before a massive wall of electricity grew up from the floor, surrounding them.

Two of the men steadied themselves, before looking across at each other and then leaping toward the group. A loud buzzing sound erupted from the wall, and the men dropped to the floor. The stench of smouldering skin filled the nave.

Dusting himself down, the leader approached them, 'I knew you weren't just kids,' he spat. 'You have interesting skills. I'll give you that. But you are no match for The Skulls. We shall return, and we shall get our revenge. Mark my words girls and boys, because you will be seeing us again.'

He turned abruptly, 'Come,' he said as the others followed him out into the darkened night. 'Let's get what we came for. Find the red-haired girl,' he instructed just out of earshot of most of the Watchers.

'It's not over yet, guys. They came for the girl with the red hair. We need to find her and fast,' whispered Ava.

$$\maltese \quad 3\,2 \quad \maltese$$

'Granville, can you hear me? We need your help again. Please show yourself,' said Nisha just moments after the fight had come to its dramatic conclusion and the Skulls had vanished.

'I will show myself only if you assure me the evil ones are gone,' he whispered back so only Nisha could hear.

'Yes, they've gone. Please show yourselves and the others. We need all of your help.'

Seconds later, the ghosts materialised.

'What can we do for you, lovey?' said a completely different ghost, a stocky middle-aged woman with curly brown hair whose hands appeared to be dripping with blood.

Curling up her face in disgust, Lana braved it and spoke, 'We need to know where the girl with the red hair is. We need to save her from the evil ones,' she gulped.

'Give us a moment,' the ghost replied. 'Everyone, go now. Find her before they do,' she said as they all evaporated into the air.

'What should we do now?' asked Cassie.

'We need to stick together, so we just wait for the ghosts to return,' Elliot suggested.

'It's too late,' said a voice from above. 'They've got her. I'm sorry, we didn't get there in time.' It was Granville.

'No,' shouted Emma. 'We've got to help her.'

'Wait... I think I know how,' said Imran, who stepped forward. Perhaps if the ghosts tell me where she was when she was taken, I can go back and warn her?'

'You can do that? You can go back in time?' asked Rupert.

'I can take one person with me,' he said nodding.

'I'll come,' said Emma bravely.

Once the ghosts had told them where the girl had been hiding when she was captured, Emma took hold of Imran's hand, and the two immediately began to spin. When the spinning eventually came to a stop, Emma found it difficult to regain her balance.

Swaying from side to side, Imran stood looking at her. 'Emma, there's no time for that. We've got to warn her now.'

Taking her hand, Imran pulled her around a small pathway until they faced the beautiful lion statue they'd spotted earlier.

The girl sat alone, beneath it.

As Emma and Imran approached, the sound of twigs breaking underfoot caused her to gasp, looking up. She stood quickly, staring at them, preparing to run.

'Wait,' Emma muttered before she disappeared again. 'Please, we're here to warn you. You're in danger. There are some evil, crazy guys coming for you. They'll be here really soon. You need to get away from here as quick as you possibly can or, come with us, take my hand. We're going back to the chapel to the rest of our group. You'll be safe there,' but before Emma could say anything further, the girl had vanished.

'Sugar,' muttered Emma under her breath.

'We should go back, Emma. We've warned her. If she doesn't want to come with us, there's not much we can do about that. Let's go before they come.'

Emma turned around, searching for any sign of the girl, but she knew it was pointless. She'd gone.

Taking Imran's offered hand, they began to spin again until they stood outside the chapel where the others stood waiting.

'She wouldn't come,' Emma sighed, kicking the floor in exasperation.

'But she did listen, right? She did run away?'

'Yeah, from where she was, but who's to say she didn't run right into their grasp? I just hope she's safe,' Emma sighed again as the others gathered around.

'We should get out of here,' said Moira, who was holding her arm, wincing.

'Jesus, Moira, you're injured. You should have said something. You're right, let's get out of this place before they come back,' said Lana.

'But wait... what about Joe? We can't leave without him. That's why we came, remember?' said Emma as she pushed through the others, so she stood facing them all.

'Please, we need to find him. You heard what the ghosts said. The evil ones would try and get to him. I don't even want to think about what they could do to him if they did,' she said, her face crumpling at the thought.

'He's a ghost, Em. What can they do to him that hasn't been done to him already?' Lana asked, giving in.

'You're joking, right? Did you see how terrified those other ghosts were of them? And what about poor Joe finding his way home, crossing over, where he belongs? I'm not giving up on him, Sis and neither should you. It's not about the stupid task any more. It's about helping Joe, our friend. I'm not leaving this place without him. If you all want to go, then go. I won't hold it against you. Nisha, please get the ghosts back so I can communicate with them before you go,' Emma said determinedly, turning to walk away from them all.

'Hey, wait a minute. Nobody is leaving you,' said Diarmuid as he pulled on her hand and dragged her back towards him. 'I sure as hell am not going to. I'll stay until we've found him. I promise, okay?' he said as he searched her eyes and watched as they filled with tears.

Roughly wiping at them, she nodded.

The others slowly began to step towards her, each placing a hand on her and nodding.

'I'm sorry, Sis. You're right. We're all in this together. Let's go and find him,' Lana said as she finally put her hand on her sister's back.

'You don't have to go anywhere,' said a gentle voice from nearby.

The others all dropped their hands from Emma and turned to face the sound. Sitting on a thick branch in an old oak tree, just a few metres away was the red-haired girl.

'Daisy?' asked Emma.

The girl began to climb down. When she reached the bottom, she walked up to them and smiled sadly. She nodded, 'How do you know me?'

'The ghosts told us your name. I'm glad you got away.'

Smiling nervously, she replied, 'Only because of you. Thank you,' she nodded.

'What did you mean, we don't have to go anywhere,' asked Lana.

'The ghost you're looking for, I know where he is. I've been keeping him safe for a couple of days. You called him Joe, right?' she asked.

Lana nodded, 'That's his name, well Josiah. Josiah Grimshaw. He came with us from Andilyse Island last week, but he seems to have forgotten everything.'

'Can you take us to him?' Emma asked.

The girl nodded, 'Follow me,' she whispered as the group all began to trample after her, careful not to make too much noise.

'What is that?' asked Imran as they approached a large memorial.

'It's a War Memorial,' said Daisy. 'There are catacombs beneath it. The main entrance has been blocked off, but I know a secret way in.'

'Cool,' said Liam as they walked around the memorial and then off to the side under a cluster of nearby trees. A hole in the ground had been dug and a tunnel led off towards the monument.

'He's hiding in there... with my Dad,' she said shyly.

'Oh... okay. Nisha, over to you,' Emma said with a smile.

'You want me to climb down there?' she asked a little nervously.

Emma nodded.

'It's okay. It's not as bad as it looks. It's very clean, it's just the entrance that looks a bit dodgy,' said Daisy. 'Follow me.'

Nisha rubbed her chin and followed Daisy down into the tunnel. Surprisingly, there was more room than she'd expected, and once they'd arrived at the catacombs, Nisha heard Daisy fidget around until a light was switched on.

'I always keep a few supplies down here,' she smiled as she held the torch upwards. 'Can you see Josiah? He often hides when my dad is here. And he doesn't always come when I ask him to.'

Looking around, Nisha could only see a sleeping man. The odour of alcohol drifted under her nose, making her scrunch it upwards in disgust.

'No, here's not here.'

'Josiah?' whispered Nisha.

'He doesn't remember his name, does he?'

'Oh yeah, I forgot about that. Hello, is there anybody here. Anybody ghostly? Can you show yourself?' Nisha asked, feeling a little foolish when nothing happened. 'Hello? We know you're here. We want you to show yourself.'

Daisy's father mumbled something in his sleep before turning over and snoring, his sweatshirt lifted slightly, revealing a familiar tattoo on the base of his spine. Nisha gasped but said nothing, instead turning to concentrate on Josiah.

'Look, we know who you are. We know you've lost your memory. We can help you. It's why we're here.'

'It is? You know who I am?' said a voice in the semi-darkness as a figure slowly started to emerge in the corner. The ghost of the young man sat huddled up, his face filled with confusion and fear.

'Your name is Josiah, Josiah Grimshaw. Does that mean anything to you?' Nisha asked as he shook his head. 'We're your friends. You came to London with two girls, Lana Beth and Emma Jane Morgan. Do you remember?' She asked. A faint flicker of familiarity crossed his eyes, and he sat up.

'Emma? It does seem familiar to me. Where is she?' he asked.

'She's above ground. We came here to find you. Will you return with us?' she asked.

He waited a moment before finally slowly nodding.

Nisha finally let out a sigh of relief, and her shoulders dropped back to their natural position. 'Thank you. At last.'

Climbing back out and into the cemetery, the group were huddled around each other waiting patiently for Nisha to do her work. When Joe's ghost finally appeared in front of them, they all let out a cheer, before hushing each other up in case those awful Skulls came back.

As they prepared to go, Emma suddenly remembered Daisy. Turning to look at the lonely girl, she approached her, 'Daisy, will you come back with us?'

'Back where? And what about my Dad?'

'Emma? I saw her dad down there. He's one of us; I saw the tattoo on his back. Which means Daisy is one of us too,' Nisha interrupted.

'I knew it,' said Emma, 'Look, Daisy, I can't explain exactly where we'll be going. Just know that you can trust us. And there are people there, people like you and me that would happily take you in. You can learn with us. I just know that you're meant to come back with us. There's this feeling in the pit of my stomach, and it's telling me that you should. Your dad can come to. He'll get the treatment he needs. I promise you. You won't regret it,' she said with her hands on Daisy's shoulders.

The others stood slightly back, nodding.

'I have the feeling too,' said Lana.

'And me,' said Cassie and Penny.

'I do too,' said Imran before the rest of them all agreed.

Daisy's eye welled with tears as she looked around at the friendly faces staring at her hopefully. Finally feeling like she belonged, she nodded.

The group kept quiet, but their faces lit up, and they all grinned at her before giving each other high-fives. Liam offered to climb down into the catacomb to fetch her father, but she shook her head.

'There's no need, thank you. I can do it myself.'

Within seconds, the slight girl had vanished before returning above ground carrying her father over her shoulder.

'Now that's what I'm talking about,' laughed Imran, who turned his baseball cap backwards on his head as they began their journey back to Praxos.

$$\text{❄} \quad 33 \quad \text{❄}$$

Eleanor had taken Daisy in with open arms. She was shocked that someone with her abilities had gotten by under the radar, as she'd put it. Her father was being looked after by members of the Praxos Foundation in special medical facilities beneath the UCL building not far from Praxos HQ, while Daisy was staying with Eleanor in her quarters until the right Mentor was chosen to care for her.

It was later revealed that Beau Madigan was a fallen angel, like Eleanor, who had chosen the wrong path until he had fallen in love with a human, Daisy's mother. Her name was Esther. She had died a year earlier. A fact that led to his downward spiral into alcoholism and the loss of their home. The shock of losing a mother and having to care for her father had catapulted Daisy's skills out into the open a year too soon. Her tattoo bore the words Semper Fidelis - always faithful.

The events that had occurred at Abney Park had undoubtedly brought the group closer together, and for the first time, they felt like they truly belonged. Like a family.

But the issue with Josiah Grimshaw continued, he still had no idea who he was or where he was from. The only redeeming feature so far was that he seemed to remember Emma, albeit vaguely.

On Declan's boat a couple of night's later, the four of them were sat eating a delicious meal of Chicken Madras, Bombay potatoes, rice and naan bread when Emma suddenly had a thought about why Joe seemed to recognise her.

'It's because I look like her,' she suddenly piped up after a few moments of silence as they tucked into the lovely grub.

'Hm? What are you talking about?' Lana said, shovelling a piece of garlic naan into her mouth.

'Joe. Remember when we went into his house? The photos...'

'Duh... how could we have forgotten that?' Lana replied.

'What's this all about?' Declan asked curiously as the girls proceeded to explain to him and Saleena what had happened the day Joe had died.

'That woman on the wall, she looked a bit like Emma. He did tell us her name, do you remember Em?'

She put down her fork for a second and gazed into space before picking it back up again and putting a spoonful of rice into her mouth, shaking her head at the same time.

'He told me... he said it a couple of times in the hospital. Oh, I can't remember. It was something like Ellie, Emily, that's it! Emelia!' she said, almost coughing. 'Emelia. That's the woman he spent almost his entire life searching for. She went missing in the storm of 1953.'

'Poor bloke,' said Declan. 'But how come he's a young man?'

Lana and Emma shrugged.

'It was weird. The day he died, his body was found, barely alive, out in the North Sea. The same morning, his young body was found washed up on the beach at Andilyse. It was like there were two of him. A young man and an old man. We never understood how that was possible, but now, after all we've learned over the past few weeks, we realise anything is possible,' said Emma as she polished off the Madras on her plate.

'Help yourself to more, Emma,' offered Saleena.

'I couldn't eat another thing, thanks. I'm so full,' she smiled. 'It was absolutely delicious.'

'It sounds to me like this woman is the key. You need to find out who she was and exactly what happened to her,' Declan suggested. 'Hopefully, that will bring back his lost memories so he can move on. Maybe I can use my contacts and get some of those photographs scanned and emailed to us?'

'You can do that? But wouldn't Dad find out? Wouldn't he ask questions?' asked Lana, surprised.

'I was planning on going directly to your dad, actually. He knows I'm an investigator so he wouldn't ask any questions at all,' he smiled cheekily.

'Excellent,' Emma said as she gave in and scooped up a little more Madras on to her plate with a grin.

The following morning, true to his word, the girls sat waiting for the email. Patrick had sent one of his officers up to Mr Grimshaw's home to obtain several of the photographs that were on the wall in the strange immaculate little room towards the back of the house. They'd been scanned in and emailed immediately to Declan.

Patrick had made a comment in the body of his email about the young woman looking a little like his daughter, but it was apparent he'd thought nothing more of it.

As Declan opened the photos, he could see the similarity in the same wavy chocolate brown hair and intense green eyes. They shared the same slim face shape and high cheekbones. It was easy to see why Joe had seen Emelia in Emma when he was on his death bed.

Declan and Saleena stood leaning over the girls, as they flicked through the four photographs that had been sent. 'I wonder who she was,' muttered Saleena.

'That's what we're going to find out,' said a determined Emma, as they printed off copies to take to Praxos with them.

The rest of the group had already completed their tasks. Some were hanging around the HQ, chatting and playing board games. Others trained in the gym and some had even gone sightseeing in the city with a few Mentors.

Liam was one of the ones working up a sweat, while Diarmuid was determined to give the girls a hand in carrying out their task in assisting Joe to cross over.

Joe was pleased to be surrounded by friendly folk in a comfortable environment, and so he had no reason to stay hidden as he had done at Abney Park. He drifted from room to room, watching what was going on, sometimes talking to others, but mostly staying quiet, hoping that his memories would return to him.

When Emma, Lana and Diarmuid approached him that morning, he beamed happily, enjoying being part of the conversation.

'Hey Joe,' said Emma as he floated towards them in the room with all the lovely soft bean bags. Lana let herself drop into one as Emma took the photos from her satchel.

'I have some photos for you to look at, Joe, and I want to know if they're familiar to you at all,' she said as she laid them out on a small table in the centre of the room.

He drifted closer and looked down. His eyes flicked from one to the other for quite a few minutes before Emma finally spoke again, 'Well, Joe? Do you know her?'

He glanced up and nodded, 'I think so,' he said.

'Yes!' shouted Lana from the other side of the room. 'At last!'

'Who is she?' asked Diarmuid.

'I... I don't know,' he said.

'Doh,' Lana cried.

'Think Joe, think long and hard. We got these photos from your home – your little house on Andilyse Island. You have a room there completely dedicated to this woman. The walls are covered with photos of her.'

'I do?' he asked. 'She looks like you.'

'Yes, she does a little bit. But it's not me. This is a woman who disappeared in 1953. You've spent years searching for her, hoping she'd come back to you. Does any of this bring back any memories? Anything at all?'

Joe held out his hand and gently tried to stroke the face on the photos, his fingers going straight through her.

'I do... I do remember her face.'

'We believe her name was Emelia,' Lana said, hoping it might help.

'Emelia?' he said all of a sudden. 'Emelia. Yes, I remember I loved a girl named Emelia,' he whispered excitedly.

'Yes!' yelled Lana for the second time.

'Now think back... who was she? What was her full name?' Emma asked.

But his face went blank, and he shook his head. 'I'm sorry, I'm so sorry... but I don't remember.'

Lana leaned forward with her head in her hands, shaking it.

'That's all right, Joe. At least you've remembered something. That's great for now,' reassured Emma.

'I have an idea,' Diarmuid said just as Liam walked into the room with a towel around his neck.

'What did I miss?' he asked as he walked towards Lana who curled up her nose when he leaned over to kiss her.

'Ew, you're all sweaty,' she said. 'Joe can just about remember the girl in the photo. We know her name was Emelia, but that's it, so far.'

Diarmuid, who had run out of the room after he'd announced he'd had an idea, returned, carrying a laptop.

Sitting down, he opened it and connected to the internet. After a few moments of typing and clicking away, he turned the screen towards the ghost.

'Joe, have a look at this... do any of these images ring a bell?' he asked.

If Joe had been alive, his face would have drained of all colour. His expression changed, and fear filled his eyes.

'The storm,' he whispered. 'People died. The old church was ruined, as was the... the pier. Emelia... was lost in the storm,' he cried. 'Oh, Emelia, where did you go?' he said as he drifted back to the photos, sobbing. 'Emelia, my love, oh Emelia.'

'I think it worked,' Emma said quietly. 'But I think it's brought him too much pain.'

'Unfortunately, he needs to remember everything,' Diarmuid said sadly.

'Joe? Do you remember us now? Do you remember how you came to London?'

'I came with you. You were the only ones who could see me. Emma, you were there when I died. Yes, I remember everything.'

'Do you remember yourself as an old man?' Lana whispered.

Slowly he looked up at them and nodded. As he did so, his features began to change. His eye sockets deepened, and little wrinkles started appearing all over his face. His brown hair faded and thinned, while his pink lips became less full and bright. The ghost of Josiah Grimshaw became old in a matter of seconds.

'What's happening?' asked Lana as she gasped at the sight of him changing.

'I'm an old man again,' he whispered. 'I've lost my youth. I can't be dying. I'm already dead,' he said mournfully as he faded from them.

'Don't go, Josiah,' Emma yelled, 'Don't leave us again,' she said, almost sobbing.

He returned momentarily to say, 'Don't worry, I want to be alone for a while, that's all. I won't leave. Whenever you want me to come back, call. I promise not to leave Praxos,' he said with the saddest smile she'd ever seen before he turned his back on them and disappeared into the air.

When he was gone, Emma's eyes filled with tears and she sobbed into Diarmuid's shoulder, 'What have we done to him? What have we done?'

Determined more than ever to help poor old Josiah Grimshaw come to terms with what had happened to him and find his true love so he could cross over, Emma and Lana were now on a mission. Mission Josiah.

Meanwhile, the other Watchers spent time with Eleanor and their Mentors, detailing what had happened at Abney Park that night, describing the Skulls in as much detail as possible. Occasionally, Eleanor would appear and ask Lana and Emma questions, but she understood that their need to complete their own task was much more important to them at that time.

They spent hours online researching the Great Storm of 1953 and, although they had failed to discover Emelia's true identity, they were shocked to uncover that on the night of 31st January all those years earlier, all hell had broken loose around the coasts of England, Holland, Belgium and Scotland. There were nearly 2000 deaths in Holland alone, over 300 in the UK, 28 in Belgium and more than 230 people died on board sea craft in the North Sea after many fishing trawlers sank. The Princess Victoria ferry was lost in the Irish Sea with 133 fatalities. Thirty thousand people were evacuated in England and 30,000 animals drowned. It was the mother of all storms.

Emma couldn't stop herself from sobbing while they read and

so Lana kept her hand across her sister's shoulders in an almost maternal fashion.

'Does it have the names of the dead anywhere?' asked Emma, in between sobs.

'Not that I've found so far. But I'll keep looking...' answered Lana sadly.

Several hours later, the girls sat disappointed and tired when Eleanor approached them quietly.

'Girls, I have some news. I've been in touch with some of our special contacts who have managed to obtain a list of the victims of the Great Flood. I'm afraid to say that, of all those who perished on Andilyse Island, nobody matched that of this Emelia character. We also checked the list of those from England, Scotland, Belgium and Holland, and there is no match for her anywhere.'

'Do you think she's still alive?' asked Lana hopefully.

Eleanor shook her head, 'I think it's unlikely, due to how she vanished. It was during the night of the storm; she was on a small island in the middle of the North Sea. There was nowhere for her to go.'

'I don't understand,' sighed Emma. 'What could have happened to her?' she asked.

'I'll leave you to ponder that question,' she said with a smile before turning and walking away.

'I need to stretch my legs,' Lana yawned. 'Shall we go for a walk?'

Emma nodded, and the two stood up, stretched and headed to the elevator.

Outside, the day was cold and blustery, the pavements a little slippery after a summer shower. Linking arms, the girls sauntered down the road, each deep in thought about the elusive Emelia.

'Maybe she faked her own death?' suggested Lana.

'Really, Sis, that's the best you can come up with? If she'd done that, she'd have made sure that her name was on the victim's list, surely? And why would she do that? You can tell by those photos that she was so happy with Joe.'

'Yeah, I guess,' mumbled Lana in response. 'Maybe she was a spy?'

Emma rolled her eyes and shook her head, her face breaking into a little smile.

'For who? The Russians? Americans? Germans? It was 1953; the war was over.'

'I suppose,' sighed Lana.

As they walked along the pavement, barely noticing where they were going, Emma finally looked up and realised they were right outside the British Museum.

'Ooh, look Lana. Shall we go in?'

'Yeah, it might do us good to take our minds off Joe and Emelia for a while,' she said as they turned to face the grand building and walked up the stairs and through the entrance.

'Wow,' uttered Emma, 'It's seriously impressive.'

'Yeah, I guess so.'

As the girls made their way through the museum, room after room, taking in the majestic architecture of the building and the historical delights on offer, Lana soon grew tired and bored, moving along quicker than Emma had the chance to read about any of the exhibits.

'Lana, let me just read this,' she said time after time as Lana stood, arms crossed, tapping her foot impatiently.

'Can we go now?' asked Lana eventually. 'I'm bored stiff.'

Shaking her head, Emma smiled, 'God you're so predictable, Lana. What do you want to do, go shopping?' she said sarcastically.

'Now there's a thought,' Lana replied with a laugh. 'Oh come on, I was only joking. There's only so much history you can take in in one day.'

'No, actually there isn't. This place is like a treasure trove, it's amazing. I could spend days in here.'

'Not with me, you couldn't.'

Emma raised her eyebrows and laughed. 'Too right.'

Lana pouted and put her hands on her hips just as an attractive young man strolled past, cheekily smiling at her.

'Erm, actually, maybe we could stay a little longer,' she said as she watched him stop over by a North American feather bonnet, reading the facts with a smirk still on his face.

Emma just shook her head and continued to pore over the artefacts as Lana wandered over to him.

'Hi,' she said, leaning against the wall.

'Hi yourself.'

'Ooh, you're American,' she breathed.

The young man laughed.

'I expect you already know about all this stuff,' she said, pointing to the North American artefacts in front of them.

'Yeah, you could say that. But you can never tire of this kind of history and culture, can you? This is one awesome museum you guys have here. If I lived here, I'd never want to leave,' he smiled, revealing a set of bright white teeth that wouldn't go amiss on a toothpaste advert.

Instantly put off, Lana's shoulders drooped.

'Yeah, I guess,' she said, adding, 'Sorry, I really need to get back to my sister. See you around,' she said without even giving him a chance to speak.

'I don't believe you,' Emma said, so embarrassed that she dragged her away from the North American exhibition and far away from the poor guy, heading into the Asian exhibition where a massive group of tourists were circling a tour guide.

'Come on, let's get out of here. It's getting too busy, and I don't want to bump into that poor guy again. How embarrassing, Lana,' she sighed as they rounded the corner without looking where they were going, smack right into a woman who appeared to be an employee of the museum.

'Oh sorry,' said Emma. 'Are you okay?' She asked. As she moved her eyes from the women's feet up towards her face, Emma suddenly felt like she'd been slapped. Standing in front of them was the dread-locked woman from Abney Park.

'I'm fine. I'm fine. Don't worry. Sorry I'm in a hurry. Must dash,' she said in a very posh English accent as she rushed away without even glancing at them.

'Th...th... that's her from the graveyard,' whispered Lana. 'What is she doing here?'

'More importantly, do you think she recognised us?'

Lana shook her head. 'She didn't even look at us. Do you really think she works here? It's just so... weird. And did you see her eyes? They weren't all yellow and glowing this time, they were just, you know, dull.'

'Yeah, I know. Let's get out of here and tell Eleanor. She'd want to know.'

As they exited the building, thunderous clouds hovered overhead threatening to empty their load. The sisters looked up just as a great clap of thunder echoed throughout the sky before droplets of rain began to drop one by one on top of them. As they walked huddled beneath their jackets held over their heads, the rain gradually became heavier and heavier until their small steps turned into a sprint. They rounded the corner and headed down the road until they reached the external front door with the Praxos emblem on it.

The moment they arrived, it was pulled open by Wilbur who stood waiting with a couple of towels for them.

'Aww thanks, Wilbur,' said Lana as they roughly towel dried themselves and followed him through the house, taking a different route this time. Eventually, they found themselves in an old kitchen.

'Where did this room come from? We never found it the first time we were here?' asked Emma in amazement as she slowly walked around the large room, fingering the old fashioned aga covered in dust.

Wilbur smiled secretively, 'There's lots here at Praxos that you haven't seen yet, ladies. Come on, follow me,' he said as they ducked down and walked into a tiny pantry. When he closed the door behind them, the pantry transformed into an elevator, and they quickly began their descent to HQ.

'That's amazing,' sighed Emma. 'A pantry lift. That's just cool.'

After Wilbur left, taking their damp towels with him, the girls walked into the main hall and spotted Liam sitting beneath the angel statue with his computer on his lap.

'Hey you,' said Lana with a grin as she flopped down beside him and laid her head on his shoulder. He put his arm lazily around her and carried on what he was doing. Lana closed her eyes.

Emma, feeling like a gooseberry, just stood for a moment and took in the beauty of the statue above her when she suddenly realised something.

Slapping her forehead with her hand, she turned to look at Lana and said, 'It's been right in front of us the whole time.'

Opening one of her eyes, Lana raised her eyebrows, 'What has?'

'Emelia. What if she's an angel?'

Slowly lifting her head from Liam's shoulder, Lana gently bit her lip and thought about it before nodding. Climbing back up, she and Emma stood side by side, looking at the statue.

'What do you reckon?' asked Emma. 'Do you think it's possible?'

'It's more than possible. It would explain a heck of a lot. We need to get our heads around this paranormal malarkey, you know. We have to stop thinking like humans,' laughed Lana. 'If you know what I mean?' she said, knitting her eyebrows together with her finger in mouth.

Emma nodded, 'Yeah, I know exactly what you mean. Come on.'

Turning away, the girls excitedly ran towards Eleanor's office, knocking and waiting for a response before entering.

Eleanor stood facing the huge screen with her arms crossed, watching a crime unfolding. An armed man had punched a young woman and dragged her into his car.

Lana and Emma both stood with their mouths agape.

'Shouldn't we do something?' asked Emma.

Eleanor turned and smiled at them briefly.

'Don't worry. It's all under control,' she said, turning back to the screen just as a woman appeared seemingly out of nowhere and dragged the man out of his car window. She grabbed his gun and punched him in the face with it. She then handcuffed his hands behind his back and turned her attention to the poor, stunned woman who sat cowering in the back seat.

After a few moments of coaxing, the woman gingerly climbed out, tears streaming down her face. Her defender hugged her, said a few more words, turned to look at the secret hidden camera and gave a thumbs-up signal before disappearing, leaving the shocked woman alone to call the police.

'Wow... was she... one of us?' asked Lana as Eleanor nodded and finally turned her attention to the girls.

'Yes, she's actually one of the professors at the academy. I believe today is her day off,' she smiled. 'Now, what can I do for you?'

'Two things actually,' offered Emma. 'We went to the British Museum earlier and bumped into one of those evil people from the other night.'

Emma had certainly caught Eleanor's attention. 'One of the Skulls? At the British Museum? Are you absolutely certain?' she asked as the girls nodded. 'Did she recognise either of you?'

The girls shook their heads, Lana continuing, 'She was focussed on something. She was in a hurry.'

'That's good. Which of the women was it?'

'The one with the dreadlocks,' replied Lana.

'Right. Just give me a moment,' Eleanor said as she picked up her phone and dialled.

'Bryn? Eleanor here. We just received word about the whereabouts of one of the Skulls. It's believed she works in the British Museum, yes, that's right. Dreadlocks, blonde, about... approximate age girls?' she asked.

'Nineteen or twenty, more or less,' Emma replied.

'About twenty, Bryn. No, we don't have any names. The only name that came to light the other night was Grycan, a wolf - possibly a Lycanthrope. Yes, fine. Excellent, I'll leave it with you. Thank you.'

Putting down the receiver, Eleanor returned her attention to the sisters.

'And the other thing. We were wondering whether Emelia can be an angel?'

The idea seemed to please Eleanor for some reason, and she stood with a smile.

'I knew you'd eventually come to the probability of paranormals, and yes, I do believe it is a possibility.'

Lana pulled a funny face, 'Why didn't you say something?'

'This is your task, Lana. You must come to the conclusions, not me,' she smiled warmly. 'It's how you will best learn to use your skills. Remember that.'

'If Emelia is an angel, wouldn't you have known her though, Eleanor?' asked Emma as their guardian shook her head.

'I'm afraid not. I don't know of all the angels that roam the earth. I know many of them, but not all. It is up to you now to delve further into this possibility. You must ask the right questions to the right people, and soon, you will get your answers,' she said as she wandered slowly over to the door and opened it, indicating their time was up.

❧ 35 ❧

'We should ask the Mentors,' Lana suggested as they walked out of Eleanor's office and back towards the main hall. 'And Wilbur...'

'You called?' said a voice behind, startling them both.

As Wilbur stood over them waiting for them to speak, Lana shifted from one foot to the other, putting her hands in the back pockets of her jeans.

'Erm, yes. We have a question about a possible angel?'

'Yeeesss,' he said slowly.

Emma delved into her satchel and pulled out the photographs of Emelia. 'Do you know her, Wilbur?'

Gazing down at the images, he stroked his chin with his fingers before turning to Lana, then Emma, and shaking his head.

'Sorry, she's not particularly familiar. I don't think I've seen her before. But then, I've had to deal with countless people and paranormals in my time. She looks a little like you though, don't you think?'

'Yeah, I've been getting that a lot. Thanks though, Wilbur,' Emma replied as they left him standing behind them.

'We already know Declan and Saleena don't know her, so who next?'

'Let's ask Zane and Marian. Diarmuid and Liam will know where they are.'

Liam was still deep in concentration on his laptop, sitting in the same spot, beneath the statue of the Praxos angel.

'Liam?' asked Lana as she approached.

'Hm-hm?' he responded without looking up.

'Do you know where Zane and Marian are?'

'They're out with Diarmuid,' he said flatly.

'Do you know where?' asked Emma.

He just shrugged his shoulders. Lana leaned forward to see what he was doing. When she saw that he was playing a stupid game, she became irritated, pushing the laptop shut.

'Babe... I was right in the middle of, oh never mind,' he said, shaking his head, a bit peeved.

'We need to know where they are,' she demanded.

'They went to the Tower of London, ages ago.'

'See... that wasn't so hard, was it?' she said flirtatiously, making him laugh. 'You wanna come with us?' But he shook his head and reopened his laptop to continue playing the game. Before they walked away, he winked, 'Practise makes perfect.'

After trying to phone Diarmuid, they found his mobile was switched off. He must be in the middle of a tour, they figured, and so they moved on to find the other Mentors.

With none of the other Watchers in the immediate vicinity, the girls had to phone them to find out where they all were. Moira and Imran were on a boat trip with Brody and Oksana, Ava and Rupert were shopping with Megan and Rhydian, Penny and Nisha didn't know where Habika was, and Bryn was busy sorting something out for Eleanor.

'Great. Now, what do we do? Time's running out. We're going home in a couple of days,' sighed Lana as they sat down in the dining room with a cup of tea.

'Let's talk to Joe. See how he is. Joe. Josiah. You there?' asked Emma quietly looking around the large room.

Within moments, the ghost of an elderly man hovered before them, his face filled with sadness.

'I'm here,' he said slowly.

'How are you doing, Joe?' Emma asked, feeling guilty.

Sighing heavily, the old ghost approached her and looked at her face. He attempted a smile but failed terribly. 'Same, same,' he uttered.

'Joe, I'm so sorry about everything. We didn't mean to bring you so much grief.'

'You didn't bring me grief, Emma. I've lived with this grief my entire life. Ever since... ever since...'

'1953?' Lana interjected, and he nodded slowly.

'Yes, that's right. Ever since she vanished. My Emelia Doris,' he sighed.

'Sorry?' Emma said suddenly, her attention captured. 'What did you say?'

'Ever since she vanished,' he murmured.

'No not that. The bit about her name. You just said her name, her full name?'

'Emelia... Doris,' he whispered, his eyes widening. 'I'd clean forgotten her name. It just came back to me now. I didn't even realise I'd remembered it. Emelia Doris,' he sighed.

Emma and Lana had immediately jumped up and disappeared out of the room, leaving Joe and their cups of tea behind.

'Sorry Liam, you're just going to have to practise later,' Lana said as she ripped the laptop out of his hands and plonked herself down on the ground with Emma besides her.

Liam barely said a word; he just stood up and walked away, shaking his head.

After twenty minutes, Lana let out a high pitched squeal, 'I think I found her, I found her. Look here, look. Emelia Doris, born to the wealthy Doris-Baxter family in 1827. Oh, she died in 1845, just 18 years old. There's a sketch of the family,' she said as she waited for the image to open. When it did, the girls just sat motionlessly. It wasn't her.

'I thought it was going to be her. I mean, how many women are there out there called Emelia Doris? I'm so bummed,' sighed Lana as Joe appeared suddenly by their side.

'What's going on?' he asked.

Glancing at each other, Lana leaned over and closed the laptop.

'Oh, it's nothing. We're just doing a bit of research. Nothing that would interest you,' she said. Looking somewhat downtrodden, he vanished as quickly as he'd appeared.

'Why didn't you tell him we were looking for her?' asked Emma, a little put out.

'I don't think we should until we find out exactly what happened to her. Let's just wait. All we know is that she probably wasn't human. We shouldn't say anything until we know for sure.'

Emma reluctantly agreed as they heard the grandfather clock in the living room strike five o'clock. Moments later, Eleanor came bounding out full of energy, wearing black leather jeans and a pink t-shirt covered in sparkly sequins.

'Hey girls, any luck?' she asked as she whizzed over to them, grinning, stretching her arms high above her head.

Lana and Emma both nodded their heads and explained that Joe had finally remembered Emelia's full name.

'Perhaps now would be a good time to show you our special archives,' she said as she motioned for them to follow her. Leading them down one of the tunnels, Eleanor pulled a necklace out from underneath her t-shirt, revealing a key dangling from it. As they approached an old wooden door, she bent forward and unlocked it, pushing it open. The girls followed her inside before she closed and locked the door behind her. The flick of a switch revealed a small room with two doors either side. Turning to the right one, Eleanor used the same key to unlock it. When it was pushed open, and a light switch turned on, Emma and Lana were gobsmacked by the sight before them. It was a massive room, not unlike the main hall, and it was full of filing cabinets, vast book stands and boxes upon boxes were neatly placed among them.

'What is this place?' asked Lana as she stood staring around her.

'It's our filing system. It goes back hundreds of years. Here you'll find everything you'll ever need to know about the Paranormals, the Elementals, the Others, even the Watchers, Mentors and Guardians... not that there have been too many of those. Not in England anyway.'

'But it's so... so... so big. It would take months, if not years, to go through this lot,' Emma sighed, with a gulp.

'Not necessarily,' Eleanor smiled as they followed her through the mass of paperwork until they stood in front of a smaller door that was already unlocked. As she pushed it open, there was a little desk with a modern computer on it.

'It might seem like an awful lot of paperwork, but we keep it all backed up on the archive computer. Wilbur and a few of the others keep it up to date.'

'Wilbur certainly keeps himself busy,' smiled Lana as she walked up to the computer. 'Can I switch it on?' she asked.

'Of course. You know what to do. I'm going to leave you now. I'll give you the key. Now, use your heads. Think,' she said, tapping the side of her head. 'As Watchers, you have remarkable brain-power that you just haven't tapped into yet. The answers you are searching for may well be here. If they are, I believe that you can find them. Think about Josiah,' she said with a smile before turning around and closing the door behind her.

'Wait,' shouted Lana as Emma rushed to the door and opened it. 'What about the password?' she yelled, but Eleanor had already gone.

'Great.'

'It's okay, Lana. We know what it is, we just have to think,' she said, tapping the side of her head with a chuckle.

'Okay, then. Let's try Praxos,' she said as she typed.

'Too obvious,' Emma said just as the computer flashed back, ' Access Denied'.

'Watchers?'

Access Denied.

'Eleanor?'

Access Denied.

'Hayden-Jones?'

Access Denied.

'Wilbur?'

Access Denied.

'Angel?'

Access Denied.

'Skulls?'

Access Denied.

'I know,' Emma smiled as she leaned forward and typed in the name Tarquin and pressed enter.

'Access Granted.'

The girls squealed before Lana turned to her and asked, 'What's Tarquin?'

'You don't remember?' Emma asked as Lana shook her head, confused.

'Tarquin was the name of the man Eleanor loved,' she said sadly.

'Oh, that's so sad.'

'So what do we look for now?' Emma asked.

'All we know is the name, Emelia Doris.'

'Let's just search for that then,' Emma said as she typed it in and pressed enter.

There were several Dorises, most of whom were fallen angels, although there was one reference to a Doris who was married to a man called Nereus and had something to do with Greek Mythology. There were also a few Emelias. One Emelia Hilton was an Elemental who was killed by the Skulls in 1949, another was a Watcher who currently works in New Orleans, and the third was something called a fae who lives in Nairn in Scotland.

'What's a Fae?' whispered Lana.

'Let's have a look,' Emma said as she clicked on it. Immediately several images popped up of innocent-looking beautiful people, with a long description which began 'Fae, also known as fairies, faeries or fay are human in appearance with magical abilities and sometimes wings (it remains unknown why some grow them, and some don't). Generally, the fae work alongside Praxos, but there have been several who have been tempted by the darker side of paranormal life. Mirelia Murdoch, for instance, was infamous for having been involved in the kidnapping and torture of Tabitha Collins and her family in 1659. Fortunately, Praxos was able to contain Mirelia before further wrongdoings could be carried out. Mirelia perished in the Great Fire of London in 1666. Further reading can be found here...'

'Fairies are real?' breathed Emma dumbfoundedly. 'That's so cool.'

'This is freaking me out, Sis,' said Lana. 'If fairies are real, what else are we going to find here?' she asked nervously.

'We need to know. This is part of our world now. There's no point in freaking out. It's too late for that.'

'What else is there?'

'An Emelia Roundhead who was a known Shifter worked with the Skulls.'

Lana gulped, 'A Shifter? Is that what I think it is?'

Emma continued to read the description to herself before nodding, 'Yeah. It's a creature that looks human that can change its form to look like someone else,' she shivered.

'Is that all the Emelias and Dorises?'

'Yeah. What should we look up next?'

'Try Nameless'

'No, nothing,' Emma said as she thought for a second and typed in, Unidentified.

A list with the title, Paranormal Individuals who remain Unidentified, appeared on the screen. Scrolling through them, the girls subconsciously inched closer together.

'Amazons, Angels, Banshees, Changelings, Demons, Djinns, Elementals, Fae, Ghosts, Ghouls, Harpies, Mothmen, Mermaids, Ogres, Shifters, Sirens, Wendigos, Werewolves, Witches, Vampires, Zombies ... the list goes on, Sis.'

But Lana had gone white.

Turning to look at her, Emma couldn't help but laugh a little, albeit somewhat nervously herself. 'Might as well get used to those names because we're going to be dealing with this kind of thing a lot in our future,' she joked half-heartedly.

'I... I'm not so sure I want this future,' she gulped.

'Really, Lana? You don't mean that, do you? Remember how we felt when we attacked those guys in the alley? Yeah?' she said as Lana nodded. 'Remember that rush of adrenaline. That kick we got? Well, we get to feel like that all the time once we pass this task and go to the Academy. This is what we're meant to do with our lives, Lana. It might sound scary now but look how lucky we are. This is phenomenally awesome,' she laughed.

'I... I guess so,' Lana said, calming down. 'It's just a bit freaky, that's all.'

Emma leaned her head momentarily on Lana's shoulder, 'I know Sis. I know.'

❧ 36 ❧

Thirteen hours later, the girls hit the jackpot. Lana, who was asleep on a mattress on the floor (kindly brought in by Wilbur along with plenty of food and drink), awoke with a start by the sound of high pitched squealing and laughing.

'Wh..what... what is it?' she said, rubbing at her eyes and trying to straighten her unruly bed head.

'I found her, I found her...'

'What?' Lana said, jumping up and staring down at the computer screen where the image of a woman who looked remarkably like Emelia stared back at her.

'Oh...My...God. What did you find her under? What is she?'

'Well, we were certainly right about her not being human. Emelia Doris was a Nereid,' she said, feeling very pleased with herself. 'And we should never have disregarded the Greek Mythology link we read earlier on. Doris is actually the name of her mother!' she squealed.

'But what's a Nereid?'

'Kind of like a Mermaid, a Sea Nymph.'

'Really? A Sea Nymph? It just sounds so, well, bizarre. What happened to her?'

'Unfortunately, we don't know the answer to that. All we have here is a photo taken of her in 1952 by a fisherman off the coast of Norfolk. Locals thought it was just a hoax, but the image eventually made its way to one of the Praxos offices, which confirmed its authenticity.'

'So we know who she is and where she was spotted before she came to Andilyse and met Joe, but where is she now?'

'Well, according to this, the Nereids originate from the Aegean Sea where they live with their elderly father, Nereus.'

'Is this for real?' asked Lana astounded, 'It's like Greek History all over again,' she shivered, making Emma laugh.

'Well, according to this, it is real. I wonder if she's still alive? I want to know why she disappeared and never returned to the island.'

'Yeah, you and me both,' sighed Lana. 'Come on, now we know for sure, let's shut the computer down and tell Eleanor,' she said with a long yawn and a stretch. 'You must be exhausted?'

Emma nodded and yawned too, rubbing her eyes and revealing dark circles beneath them. 'What time is it?'

'7am,' Lana said, looking at her watch as they exited the small room with the tray of empty plates, glasses and mugs. Walking through the maze of paperwork and filing cabinets, the girls jumped, nearly dropping the tray at the sight of Wilbur standing on the other side of the door at the very moment that they opened it.

'Wilbur!' exclaimed Lana, 'You're always one step ahead of us,' she smiled as he took the tray out of her hands with a grin.

'Don't forget to lock the door,' he said as they followed him back through the tunnel and into the main hall.

'I have taken the liberty of preparing you some breakfast. You'll find it waiting for you in the dining room,' he said. 'It's on the central table.'

Right on cue, the sounds of faint thunder rumbled around them, and Lana laughed, rubbing her tummy. 'I'm starving... thanks Wilbur!' she said, 'Oh, is Eleanor around yet?'

'She'll be out of action for another couple of hours, I'm afraid. She was out much of the night. When she awakes, I'll tell her you're looking for her.'

'Thank you,' the girls said as they entered the dining room and sat down, soon tucking into their hot breakfasts. It hadn't taken long for Wilbur to suss out their favourite kinds of food. Lana enjoyed a full English while Emma ate a more delicate balance of poached eggs on brown toast and a fruit smoothie.

Declan and Saleena walked in after they'd finished eating and were having a cup of tea.

'Good morning, girls,' Saleena said as she approached and sat down beside them, while Declan gave them one of his trade-mark grins while he headed over to the kettle to pour himself a cup of hot coffee and a green tea for his girlfriend.

'So how did it go last night?' he asked as he handed the cup to Saleena and sat down. 'I understand you found something?'

'How did you know that?' asked Emma, surprised.

But he just tapped the side of his head with a cheeky smile and raised his eyebrows waiting for an answer.

'Yes, we did find something. But maybe you already know what we found?' Lana said pouting, squinting her eyes at him. After watching him for a moment, she opened her mouth, bit down on her lip and said, 'You do know, don't you?'

Saleena started laughing.

'But how?' Emma said, 'I don't understand?'

'Wait a minute, Sis, before we tell him. I want to know if he does know what we found?' Lana insisted.

Holding up his hands, he nodded, 'Okay, okay... I know you found out that Josiah's girl is a Nereid.'

The sisters gasped, Lana's expression one of profound irritation.

'Does everyone know? Is it common knowledge? Is this just part of the task?' she said, her hands gripping the table.

'No, no, no... it's nothing like that, Lana. I assure you, I only know because I read your thoughts when we walked in.'

'You can read minds?' breathed Emma.

He nodded.

'What else can you do?' she asked.

Saleena, clutching her mug, chuckled into her tea.

'Lots of things,' he tempted.

'Oh come on... tell us, Declan,' Lana pleaded.

'I can see ghosts.'

'So you could see Joe on the first day we met?'

Declan nodded, 'And I could read your thoughts.'

Lana blushed, reminding herself how she'd thought he was handsome. Declan chuckled, and she turned her head towards him, the faint pink of her cheeks darkening.

Clear your mind, Lana, clear your mind, she thought to herself, totally embarrassed.

'What else can you do, Declan?' asked Emma, not realising what was going on.

'That's not important right now. Tell us about the Nereid,' he answered.

'But you already know,' sighed Lana.

'I do, but Sal doesn't,' he said, and so the girls told Saleena everything they'd learned about Emelia Doris.

'That's fascinating. She certainly was a long way from home. Why do you think she came to England?' Saleena asked, intrigued.

'That's anyone's guess,' Declan said. 'She might have been here for hundreds of years. We don't know. What you girls need to find out though is where she is now and why she disappeared so suddenly.'

'Do you think she loved Joe?' whispered Emma, hoping the ghost wasn't within earshot.

'Judging by those photos, I'd say so,' Saleena replied. 'It's easy to see when a person is in love, their whole face lights up, and the camera captured that,' she added, sadly looking across at Declan with the same expression.

Emma smiled as she watched them share a special look.

'Do you think the storm had something to do with it?' Lana said suddenly.

'Quite possibly,' Declan said, 'But Eleanor will probably be able to help you there. She's catching up on her sleep at the moment though. Something I think you two ought to do. Why don't you go and have a kip? Just until she gets up?'

Emma yawned and nodded, 'Yeah, I will. You coming Lana?' she asked.

The two girls cleared away their dirty plates before heading into one of the bedrooms just down the hall from Eleanor's office. As soon as their heads touched the pillows, they were fast asleep.

37

She was treading water, it was cold, but the temperature didn't appear to affect her body. The waves were getting bigger and bigger, and she sensed danger all around her. She could see land not far away, but no matter how hard she tried to get there, she was swimming against the tide, and she remained a firm distance away.

Scanning the view in front of her, she gasped at the familiarity of it all. The pier at the far end and on the peninsula that jutted out from above, the old church stood proudly. But there was a difference, the pier was completely intact, and the church stood in its entirety, no holes in the roof and no fallen steeple.

It was Andilyse Island. There was no doubt about it.

As she looked on, Lana spotted a lone figure walking along the beach. Her dark hair and knee-length red dress flowed in the brisk wind. She carried a long stick which she dragged along the sand, leaving a long trail behind her. She stopped and started to write something in the sand in huge letters. I heart J... suddenly, a massive wave came from nowhere. It was like a huge hand reaching out from the water, stretching until it enveloped the woman, pulling her into the water.

'No father... no...' the young woman screamed.

Lana's eyes widened in terror as the woman was dragged beneath the surface.

'No!' yelled Lana, letting water enter her mouth. But suddenly she was back on dry land. Looking out at the calm sea, she turned and gazed upwards. The church had been destroyed, and beneath it, the pier was no longer in one piece. Lana rubbed her eyes and dropped down to her knees, sobbing. Curling up into a ball on the shore, she closed her eyes and drifted back to sleep.

'Good morning, sleepy heads,' said a woman's voice as they eventually came round, momentarily losing all sense of where they were, and Lana forgetting all about her dreams.

Opening their eyes, the girls sat up and faced Eleanor, who stood holding two steaming cups of tea. 'I figured you'd want waking up. It's 10.30. Here you go,' she said, handing it to them.

'Thanks,' said Emma as she took a long sip and rubbed her eyes.

'We found out who she is,' Lana said before doing anything else. 'She's a Nereid, Eleanor.'

'A Nereid? Well, that's interesting,' she said, sitting down at the foot of Lana's bed. 'It's been a few years since coming across any of those.'

'I wonder...' she pondered to herself, her wrinkly hand rubbing her chin.

'What?' Lana asked as she gulped down her tea and placed the empty mug on the bedside table before sitting upright.

'I have a friend in Ireland who I believe has associations with a group of Nereids in Greece. Perhaps he might be of assistance?'

Emma's eyes widened with the prospect of finally finding out the truth.

'Really? That would be amazing,' she said, almost spilling her tea as she stood up quickly.

'Can you call him now?' she asked.

Eleanor smiled and nodded, 'Of course.' Standing up, she straightened her long full skirt before taking the two empty cups from them and turning to exit the room.

'Thank you, Eleanor,' they piped up simultaneously.

A niggling feeling kept irritating her like she needed to remember something. Whatever it was though, Lana couldn't seem to grab hold of it. When they walked into Eleanor's office half an hour later, she'd managed to push it from her thoughts. Instead, concentrating on finding out the truth about Joe's true love.

The screen was focussed on St. James Park. Emma only knew because behind it was The Mall and Buckingham Palace. Since their introduction to the Praxos Foundation, they had been learning everything they possibly could about London, including its geography, its history (much to Lana's disgust) and its beautiful buildings and architecture.

Eleanor beamed at them. 'Please sit down, girls. I have news,' she said almost bursting with excitement, like a little girl who had just been given a pony. 'I've just been on the phone to Nikolaos, and he told me a fascinating tale...'

Lana and Emma leaned forward expectantly.

'It is believed that one of the daughters of Nereus fell in love with a man somewhere in the United Kingdom. Much to her father's dismay, she made a decision which angered him terribly. She refused to return home to his side, instead choosing to marry this young man. Nereus, however, had other ideas. Because she was already promised to another, her father threatened her with a great storm to kill her beloved. Her father had always been such a gentle soul, and she refused to believe him. But she was wrong. On the night of 31st January 1953, Nereus did indeed create a massive storm so fierce that it whipped the coasts of England, Scotland and parts of Europe. As you already know, many many innocent people died. His daughter, however, was captured and returned to the Aegean Sea where it is believed, she was forced to marry the man she did not love. It is alleged that she remains there, mourning the death of her one true love...'

'Oh My God... Eleanor... I... I...'

'What is it, Lana?' she asked, standing up and walking around the desk.

'I just dreamed about that. I saw the beach on the night of the storm. There was a woman in red, and she was writing something on the beach - I heart J... - before a huge wave reached out and pulled her into the water. It must have been Emelia and her father. She must have been writing I heart Josiah,' she said, her face paling considerably.

'Yes, I think you're right. Oh the poor dears,' Eleanor said like an old lady.

'Wait a minute,' breathed Emma, 'So she's still alive? And she thinks Joe died the night of the storm? If we can find her, we can tell her the truth. Maybe then they can both move on?'

'Yeah maybe, but there is one thing here that sucks. She's alive, and he's, well, dead.'

'Yes,' sighed Eleanor, 'But she has aged apparently. Perhaps they can be together again one day in the not too distant future.'

'Is there any way of tracking her down?' asked Emma.

'I've already asked Nikolaos. He promised me that all his resources are already on the case. We just need to wait patiently.'

The girls sat back, relaxing their tense shoulders and watched as people wandered through St James Park, some of them sitting on park benches and chatting to each other.

'And the world goes on as usual,' smiled Eleanor. 'Speaking of which, you girls are going home tomorrow. How do you feel about that?'

Emma smiled, 'I'm looking forward to seeing Mum and Dad, Lucy Joe and Greg.'

'And Scott and Henry,' Lana added.

'Henry?' Emma said, confused.

'The dog!'

'Oh yeah, I'd forgotten about him. Maybe we should ask Joe what his real name is?'

'Nah, not such a good idea. How would we explain that to Lucy Joe?'

Emma laughed, 'I guess so.'

Lana turned back and said, 'I'm quite happy to be going home... because there is a possibility we'll be coming back soon, isn't there?' Lana asked curiously as she looked across at Eleanor, hoping for a response.

She smiled broadly, 'We'll talk about that tonight with the rest of the group. Oh, by the way, wear your party dresses,' Eleanor added with a cheeky smile as they walked out of the office.

After popping back to the boat for a quick shower and change into casual clothes (carrying their party outfits in bags with them), the girls walked back from Westminster where they were once again moored, towards the Foundation with Declan and Saleena. On the way there, they met up with Liam, Diarmuid, Zane and Marian.

The adults went on without them, suggesting the four of them take some time on their own before heading back. The meeting wasn't going to commence until 6pm, so they had plenty of time to kick back and relax first.

Liam casually draped his arm over Lana's shoulder, while Diarmuid and Emma firmly held hands as they walked along Leicester Square, stopping to gaze at an attractive water feature with a statue of Charlie Chaplin in its centre and spouts of water shooting up into the air.

'I can't believe the two weeks are almost up,' said Diarmuid as he squeezed Emma's hand.

'Yeah I know,' Lana added, 'But at least we're closer to the school year.'

'Yeah, that's great if we're accepted into the Academy,' Liam replied lazily. 'If not, I'll be stuck in Chelmsford. What about you, Diarmuid? Where will you go if you're not accepted?'

'Somewhere in Oxfordshire, I guess. Unless Mum wants to go back to Ireland.'

'I'm sure we've all been accepted. I hope so anyway,' Lana whispered as the sun glistened on the rippling water. 'I really don't want to go back to Andilyse for good. Not now that I've had a taste of this life.'

'Come on, let's not mope around. Let's enjoy our last few hours together. Let's get a drink,' Lana said all of a sudden, pulling them away from the fountain.

Emma's eyes glazed over as she thought about what Lana had said. Their last few hours together. The idea that she may not see Diarmuid again was the same as being punched in the stomach, and so she held back for a moment. Her sister and Liam carried on walking as she and Diarmuid stood looking at each other sadly.

'Stop thinking about what you're thinking, Emma. I can see it in your eyes. We are coming back in a few weeks. I just know it,' he said as he gently held her chin in his hand, using his thumb to stroke her cheek.

A cyclist whizzed passed them, followed by a small group of

kids eating burgers who stopped and sat beside the fountain. But Emma didn't notice them. She didn't see anything. All she saw was Diarmuid, his sweet smile revealing an almost perfect set of white teeth, just one was slightly askew. I could drown in those eyes; she thought as he leaned forward and kissed her softly on the lips.

Wolf whistles echoed behind them, but she didn't care. All she wanted was to stay in that moment, for it to never end.

But the moment passed. Lana called them from a distance, 'Come on you guys, hurry up!'

Diarmuid wiped away a tear from her cheek. 'As I said, stop those thoughts. This isn't over. This is just the beginning,' he said with a huge grin.

'You're right,' she whispered, 'This is just the beginning.'

38

'Stamus Contra Malum. Three seemingly small words that sum up the true meaning of the Praxos Foundation. We Stand Against Evil. That is what we are here for, to fight evil of all kinds. An evil that hides in the shadows of the night ready to pounce on unsuspecting innocents, whether they be human or paranormal. We vow to protect those that need our protection. And fight those that choose the wrong path in this life. Stamus Contra Malum,' Eleanor said as she stood proudly beside the statue of the angel that filled the centre of the great hall with Watchers, Mentors and a few others that Lana and Emma had never met sitting in front of her.

'The past two weeks have not only been an introduction to the Praxos Foundation for you, but it has also been an induction. The moment you were born, you were destined to join us. And the moment you grew your tattoos made you a part of this family. Your initiations proved to us that you are more than worthy, and your tasks showed us your keen abilities to successfully solve problematic riddles and in some cases, to help others,' Eleanor said as she glanced in Lana and Emma's direction. 'I know I speak for all the Mentors here by saying that you have seriously impressed us by showing your true born colours, demonstrating your unique talents in a multitude of ways. It is, therefore, my very great pleasure to welcome you all...' she said, stopping to look at Daisy who blushed, 'to the Academy in a few weeks.'

The Watchers let out a loud, wild cheer, all jumping up and hugging each other enthusiastically and yelling at the tops of their voices.

Emma looked across at Diarmuid who held up both his thumbs to her and winked, 'I told you so,' he mouthed. A grin spread across his face as he took in her appearance for the first time. Her long hair was pinned up to reveal a long pale elegant neck which was enhanced by a black lace choker, beautifully matched to the1950s gothic style dress she wore.

'But we haven't completed our task yet?' Lana suddenly blurted out when the group had quietened down a little.

Declan leaned forward over her shoulder and said, 'Yes, you have. We discussed your task earlier today, and we all agreed that you did an astounding job in tracking down Emelia Doris, girls. Your task is complete.'

Emma, who sat feeling a little self-conscious in her girlie dress, turned to look at him, 'But what about Joe? He hasn't crossed over yet. I won't be happy until he has,' she said.

Declan leaned back with a smile just as Eleanor quietened everybody down so she could speak. 'I just wanted to add how pleased we all are at how you grouped together to help one another. I think you're all aware that some of the tasks were more challenging than others. You showed us that you are indeed, already a family.

Lana and Emma, I neglected to mention this before, but your task was much more in-depth than any of the other Watchers' tasks. But, as Josiah clearly needed to be helped, I decided to give that task to you, rather than pass it on to one of the older watchers. I am delighted to announce, therefore, that the issue with Josiah is almost complete. Emelia Doris has been found. She is on her way to London as we speak. The plan is for her to travel back to Andilyse with you and Lana before you take her to Josiah's house. We believe then that Josiah will finally be able to rest in peace.'

The girls were dumbstruck, not able to utter a single word. Eleanor smiled happily, 'See? Your task is over. You passed with flying colours. It is clear that you are the stars of the past fort-night's... what do we call it? Work Experience. Come on everybody, how about a round of applause for Lana and Emma?'

Again, the group exploded with happiness and clapping, the Watchers pushed their seats back, scraping them across the floor, and surrounded the two sisters, patting them on the back and congratulating them. It was a fitting end to their first two weeks with Praxos.

'And now everybody,' shouted Eleanor above the noise, 'Now we feast!' she said as Wilbur opened the doors to the dining room, revealing a room entirely decorated for the event, with blue helium balloons floating across the ceiling and Praxos Foundation banners stuck to the walls, the winged eye looking at them from every direction.

Lana smiled, watching as everyone rushed into the room one by one. Just for a moment, she stood and patted down her black pencil skirt and an orange silk blouse and admired her brand new black heels.

Breathing in slowly, the smell of grilled chicken filled her nostrils as she then followed everyone to the far end of the room, piling her plate high with grilled chicken and sausages, salads, vegetables and what smelled like freshly baked bread. Jugs of fresh juice, homemade lemonade and ice tea were scattered among the food.

Patiently waiting for everyone to fill their plates, Emma stood against the wall when Eleanor approached her with a smile. She handed her a glass of fresh apple juice.

'Cheers,' she said.

'Cheers,' Emma replied as they chinked glasses.

'Eleanor?'

'Yes, Emma?'

'Have you told Joe yet?'

Eleanor turned to face her and shook her head. 'We thought it would be better coming from you. Perhaps you can call him tomorrow morning when Emelia arrives?'

Emma grinned, 'I'd love to.'

'Come on, Em. Come and get some food,' Diarmuid called as he made a gap for her at one of the tables.

'Go ahead,' Eleanor said, 'Enjoy.'

'Wow,' he said as she ambled towards him. 'You look amazing.'

'Th... thanks,' she said shyly, looking down at the dress. A dress she never thought she'd actually wear.

'You should wear dresses more often. They really suit you.'

Pinking slightly, she said, 'Maybe,' before they turned their attention to the feast and began filling their plates with food.

Later that night, the Mentors had allowed their Watchers to stay on at the Foundation to say their goodbyes. Eleanor had wished them all a pleasant journey home and thanked them for their efforts, telling each and every Watcher that she looked forward to seeing them back shortly and then she and Wilbur had left them alone.

The group had grown relatively quiet, sitting around the angel statue in the hall, some chatting quietly among themselves. Lana rested her head on Liam's shoulder while Diarmuid had his arm protectively around Emma's shoulders.

'Well, we should call it a night,' said Penny, who stood up and stretched, pulling Nisha up with her. 'I guess we'll see you all in a few weeks, then?' she said. 'It's been a lot of fun, guys. I'm really looking forward to studying with you at the Academy,' she added as Ava and Rupert stood up too. Rupert high-fived her before everyone else. Ava gave everyone a hug. 'Now you've all got my email address, stay in touch and I'll see you soon,' she said as the four of them walked out of the hall, into different tunnels.

Moira stood up next, followed by Imran, Cassie and Elliott who said their goodbyes and headed off down the same tunnel.

Liam, Diarmuid, Lana and Emma were left alone.

'I don't want to go yet,' Emma whispered as Diarmuid tightened his grip on her.

'We'll give you some space,' Liam said as he stood up and held out his hand to Lana. Taking it, she smiled, and they walked away, into the room with the big beanbags.

'Finally on our own,' Diarmuid said. 'I know it's only a few weeks, but I'm really going to miss you,' he whispered.

She turned so that she was on her knees facing him. 'I'm going to miss you too.' Leaning into him, she gently placed her lips on his, and they kissed like they'd never kissed before. The triple salchows were repeating themselves in the pit of her stomach as she rubbed her hands over his back, feeling the muscles rippling beneath her fingertips.

When she eventually pulled away, she turned to see Lana and Liam standing awkwardly waiting for them.

'I guess we should go,' he breathed, pushing a strand of hair behind her ear.

She kissed him gently just one more time and then hopped up, walking towards her sister. She gave Liam a quick hug and then pulled Lana away towards the elevator where she pressed the button, and they stepped inside, turning just one last time to look at him.

'I'll call you,' he shouted just as the doors closed.

Lana gave her sister a hug before gently rubbing her arm. 'You'll see him soon. The next few weeks will go by so quickly.'

Emma gulped back the tears, 'I know.'

'Liam and I broke up,' she said suddenly with a smile.

'Wh...what? Why?' Emma replied astounded.

Lana shrugged her shoulders. 'It was just a bit of fun for both of us. It was great while it lasted.'

'I don't understand.'

'Come on... you know me. I'm the world's biggest flirt... and he's kind of like the male version of me,' she laughed. 'We're still good pals though. It's cool,' she winked, glad to have made Emma think of something else.

39

An elegantly dressed elderly lady with bright white hair and a kind smile approached them as they stood to wait for the ferry. Saleena helped her climb down onto the pier.

Holding out a gloved hand, she said, 'You must be Emma and Lana. It's such a pleasure to meet you. Thank you from the bottom of my heart for all you have done. Is he here?' she asked, looking around as Declan walked past them carrying her suitcase, as well as Lana's and Emma's hold-alls.

'We asked him not to show himself until we're on the ferry, we can find a more private spot on there,' Emma said with her eyes already glazing over.

The old lady nodded, 'Yes, yes, of course.... so you live on Andilyse?'

Lana nodded, 'We grew up there. Our dad is the Chief of Police and Mum's a nurse there.'

'That's lovely, that's lovely. It was such a beautiful island. I loved it the moment I stepped foot on it,' she sighed. 'I never stopped... if only things had been different.'

'Can I ask you a question, Emelia?' Emma asked nervously.

'Of course! Anything.'

'Is Emelia Doris your real name?'

The woman dropped her head back and let out a throaty laugh, dabbing at her eyes with a cotton handkerchief, 'No, but I needed a, erm, a common name. My real name is Laomedeia. I always loved the name Emelia, and my mother's name is Doris,' she explained.

'Laomedeia? It's pretty,' Emma replied. 'Why have you... aged? I thought someone like you would stay young forever?'

Again the woman chuckled to herself. 'It was my father's way of punishing me for what I did. My sisters are all still young and beautiful,' she said, shaking her head. 'It was silly of him because once he'd cast his spell, he couldn't take it back and the man he wanted me to marry didn't want someone who was going to age. He went on to marry Menippe,' she sighed.

'I'm sorry.'

'Don't be sorry, my dear. My entire life, I've wanted nothing more than to die so that I could be with Josiah. At least now, I'm one step closer to getting my wish.'

As they'd been talking, the ferry had arrived, and a few people had disembarked before Emelia, Emma, Lana and Declan had climbed aboard.

Saleena had hugged them tightly before she headed back to her own boat, but not before giving Declan a loving kiss.

Emelia sighed as she watched them, 'How I miss that,' she said as they took a seat in a corner away from prying eyes, and she very carefully removed her gloves, revealing perfectly manicured fingernails beneath.

'Emelia?' said a quiet voice out of nowhere as Josiah finally revealed himself to her.

Gasping, her hands shot to her mouth and tears began to fall down her cheeks.

'Josiah? Is that you? Oh, how I've longed for this day to come. I'm so sorry, my darling...'

⚜

SEVERAL HOURS LATER, THE GIRLS STOOD ON THE FRONT OF THE ferry watching a thick fog hanging over the island with the sound of seagulls racing and squawking overhead.

Once they'd finally come to a halt, they hopped off the ferry and straight into the waiting arms of their mum, dad, brother and sister who squealed and jumped up and down at the sight of them.

'I hope they've not been too much trouble, Declan?' Patrick asked as he shook the hand of his good friend.

'They've been as good as gold. I'd be happy to look after them any time,' he said, 'And Sal just loved them both.'

'Oh thank you so much, Declan. We are indebted to you, we really are. I'm so pleased that the girls finally got to experience some London culture and history. Now tell us a little more about this Academy...'

Lana yanked Emma away the moment she laid eyes on someone else who'd come to welcome them home.

'Scott!' she yelled as the two girls ran straight into him and hugged him, laughing. 'We missed you!' she squealed.

'So what did we miss? What have you been up to? What was it like working on the Nutter's farm? Are you and Lottie going out yet?' she asked, barely taking a breath.

'Woah. Woah... I should be asking you all the questions. You're the ones who've been out gallivanting in the big city, not me!' he laughed, his cheeks bright pink from happiness.

'We'll tell you about it later,' Emma said as she glanced across at her sister knowingly. 'But we've got something important we need to do first though. Can we meet up in the morning?'

'Sure,' he said, grinning, 'Just give me a buzz, and I'll come round.'

After saying goodbye to Declan, Audrey and the younger kids headed home in her car while Patrick took Emelia, Emma and Lana up to the old Grimshaw house, after he'd been told that she was a long lost relative who had inherited the place.

'Thanks Dad,' said Emma, 'We'll take it from here. We'll walk home in a bit.'

Patrick had nodded, given Emelia his card and suggested she call him if she needed any assistance, and then he'd left them by the old wooden gate.

The moment he was gone, Josiah showed himself.

'I wish I could carry you over the threshold, my love,' he said as she gazed at him with such an abundance of love that the girls had to look away.

'Erm, shall we just come inside with you and see if there's anything we can do before we leave you to it?' asked Lana, breaking the silence.

'That would be lovely, my dear. Thank you so much.'

Emma picked up the lady's suitcase and pushed open the gate.

'I remember it like it was yesterday. This was the house you grew up in. You brought me a couple of times. I never forgot it...'

As they walked indoors, Lana cringed, expecting the disgusting mess they'd stumbled upon before but there was nothing of the sort. The house was absolutely spotless, gleaming in fact.

'Wow,' muttered Emma to her sister. 'Who?'

When they looked across at each other, realisation hit and they said in unison, 'Mum,' and smiled. The kitchen was even stocked with supplies for the newest resident of Andilyse.

'Oh, you've all been so kind. Here's a note from some of the islanders, with condolences and such like. Oh, I'm almost speechless,' she smiled. 'I should have lived this life with my love on this island,' she sobbed.

'You're here now, that's what matters,' reassured Josiah. 'I shall never leave your side.'

With that, the girls tiptoed out of the house and began their walk back home.

'So, how you feeling Sis?' asked Lana as they ambled down the lane together.

'Okay. It's nice to be home, I guess. But I am looking forward to going back,' she smiled.

'Really?'

'Of course. I miss Diarmuid already,' she said as she looked down at her shoes and kicked a stone in the road.

'I can't wait to get back to London. I can't believe we're actually going to live there!' Lana squealed.

'But there's some pretty scary stuff over there, isn't there? Aren't you worried about it, just a little bit?'

Lana pulled her cardigan tightly across her body and pondered the question for a couple of minutes before answering, 'A little, I guess. Those Skulls scare the hell out of me, of course, but I hope not to have to run into them any time soon.'

'What do you think will happen to the dread-lock girl?' asked

Emma as she remembered her glowing yellow eyes compared to the posh English girl they'd bumped into in the museum.

Lana shrugged her shoulders, 'I don't care. I just hope Bryn managed to find her and lock her up. If he did, he should throw away the key.'

Emma laughed, 'I'm with you on that one. Do you ever think about that attack on the night of our initiation?'

Glancing across at her sister, Lana nodded, 'All the time. Why?'

'It's just that we never found out who helped us out, you know. It's been kind of bugging me, I guess.'

'I wouldn't worry about it, Em. At least whoever it was, was helping us and not the other way around. I'm sure Eleanor will get to the bottom of it.'

❦

TWELVE DAYS LATER AS THE SUN SEEMED TO SHINE MUCH brighter than usual for a September day on Andilyse Island, a coffin was carried from the church to a freshly dug grave in a beautiful setting overlooking the North Sea. Just as it was gently lowered into the earth, the sea crashed onto the shoreline below. Lana and Emma watched as the hand-like waves seemed to desperately paw at the sand before pulling backwards, back into the darkness of the sea.

'Twelve days,' sighed local baker Betty Miller. 'I still can't believe she died so soon after arriving,' she re-iterated to no-one in particular as she, along with a small group of local residents, turned away from the grave, and headed back towards their cars parked up on the hill next to the church.

Lana turned and smiled at her sister, who, rather oddly for a funeral, beamed back as they watched two familiar ghosts walk hand-in-hand off into the distance until eventually, they vanished from sight.

＃ 40 ＃

Several large suitcases sat open on the two single beds. One was half-filled with strewn clothes, make-up and magazines while Lana stood beside it, continuously pulling out brightly coloured items of clothing and replacing them with others.

On the opposite side of the room, Emma sat carefully folding her three favourite pairs of black jeans and placed them gently beside several dark coloured t-shirts and Converse. Several books had already been neatly arranged down the sides of the case.

When her mobile vibrated on the bedside table, she grinned, leaning forward to read the message.

'Tell him to stop texting already, you're going to see him in a couple of days,' sighed Lana with a wink.

Swooning, Emma quickly sent a message back before zipping up her case and turning her attention to Lana's belongings.

'Here, let me do it,' she offered, nudging her sister out of the way with her hip. Pulling out various items that were totally unsuitable for the Academy, Emma shook her head and laughed.

'Really?' she said, holding up a zebra print bikini.

Lana shrugged, 'You never know... we might go swimming one day?'

'In an animal print bikini? If we do go swimming, you'll need a swimming costume. You know, an all-in-one?' she laughed, putting it back in the drawer behind her and taking out a slightly more sensible bright pink one piece and putting it at the bottom of the case.

One by one, Emma pulled out clothes that would be far more suitable for nights out clubbing than college classrooms, replacing them with slightly more apt versions. But Lana just sat back and watched Emma do her magic. She'd always been better at packing than Lana had so she just left her to it, keeping an eye on a couple of pieces that she would shove back in later on.

A creaky sound alerted them to the fact that someone was climbing the stairs. Opening the door, a whiff of freshly baked pies entered the room, and Audrey appeared with cups of tea for her two girls. She'd been crying.

'Oh, Mum, what's up?' asked Lana with genuine concern.

'I... I... I'm just going to miss you, that's all...' she said as the tears began to flow again.

Lana chuckled while Emma rushed forward to take the cups from her mother's hands, placing them on the chest of drawers before turning back and hugging her tightly.

'I...I... I can't believe how fast you've grown up and now you're off to... to... c...college... in... London,' she wept.

'You'll see us every holiday, and parents open day is only a month away. Plus, you're going to come to London to see us every now and again, aren't you, Mum?' Lana asked as she gently stroked her back.

Audrey nodded with a smile, wiping her eyes with the apron she'd been wearing all morning as she tried to take her mind off the girls' imminent departure.

'See, you'll probably see more of us there than you do now!' she laughed.

'Yes, I suppose you're right,' Audrey chuckled sadly. 'Well, drink up your tea and then come downstairs. I've made your favourite pies for dinner,' she said as she walked out, stopping and taking a long look at them before wiping at her eyes again.

Something banged on their bedroom window, making them jump. And then again, they noticed a little stone tap against it.

Pushing it open, Lana leaned out. Looking down, she saw Scott straddling his bicycle with a grin.

'We'll be right down,' she yelled as she shut it again and the two rushed downstairs, through the hallway and out through the back door.

'Hey!' he said as they walked up to him, all grinning like children.

He let his bike drop to the ground as they turned away from the house and sauntered to the bottom of the garden, where they sat with their feet dangling over the edge, looking out across the sea.

Nobody said anything for a while, but they were all thinking the same thing. Scott was being left behind, and they were really going to miss each other.

'S...so,' he stuttered, 'Just one day left.' His voice cracked slightly, and he looked away from them, embarrassed.

'Will you come and visit, Scott?' Emma asked quietly, picking up a stone and flicking it over the edge.

Lana sniffed loudly.

'If I can get time off, I will. I promise.'

'I still can't believe you're going to be working full time on the Nutters farm,' Lana said, sniffing again.

'I never was cut out for college. I much prefer to be outdoors working, always have. You know that.'

'But on a farm?' she almost shrieked, shuddering at the thought, making him laugh.

'I really enjoyed doing the work experience there... it's hard to believe they actually offered me a job.'

Emma turned to face him, 'It's not hard to believe at all, Scott. You've always been a really hard worker. You could get a job anywhere... anywhere you wanted. And you're just so... you know... likeable,' she said, blushing as Lana agreed, nodding avidly.

'You think?' he asked, his cheeks turning pink. 'Thanks.'

After they were silent for a few more minutes, he opened his mouth to say something but then shut it again. He tried again but then stopped and sighed.

'What?' Lana asked.

'I've been trying to work out what happened before you left, you know? The...the... ghost? And you... jumping off the cliff. I know you've been avoiding my questions. I just want the truth.'

Lana was reminded of Tom Cruise and Jack Nicholson, 'The

Truth? You want the truth? You can't handle the truth.' But she kept her mouth shut and looked at Emma whose pink cheeks burned as she gulped.

'There's nothing to tell,' Lana said totally unconvincingly.

'Really? You expect me to believe that? You're my best friends, we've never kept secrets before. Why start now?'

Lana let her head fall backwards, and she looked up at the intense blue of the sky, sighing loudly, not knowing what to do.

'Scott, we can't tell you,' Emma whispered. 'I'm sorry.'

He shook his head, looking out at sea, before biting his bottom lip. 'Can't or won't?'

'Both Scott. Look, it's for your own good. Honestly.'

'I don't believe this,' he said scrambling to his feet, stumbling backwards. 'Look, I'm going home. Tell your Mum I'm sorry I can't stay for dinner after all. Good luck in London.'

The girls sat still, Lana putting her head on her knees while Emma lay back onto the dirt, looking up at the sky.

'Well, that went well,' Lana sighed. 'Now what are we supposed to do?'

'Nothing we can do. We promised we wouldn't tell a soul and that includes Scott.'

'But he's our best friend. It hurts to keep secrets from him,' she said, wiping her eyes.

'Are you crying, Lana?' asked Emma, who sat up looking at her sister's face.

'No,' she croaked.

Emma put her arm across her shoulders, 'Well I never,' she said, smiling slightly. 'I never thought I'd see the day.'

Lana shook her head and smiled at her, 'Oh shut up.'

41

Through the fog, Declan stood waiting patiently as the family said their goodbyes. Patrick, Audrey, Lucy Joe and Greg stood around the girls, all were sobbing slightly. Even little Greg pretended to have something in his eye.

Lana and Emma kept scanning the harbour, hoping that their best friend would have had a change of heart and would turn up to say goodbye, but there was no sign of him.

Reluctantly, they boarded the vessel after giving their family members one last hug, promising to call regularly. As it chugged into motion, Lana and Emma held hands, tears free-falling down their cheeks. Shivering, they turned to go inside when a voice pierced through the foggy air.

'Lana... Emma...'

'Scott!' yelled Lana as she released her sister's hand and ran right to the back of the ferry, Emma following behind.

'I'm sorry! I'm really sorry, I didn't mean it,' he cried as he threw his bicycle to the floor and ran as close as he could to the edge of the water without falling in. 'I'm going to miss you! Call me, text me, email me, okay?' he shouted.

'We will. We're sorry too, Scott! Come visit us,' Lana shouted at the top of her voice, 'We're going to miss you so much!'

Both girls stood waving frantically until both he and their family disappeared, enveloped within the misty air.

'He came,' sighed Lana as they turned and headed back indoors into the warmth, where they sat beside Declan smiling, knowing that everything was going to be okay. Knowing that they hadn't lost their best friend. They just wouldn't see him for a while, that's all.

Sitting down beside Declan, he turned to look at them with the most prominent, cheesiest grin in the world, 'So girls... are you ready for the Academy?'

THE END

42

THE TEMPORAL STONE
EXCERPT 1

Stretching her long pale limbs beneath the warm duvet cover, Emma let out a deep yawn and climbed out of bed. She strolled over to Lana and shook her vigorously just as Moira appeared out of the bathroom towel-drying her hair.

'She'll be late again,' she chuckled as she walked past.

Emma rolled her eyes.

'Come on, Sis. Time to get up, we've got to be ready earlier this morning, remember?'

A faint moan could be heard from beneath the covers. Emma shook her head.

'Come on, get up, lazy bones.'

'No, it's too early,' grumbled Lana who rolled over languidly.

'Well, if you're not up and ready soon, you'll miss out on our trip to Somerset with the rest of the class,' Emma replied with her eyebrows raised as she slowly made her way to the bathroom, a towel slung over her shoulder.

The covers were immediately flung back and Lana groaned with an excited grin. 'Somerset here we come,' Lana groaned. She threw back the covers immediately and hopped up with an excited grin. Throwing on her dressing gown, she began frantically emptying her wardrobe, trying to find the perfect outfit to wear.

oOo

Hand in gloved hand with her boyfriend, Diarmuid, Emma stood dressed entirely in black and purple, her dark hair tied back in two simple plaits and a checked woolly hat perched on top of her head. Noticing she was shivering, Diarmuid pulled her close and rubbed her arms up and down while she laughed. He then pulled her into a more secluded spot, allowing a faint glow to emanate from his body. Warmth immediately embraced them both.

'Better?' he asked.

'Hm hm,' Emma nodded as she leant her head on his shoulder.

As they waited for the rest of the gang, Lana walked up the steps that led from the academy. With a huge grin plastered across her face, she walked over to her sister where she turned this way and that. Emma shook her head, laughing.

'Well?' asked Lana.

'Yeah Sis, you look amazing. Is that the new dress you bought last week?'

'It is. It's gorgeous isn't it?'

'Let's just say - it's very you. I wouldn't wear it though!' laughed Emma as Diarmuid wolf whistled from behind her.

'Well of course you wouldn't. It's not black or purple and it's a dress,' she joked as she put her long brown coat back on over the long-sleeved leopard print dress which was a little inappropriate for a field trip across the country.

Moments later, Declan Alexander appeared from within the building, rubbing his hands together. A group of teens trailed behind him.

He turned as he approached, 'Come on guys, gather round. We're walking round to Russell Square where we'll be hopping on to the Tube to Paddington Station. From there we'll get the train to Bath, so make sure you've all got your Oyster cards ready before we leave.'

When they'd finished fishing around in their pockets and handbags, and Declan was content everyone had what was needed to take the trip, they exited the well hidden entrance to the Academy and joined the rest of the commuters within the capital.

oOo

'I STILL FIND IT HARD TO BELIEVE YOU'RE NOT THAT BOTHERED about Liam dating Ava,' said Emma as Diarmuid stretched his legs, stopping for a chat with his friend who sat with his arm draped across the exotic beauty at the other end of the carriage.

Lana shrugged her shoulders.

'Why would I be? It's been months since we broke up and we weren't exactly serious. Not like you two,' she replied, following Emma's gaze.

'Besides, there's plenty more totty at the Academy now.'

Emma choked into her now tepid green tea, 'Totty? You can't call them that!'

Lana looked at her sister as if she was mad, 'Why not?'

'Well... it's... it's derogatory.'

'Sis, you really need to get out more,' laughed Lana, standing up as Diarmuid returned.

'I'll leave you two love birds to it. I'm going for a wander.'

Passing Declan a few seats down, she wondered how long it would be until they arrived in Bath.

'About twenty minutes,' he said.

'Huh?' she muttered, having completely forgotten he could read minds.

'Oh right. Thanks,' she answered, blushing slightly. He chuckled, brushing his hair out of his eyes before turning his attention back to his newspaper.

'Don't wander too far,' he added as she walked away.

But Lana was bored and she'd already decided to walk through the rest of the carriages to the end of the train, regardless of how long it took. Surely the train wasn't that big, anyway?

Before she'd given it another thought, she was already several carriages away from the rest of her classmates. Intrigued by the suited businessmen who tapped away at their laptops, oblivious to the world around them, Lana had walked slowly past each and every one, watching them until she'd reached the end. Sighing, she turned around and spotted a couple of empty seats just ahead of her.

As she bent to sit down, the carriage became darker. Gazing

out the window, she realised they were going through a tunnel. A rather long and very dark tunnel.

She closed her eyes, just for a moment.

When she opened them, she was no longer on the train. Instead, she found herself outside in a dusty, dirty environment surrounded by sounds of hammering. Bang after bang like some kind of one-sided symphony. She watched as sweaty men worked hard digging a strange tunnel with picks. The stench of horse manure and sweat made her eyes water.

Swallowing loudly, Lana closed her eyes again, trying to calm herself.

'It's okay, it's just a dream,' she whispered. 'I can control this, just breathe, Lana, breathe.'

Opening her eyes again, she found she was still in that dirty place. Her only real concern, though, was her new dress.

'Great, it better not get dirty in this filth,' she muttered as her eyes scanned the crowd, eventually stopping on a rather important looking man in the distance, who sat on a beautiful black horse. His clothes were spotless.

Sighing, she began to walk towards him, through the stream of workers who continued to bang, bang, bang at the seemingly solid ground beneath their feet. They were oblivious to the rather oddly dressed 16 year old who strode through the dustiness in her tan leather boots, brand new dress and brown coat, cursing, wishing she would return to her own time and place.

The odd sound of a manly scream broke through all the noise, causing almost instant silence.

'There,' pointed a man dressed in a 19th century suit.

Lana followed his pointed finger towards a fallen man. Several others rushed to his side but it was too late.

'He's dead, I'm afraid,' said another suited gentleman.

'Another? We're nearing 100 deaths,' whispered the impressive man on the horse who had ridden over to see what the commotion was about.

Removing his hat, he nodded towards a small group of men that seemed to appear out of nowhere. As instructed, they walked forward and lifted the still warm corpse, carrying him away.

No matter what Lana had been through since her 16th birthday, she knew she would never be able to come to terms with death.

'But why? The heat isn't overbearing, they are being fed quite well I think, and they're all of good strong build. What's causing so many to perish?' asked another man, a pair of spectacles sitting at the end of his nose and a large ledger in his hands.

The man on the horse simply shook his head, 'I wish I knew.'

A tear escaped from her eye which she quickly brushed away, as the sound of screeching deafened her. Placing her hands over her ears she was suddenly catapulted forward, banging her forehead on something in front of her.

Opening her eyes, she realised she was back on the train, but it was still dark.

And they were no longer moving.

43

THE TEMPORAL STONE 2

'What's going on?' several voices came from behind her as people stood up to peer through the glass.

'I think we're in the Box Tunnel,' said a woman's jittery voice from nearby.

'But what's happening? Why have we stopped?' asked another.

'There must be something wrong with the line. I shouldn't worry. I'm sure we'll get moving in no time,' a man said a little more confidently.

'We'd better. I've got an important meeting in half an hour,' said an agitated voice.

To make matters even worse, the lights on the train began to flicker on and off.

'Oh great,' he added.

'Lana?' asked a sweet voice from the back of the carriage as the lights went off again. A few moments passed and she continued to stand in darkness, waiting for them to come back on again.

When they didn't, it was as if someone had held up a sign saying 'panic'. Almost everyone began to shout, creating mass havoc.

'I'm here, Em,' called Lana calmly as she stood up and followed her sister's voice to the back of the carriage. 'Are you okay?' she asked as she reached her open hand and grasped it tightly.

'Yeah, we're fine. Let's get back to the others.'

When they were out of ear shot, Emma whispered, 'Do you have any idea what's going on?'

Lana shook her head, 'I kind of went into one of my weird dream thingies when we stopped. I haven't got a clue.'

'Oh?' prompted Emma.

'I'll tell you about it later. Let's just get back to the others first,' she whispered as they tried to dodge the panicking people within each carriage.

'Wow... you'd think it was the Armageddon or something,' sighed Lana as they finally arrived back to Declan and their class-mates as the lights flickered back on again.

'You girls okay?' he asked.

'We're fine. Have you figured out what's happening yet, Declan?'

'I think it's just some kind of technical hitch. The driver's trying to reach the control centre but he's having difficulty.'

Declan waited for a moment before continuing, 'No, it's no good,' he whispered. 'Communications are down.'

'Can't he just start the train back up and carry on driving, or something?' Lana asked.

'It's not that simple,' answered Imran, one of their classmates who had spent the journey busying himself with his laptop.

'Is there nothing we can do?' asked Elliott, a well-spoken member of their class.

Lowering his voice, Declan whispered, 'You know we can't use our powers in the public eye, folks. We'll just have to sit this one out and wait for the railway authorities to sort it out. Don't worry, I'm sure everything will be fine.'

'You think?' said Ava quietly. 'And in the meantime we just have to put up with all that awful wailing from those annoying people over there,' she added, rolling her eyes towards a group of women who sat huddled together crying and occasionally screaming a little too loudly.

'Don't worry, I'll sort them out,' Declan offered. 'You just sit down and stay out of mischief,' he said as he stood up.

The moment the women saw Declan, their demeanour

changed, their crying came to an abrupt halt and they began playing with their hair.

The group chuckled as the lights went out again. They waited for the wailing to start up again but Declan's reassuring words - or perhaps his good looks - had worked. Their carriage, at least, was calm.

After about 45 minutes of nothing happening at all, Declan suddenly stood up, alarmed.

'What is it, Declan?' Liam asked as he jumped up to stand beside him.

'Something's wrong. It's the driver. I've lost all connection, his thoughts have just... well, they've gone. Actually so have everybody else's. Rupert, can you use your ability and look through the carriages to the driver's cabin?'

Rupert turned to face the front of the train and concentrated hard, looking through every carriage until he could see the driver's cabin.

His face dropped as he turned to face the rest of the group. 'He's erm... he's...'

'He's what?' asked Lana.

Rupert kind of shook his head awkwardly, 'I can't describe it. He's just, well, he's...'

Lana turned to look at the ginger-haired class comedian, 'Oh for goodness sake, Rupert, spit it out. Where is he? What's the matter with him?' she tutted.

Returning his attention to her, he shrugged, 'It's not just him, it's the others too.'

'What do you mean?,' asked Liam as he pulled Ava protectively towards him.

'Well, Rupert, is the driver there or not?' Lana asked quietly.

'He's there alright. It's just that he's kind of... not there too.'

'Huh?' asked Emma as Diarmuid held her tight.

'Let's just calm down, okay? Rupert, you're really not making any sense, mate,' said Declan.

'I think you need to see for yourselves,' Rupert whispered.

The lights flickered back on again, giving the group a moment to check on the women at the back of the carriage. Declan smiled encouragingly at them before noticing something odd. It was only then that they all realised how quiet the train had become.

'Declan?' Emma whispered as she followed his gaze.

'Declan? Something's up with the women...'

As she approached them with her arm out-stretched, she held out her hand and touched one of their faces. She was stone cold and, although they were sitting in exactly the same position as before, the four women appeared to be no longer conscious. Their empty eyes stared back at her like lifeless porcelain dolls.

Declan rushed to her side and inspected them.

'The other people have stopped shouting too,' said Moira, as she took off her glasses and wiped her forehead, before she opened the door to the next carriage.

'What's going on?' she whispered. 'What's happened to them all?' she asked as she looked over all the people who seemed to have frozen, just like the women.

Following behind her, Declan and her classmates walked silently through the carriages, astonished at what they saw. It was as if the people were playing a game of Musical Statues. Each and every person was frozen, their eyes wide open, but there was nobody there.

Lana waved her hand in front of one of the middle-aged businessmen she'd noticed earlier. He was standing up, leaning over the seat in front, a newspaper tucked under his arm and his laptop on the seat next to him. His mouth was open and his eyebrows were knitted together. He looked as if he'd been shouting. She turned her head so she could look directly at his face and waved a hand right in front of his eyes.

'Hello?' she asked quietly.

The man did nothing. If it wasn't for his beating heart that she could hear quite clearly when she placed her ear against his chest, she would have thought he were dead.

'This is so freaky, Sis,' she said as she stepped backwards and turned to see her sister waving her hands in front of an old couple who sat cowering in their seats. Fear was etched into their faces.

'You can say that again,' Emma gulped as she too, stepped backwards just as Declan rounded up the Watchers.

'There is definitely something supernatural going on.'

The Temporal Stone is available from most online book retailers

The Ghost of Josiah Grimshaw is available from most online book retailers

ACKNOWLEDGMENTS

Huge thanks to Jill Ibrahim, Brittany Willis, Poppet, Mary Endersbe and Andrea Baker for reading and correcting my work. I'm hugely grateful to you all. A special thanks to all my friends, social networking pals and readers for the constant support they always provide.

And of course to Michael, my rock and best friend. Thanks for putting up with me during the long, arduous writing process!

I want to dedicate this book to the three most important men in my life:
Michael, who turned 40 shortly after the release of this book
Dad Brian, who turned 60 just as I completed it
And to my brother Kev, whose humour keeps us choking with laughter
almost every day!

ABOUT THE AUTHOR

Suzy Turner wrote her first chick lit novel in her early twenties, but it wasn't until much later that she decided to focus on writing full time. It was during a visit to Canada in 2009 when the ravens within the dark eerie forests of British Columbia called to her. The story of Lilly Taylor was born soon after and the first novel in The Raven Witch Saga was created. Suzy has since published several more urban fantasy books (under her pen name SG Turner) and contemporary women's novels.

Having lived in Portugal since childhood, Suzy, who is originally from Yorkshire in England, loves to travel. She finds inspiration wherever she goes. Old decrepit buildings, graveyards, cathedrals and castles are just a few of the things that can be found within the worlds of her urban fantasy books, and her contemporary women's fiction novels are filled with fun friendships, ordinary people in extraordinary circumstances and quirky characters you'd want as friends.

Suzy lives in the Algarve with her husband, three cats and a dog, where she does yoga every morning and bookish stuff for pretty much the rest of the day!

For more books and updates, visit www.suzyturner.com or www.chilloutpress.com

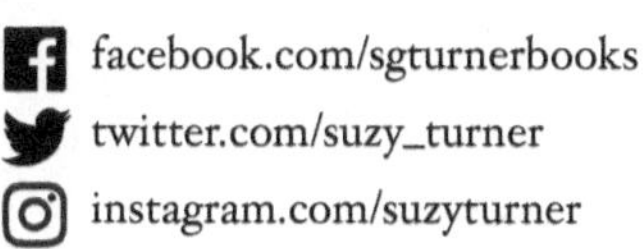

www.ingramcontent.com/pod-product-compliance
Lightning Source LLC
Chambersburg PA
CBHW020906160726
47993CB00005B/1845